# DEADPHONES

A hand twisted into Elias' hair and jerked his head straight, sending sparks of pain down through his eyes. They held his head still, and he knew with an icy shock of fright that they could now easily put the earphone on him. He bucked and writhed, trying to tear free. Then he saw the needler and stopped struggling, cold with dread. Its ugly muzzle was inches from his eyes. Beyond it, Weal's face blurred to insignificance.

"I ought to jam this down thy throat."

Elias caught movement above his head, felt a rubbery thing go into his ear. It melded perfectly with his skin, clammy and cold as dead flesh. He bit back a panicked yell, knowing he must hang on and fight, break free, or he was lost. He gathered himself for a desperate lunge. *Now!*

His body would not respond.

Other Bantam Spectra Books of interest
Ask your bookseller for the titles you have missed

# STEVEN SPRUILL

# THE PARADOX PLANET

### A Kane and Pendrake novel

**BANTAM BOOKS**
TORONTO · NEW YORK · LONDON · SYDNEY · AUCKLAND

All of the characters in this book
are fictitious, and any resemblance
to actual persons, living or dead,
is purely coincidental.

*This edition contains the complete text
of the original hardcover edition.*
NOT ONE WORD HAS BEEN OMITTED.

THE PARADOX PLANET
*A Bantam Spectra Book / published by arrangement with
Doubleday*

*PRINTING HISTORY*
*Doubleday edition published June 1988*
*Bantam edition / February 1989*

ISBN 0-553-27922-X

*Published simultaneously in the United States and Canada*

*PRINTED IN THE UNITED STATES OF AMERICA*

O      0 9 8 7 6 5 4 3 2 1

*To Mrs. Elsie Rose Camp,*
*1894–*
**GRANDMA**
*For all the good stories you read to me*

# THE
# PARADOX
# PLANET

ELIAS KANE WAS ABOUT TO PROGRAM THE FIRST PARA-space jump when he noticed the strange odor. He sniffed along the *Wager's* starboard until he'd traced the smell to access panel #4. A faint smell, not unpleasant, but oddly menacing. His spine crawled.

He closed his eyes, concentrating. Where had he smelled this before? His brain felt thick, resisting his effort to remember. *Not overheated microchips, not insulation either; an organic smell, like chopped walnut.* He shuddered.

"Is something wrong, Elias?" Pendrake's voice rumbled above his ear, making him jump. The pumpkin-colored face was calm, but Pendrake's hand betrayed him, tugging at his thick, white ponytail in a telltale gesture of unease.

"Nothing a vacation won't cure." Elias felt a sour distaste at the lie. Vacation hell. He was running. And it wasn't going to *cure* anything.

So what about panel #4? He could pop it and check the circuits, but it would mean delaying the jump. He wanted to get going, put Earth as far behind as he could, as quickly as he could.

He sniffed again and realized with relief that the smell was gone. Good. Probably hadn't been there in the first place—just his nerves playing up.

1

•

He turned from the panel and found Martha and Pendrake peering at him with anxious expressions. He forced a smile and squeezed between them to the bridge. Sliding into the pilot's chair, he scanned the green-lit instrument board, then looked up to the forward screen, getting a visual fix on Luna. It hung in the velvet blackness, curved full as a womb, glowing with intimations of life.

*What if the rumors were true?*

Elias felt a grim annoyance. What if they were? A woman with Briana's appetites—and power—could have as many different lovers as she chose.

*Yeah, but why did you have to be one of them?*

He felt indignant. Why did he have to suffer through these feelings all over again? He'd tormented himself enough about Briana. If she'd seduced him before Beth, he'd have brushed it off with no more than a bad taste, but it'd been after Beth—much too soon after —and it didn't matter that Briana had preyed on his grief in the most unconscienable way. He was still a grown-up man, and he could have said no.

Enough! Elias thought with exasperation. It's just a rumor, and even if it's true, you're probably not the father, and even if you are—

"Elias, something *is* wrong, isn't it?"

Martha's reflection gazed at him from the forward viewscreen of the cockpit. The warm-lit cabin dwindled behind her, superimposed on the frigid black of space. Her perceptiveness rattled him. It was not something he could talk about, the dark center of his fear: *No child could ever belong to both Briana and me. And Briana is Imperator.*

"Thought I smelled something funny," he told her. "But now it's gone. And so are we—the second we pass Luna's orbit. You ready?"

"You kidding? A month without VD lectures to simpering praetorians, without having to pluck whiskey glass out of their rumps or stitch up their lips. Know what my number one surgery is? Rebuilding praetorian fists. It's worse than the VD. I can't seem to teach them that mandibles are tougher than phalanges." She gave him one of her lopsided grins, and he felt better.

He was starting to like that smile a lot.

He looked at her, wishing he could forget everything else and just stare until he understood what about her looks so endlessly fascinated him. Other women were more beautiful—Briana, for example. But Martha was unique. Her face was intriguingly asymmetric. She had an awkward, girlish look that vanished when she moved; he loved her walk—her long stride, her unselfconscious, loose-jointed grace. Her auburn hair would be gorgeous long, but she kept it short—easy to tuck under the cap in surgery. He liked it that way, a soft, tawny shag, because she'd rather have an edge in OR than look gorgeous. He liked her eyes too, even though they were a nondescript gray. They could look incredibly vivid and striking between a surgical mask and cap. They seemed to take on other colors like a chameleon. Now there were points of green in them from the side-panel instrument lights—

Elias realized he *was* staring endlessly, and that Martha was aware of it. He flushed and busied himself with a final check on the jump solution. Martha must know about Briana, he realized as he worked. She's not ob/gyn, but she'd be in charge of assigning one.

I could ask her—

*Don't be an idiot!* He winced inwardly, remembering how he'd made Martha his mother-confessor after Briana—a bonehead mistake, if ever there was one.

"Pendrake's been telling me about Cephan," Martha said. "I can't wait to see the chartreuse seas, and those ancient tents on the plain of Roon."

"The Mardandris dwellings," Pendrake supplied, his powerful, three-fingered hand probing at access panel #4. Pendrake went on talking about Cephan, but Elias couldn't concentrate on his words. Instead, he imagined himself holding a small, warm bundle wrapped in blankets, gazing at its perfect little face, feeling its chubby fingers grip his nose. His throat constricted. A girl—he'd like a girl best, though he wasn't sure why. A wave of longing passed through him and a sense of futility.

*No child could belong to both of us.*

He tried to shrug off his gloom, tuning in to Pendrake's conversation with Martha.

". . . an ancient race, thought to inhabit the central plain of the northern hemisphere of Cephan fifty thousand years before we Cephantines existed. The climate there is so mild, the Mardandris were able to live in tents. The fabric of them is thin as a butterfly wing and clear as crystal, yet they are indestructible. At night, when the wind blows from the north, the tents sing. It is very beautiful and very sad."

Elias heard the longing in Pendrake's voice, and was ashamed at letting his own preoccupations taint the start of the trip. Pendrake had not been back to Cephan since he was captured there by outlaw slavers almost ten years ago. This would be a joyful homecoming for him. So cheer up, Elias told himself, or you'll spoil his fun.

The ship plunged into darkness.

Elias heard Martha's nervous laugh, and then the thunk of an access panel popping free, and he knew with a sinking feeling that it must be the panel he'd decided not to check. It was a nexus for the ship's lights. The ship was still under power, but there'd be no illumination until he fixed it.

He reached under the control console for the handflash. The strange smell hit him again, much stronger.

*S'uniphs!*

Panic surged through him. He thumbed desperately at the switch of the handflash. Nothing happened. The deck remained pitch dark.

Elias' stomach twisted into a knot. "Come forward," he shouted. "Now!"

"Elias?" Martha's voice was tight with fear.

"It's all right," he said, forcing calm into his voice. "Be careful. *Don't fall.*"

He groped for the rotational control, feeling Pendrake brush by him, hearing Martha grunt and knowing with relief that Pendrake must have grabbed her. Elias found the control and rotated the ship, at the same time locating the viewport controls, punching them all down. The overhead viewport shields hissed open, dropping slivers of moonlight onto the deck. Elias focused on the one nearest their feet, watching it widen out to a large rectangle as the ship's rotation aligned the viewport with Luna. When the rectangle of moonlight started to narrow again, Elias killed the *Wager*'s rotation.

He stared down with cold dread at the patch of milky radiance. A creature the size of a rat crawled into it. For a second he hoped that it *was* a rat, and then he knew it wasn't—no tail, a gleaming brown carapace, the tilting, beetle-like crawl. His heart began to hammer with fear. It was a s'uniph all right, and unless he did something fast, they were all dead.

Damn, another one, and then more, crawling toward them through the moonlight. There must be a hundred of them! The first was only a meter from their feet. Someone must have planted them behind the panel, along with a small, timed charge that would simultaneously kill the lights and free the insects.

Outrage burned through him. Who? *Why?*

His anger turned against himself. *If you hadn't been in such a hurry—*

"Elias," Martha yelled. "What *are* they?"

"Insects. The Ornyl use them as a weapon. They can bore through almost anything. They deposit larvae that migrate through the bloodstream and feed on heart tissue. If we want to be alive tomorrow, we can't let even one of them too close."

Elias saw that the rectangle of moonlight was full of them now, a horde, crawling toward them slowly, inexorably. They smell us, he thought, just like I smelled them, but *they* know what they're smelling. *Hosts.*

He shuddered. A thousand squirming larvae, crawling through your veins—

Martha said, "Can't we just smash them with something?"

"Carapace is too hard. You could drive a tank over them and they'd keep right on crawling."

Burn them! he thought.

With what? The *Wager* was engineered nonflammable, and there was no provision for making a fire, too damned deadly on a ship in space.

An inspiration struck Elias. "Martha, your medkit."

"I stashed it under the console." He heard her groping for it. "Here!"

"Good. Has it got a cauterizer?"

"Sure."

"Turn it on and give it to me, quick!"

Seconds crawled by. Elias could hear the soft tick of s'uniph legs on the deck. A pinpoint of light from the cauterizer glowed to life a few feet away.

"Elias, I'm holding the iron straight up. Grab it about ten centimeters down. Careful!"

"Right." His fingers closed around hers. He could feel her hand trembling as he took the iron from her. The glow swelled into a soft halo as the cauterizer heated up. As a handflash, it was pitifully inadequate— the thing was designed for heat, not light. But heat was what he wanted most—fire, *burn the ugly things!*

He held the cauterizer out and down. In its dull, reddish glow he saw a s'uniph inches from Martha's ankle. The hair stood up along his neck. He swore and kicked out, flipping the creature back into the darkness.

"Get back! Pendrake, help her up onto the console! Get as high up as you can, both of you. The bloody things can jump!"

Elias held the iron out, waving it in front of him. The floor was a brown mass of movement. His throat went dry with fear. With a yell, he plunged the tip of the iron into the back of the lead s'uniph, pinning it to the floor, feeling the hardness of its carapace through the handle of the cauterizer. It squirmed, its shell glowing, then smoldering—

God, one was on his wrist!

He twisted away in panic, flinging it off before it could bore into his skin.

He realized with a sinking feeling that the cauterizer was no good, there were too many of them, the point of heat was too small. As he tried to hold it on one, the others would get him.

He needed a damned blowtorch. . . .

*Gas!*

The recycler. One of the by-products from ship's hydroponics tanks and waste recycling was methane gas, periodically piped out to the outer hull, where it could be manually vented when the ship was in space. Had he vented recently? Please, God, no!

Two s'uniphs—at his ankles!

He kicked in a fury, trying to visualize the correct access panel. Number six? Or was it seven? He gasped a deep breath and launched himself across the sea of crawling insects.

"Elias!"

He did not answer, needing all his concentration to stay upright. The insects rolled under his feet, treacherous as flattened ball bearings. He felt himself slipping, pitching forward. He grabbed the molded surface of an access panel, clinging to his balance, kicking, feeling the weight of one fastening itself to his boot. *Damn, hooking in with its borer.* He held the tip of the cauterizer against it and it recoiled, dropping away.

He tore at the access panel in a frenzy, popping it, throwing it onto the squirming insects behind him. *Chew on that, you bastards!*

He held the tip of the cauterizer into the exposed panel, illuminating the relays and circuit panels, but the vent hose did not pass through this panel. Damn! Next panel—quickly! He jerked and tore at it, hurling it down, feeling a drag on his boot and kicking out in revulsion.

He found the vent hose. Good! There—below it, the trip handle, used to flush out the gas. But first he had to tear the hose loose from the safety ring that locked the end of it to the outer hull. Then he could reel it back inside the ship, flush the tanks and use the hose as a sort of flame thrower—

*If* there was enough methane!

He grabbed the hose in an agony of hope and fear, and pulled with all his might. The line wouldn't budge. He swore in frustration, kicking, thrashing his feet as the insects closed around him. He bent and grabbed the fallen panel, using it to scoop and shovel them away from him.

"Elias!"

"Stay back!"

But he heard Pendrake pounding toward him across the deck. Holding the cauterizer out like a hand-flash, he saw Pendrake's boots crawling with insects, knew there were too many, that they'd already started boring.

"Quick! Can you pull this free?"

"Certainly, Elias."

Elias bit back a hysterical laugh. Pendrake would be polite at his own execution! The big alien grabbed the line from him and heaved on it. It tore free. Elias flushed the vent lever and the rotten eggs stink of methane rushed from the end of the hose. Sweetest damn thing he'd ever smelled!

His hand shook as he held the glowing tip of the cauterizer to the end of the vent hose. The spewing gas puffed into a huge fireball, filling the cabin with orange light, singeing his eyebrows. He gulped and pinched down on the plastic, cutting down the gas flow. The billowing flame shrank back a little. Excitement surged through him. It was going to work! He plunged the end against Pendrake's boots. In seconds, the s'uniphs burst into flame. They sloughed away with a screeching sound that chilled Elias' blood. Pendrake slapped at his boots, snuffing the fire.

Elias bent forward and thrust the torch into the writhing mass of insects. The front line of them caught fire, and then the flames spread back across the writhing mass, throwing the interior of the *Wager* into a hellish orange light. He looked for Martha, saw her standing on the control console, one leg drawn up, her back hunched into the curve of the overhead. He saw that a knot of s'uniphs had jumped to the console. One was closing on her foot. No! A savage yell tore from his throat. He dashed through the flaming sea of insects, pulling the vent line with him until it brought him up short, still two meters from her.

"Martha! Jump!"

She sprang down to him, the insects following. He thrust the flaming end of the line at them, watching with fierce satisfaction as they crisped and curled in the flames. The nutty smell turned sweetish and foul as they burned. He choked on the stink, coughing. The cabin was filling with smoke, noxious, asphyxiating.

Worse, it was getting very hot. Every kilo of heat shielding was on the outside of the *Wager*, where it had to be for reentry. The ship wasn't designed for such hellish heat inside. If the fire got much worse, it'd start fusing circuits all through the inner skin of the ship. Fuse the wrong relays, and the conventional launch fuels could blow out of sync and send them cartwheeling on a long funeral voyage of no return, or—if they were lucky—smash them down against Luna.

Elias felt a cold wave of fear. He did not want to die, not if there might be a child—hell, not if there wasn't one, either.

He realized there was no point worrying about the fire—not until he'd killed all the insects. He searched the deck, coughing, looking for intact s'uniphs. There— six or seven of them to the side of the others, not burning. He skirted the flaming mass in the center of the deck and held the burning hose out toward the survivors.

The flame guttered and went out as the last of the methane burned away.

He swore and dropped the nozzle, flanking the insects, kicking them into the burning mass in the center. He looked up and saw that Pendrake was standing by with the fire extinguisher. Good!

"Wait," he said. "We have to be sure!"

Pendrake nodded. The fire was at its height, blazing hot. Elias saw the struts of the overhead shimmering in the heat. "OK, go!"

Pendrake emptied the extinguisher into the fire; steam rose, bits of foam swirled around the cabin. The fire shrank but burned on. Martha brought a cannister of water from the head and dashed it into the heart of the flaming mass. Pendrake grabbed a galley pan and Elias joined in, snatching a big steam pot, helping form a relay.

His mind went blank. He was aware, dimly, of his muscles laboring—*fill, pass on, take the empty, fill again*—and then he couldn't see and he realized the fire was out.

He slumped down against the toilet, shaking with relief. The relief faded, turning to fury. "Those *bastards!*" He felt Martha's hand on his shoulder.

"Who, Elias?"

"I don't know." He tried to think. Who would want us dead? *Why?*

He got up and felt his way back into the main cabin, still quaking with reaction. Pendrake had already rolled the ship, centering a square of moonlight on the panel that had been sabotaged. The moonlight leached Pendrake's face of color. "They removed several circuit boards, Elias. Do you have others?"

"I did, in the overhead storage—but don't be shocked if they're gone."

Pendrake disappeared from the shaft of moonlight and Elias heard the storage door slide back. "It appears you are right," the alien said gravely. "Can you fly this ship in the dark, Elias?"

"To get back to Earth right now, I would fly this ship hanging by my heels from the overhead with my hands tied behind me."

Martha laughed and he heard the giddy release of tension in her voice. "Using your nose, no doubt," she said.

"Right. Hunt and peck." Elias remembered Pendrake and felt a rush of sympathy. "I'm sorry about Cephan, my friend."

"Forget Cephan! I just want to plant my feet on solid ground again. We will go to Cephan another time."

Elias knew that Pendrake was hiding disappointment. He felt another surge of fury at whoever had done this. He would find out. They would pay.

With a crackle of static, the communicator burst to life. A male voice began to drone the usual hailing code; then an angry, female voice broke in: "Forget all that twaddle. Elias Kane, this is the Imperator. Are you reading me?"

"I'm reading you, sir," Elias said. She'd called herself the Imperator, not Briana. Formality seemed to be called for.

"How dare you sneak off like this?"

"I'd hardly call it sneaking off, *sir.*" *Except that's exactly what it was.* Elias felt dread welling up inside him again. Why was she calling?

He made an effort to bluff it through. "May I remind Your Highness that she does not presently hold me under contract?"

"Don't split hairs with me, Kane. I'm ordering you home at once, do you understand?"

"Yes, sir."

"You are to report to me the second you land. Your little pleasure cruise is over."

Elias looked with disbelief at the smoldering embers of the s'uniphs, then burst out laughing.

## 2

"S'UNIPHS!" THE IMPERATOR MUTTERED. "YOU KNOW what that means?"

Elias tried to form an answer, but all he could think of was her belly. He fought a compulsion to stare at it. Was she showing or not? He knew he must have glanced down a dozen times already, and yet he had no clear impression. His head buzzed with anxiety.

*What did she just say? S'uniphs—asking me what it means.*

Elias fingered his chin, pretending to consider. *Just one good look, slow and calm.* He glanced at her bodysuit, a soft, brushed material, black and glossy as raven wings. On its front, stitched in silver, was the tree emblem of the Amerdaths. He let his eyes follow the tree down—foliage over the breasts, trunk descending over her stomach, roots spreading suggestively below her belt. Lust swelled through him. He suppressed it, annoyed with himself. Her waist seemed slim as ever— not the slightest thickening to suggest she was bearing a child.

He felt no relief. She could be several months pregnant and still show nothing in her waist—

"Are you going to stand there gaping at me?" Briana snapped. "I asked you a question."

"I'm afraid I don't know."

She gave a delicate snort. "The great Elias Kane, intergalactic detective, stumped by the obvious. What's the most likely way anyone could get ahold of that many s'uniphs?"

"On Ornyl," he said.

"Or *from* an Ornyl," she amended.

She turned her back, mounting the steps to her throne two at a time, whirling to sit. She stared down at him with an intensity that made him uncomfortable. He remembered seeing that same look on her father's face—a hungry, prying eagerness to enter your mind and paw through whatever was there. He did not like Briana up there staring down at him. He was suddenly repelled by this vast, overrich throne room, with its statues, marble pillars and gold gilt, its nymphs and satyrs chasing across the frescoed ceiling. When it had been her father's, this room had shown a Spartan restraint. But now it reeked of both power and excess.

"Either an Ornyl tried to do you in," Briana said, "or someone who counted on an Ornyl contact to supply the s'uniphs. Find the Ornyl, and you find the saboteurs. And I don't think we have to look very far."

He saw where she was leading. "Chuddath?"

"It makes sense, doesn't it? Your ship is housed in one of the palace's private berths. The sabotage must have been done there. Chuddath's the only Ornyl warrior in the palace, not to mention the rest of Earth."

"That we know of."

Briana gave a derisive laugh. "Come on, Elias. An Ornyl is not exactly hard to spot. And I've not rescinded my father's decree. They're banned here, you know that—except for Chuddath." Her voice softened. "When Papa got Chuddath, he decided the only thing that could beat his new bodyguard was another Ornyl. He was wrong, of course. Poor Papa."

Elias found himself resisting what she was saying. He had no great love for Gregory Amerdath's bodyguard—how could anyone? But Chuddath and he had been through hell together, and that ought to count for something. He said, "How could it be Chuddath when he never leaves the vault door? He even has his food brought to him."

"*It*, Elias. *It* has *its* food brought to *it*."

Elias recoiled inwardly from the heat in her voice, the racial hatred, so quick to ignite. He felt an involuntary disgust for the flawed heart inside the perfect young body. *Please. Don't be bearing our child.*

He suppressed a bleak laugh. I'm obsessed, he thought. Why do I keep coming back to it?

"Just because Chuddath doesn't leave that vault door," Briana said, "doesn't mean other people can't come to it."

"Don't Alvar Sabin's men keep watch too?"

"At a distance," Briana conceded. "It won't let any praetorians closer than thirty meters. As if they would harm my father—what's left of him," she added bitterly.

"The most important part of him is left," Elias said more sharply than he had intended. "And it was a praetorian who attacked him the first time."

Briana's face flushed. She sprang up from the throne and stalked down the curving steps as if she wanted to strike him. He held himself still, determined not to back away. She pulled up inches from his face. "Yes," she hissed. "But what about all the other times? It's rather like the fox guarding the chickens, don't you think?"

"Chuddath is incapable of the slightest disloyalty to your father. He always was and always will be. You know that."

"And *you* know, if you'll let yourself think about it, that Chuddath might have some very good reasons to want you dead. It mightn't consider you the folk hero portrayed in the synpapes. It might even feel that you thwarted my father's will. Exposed him to shame."

The suggestion made Elias uncomfortable. "No human can know how Chuddath feels," he countered, knowing he was being stubborn.

"Except for one," Briana said softly. "My father. He can see into Chuddath's mind through the S'edhite link." She shuddered and hugged her arms, then quickly crossed them as if ashamed of showing weakness. "I'm going to open the vault," she said firmly. "And bring my father back."

Elias looked at her, appalled. *God, and I walked right into it.*

"My father is the one human alive," she went on defensively, "who could tell us whether Chuddath tried to have you killed."

A wave of sickness passed through Elias. He put a hand on her shoulder. "You mustn't."

She gazed speculatively at his hand and he pulled it back, wondering what had possessed him to touch her.

"Why not, Elias?"

"You know his final orders to us all. We were not to bring him back, except to restore him to a body."

"Do you also remember my reply?" she said in a low voice, "when he tried to give me other 'final' orders. I told him that I was Imperator now. You should enshrine his answer to that in your heart. He said, 'That's the only answer a true Imperator could give.'" For a second her eyes looked weary and pained. But her voice remained firm. "I am your Imperator now, Elias. In all things, I must do what I think best."

Elias was filled with sick dread. To revive Gregory Amerdath from his dreams, to expose him once again to his unbearable reality, just so he could answer a question? It was cruel, unthinkable. He said, "*I* am one of the people who was almost killed. I want to know who and why at least as much as you do. But even if I knew it would prove Chuddath guilty, I would not want your father awakened."

She touched his face gently. "You don't value your own life enough, Elias. That saddens me, but it changes nothing. *I* value you. I want to know who tried to kill you, even if you don't."

Elias felt a deep uneasiness. *I "value" you*—it was not what he wanted to hear right now.

She strode to the towering doors of the throne room, leaving him behind. Her touch lingered on his cheek, chilling him with foreboding. She turned. "Come on," she commanded. "We'll get it over quickly."

He looked at her, seeing suddenly a human panther, the same muscular, green-eyed beauty, the same lethality. He could smell an aura of blood around her. His mouth went dry. "Chuddath will never let you open the vault. People will die."

"Then so be it."

Elias stood with Martha and Pendrake before Amerdath's vault. A few paces in front of them was Briana, flanked by two praetorian captains. They faced the Ornyl warrior, who stood with his back to the bronze doors of the vault, immobile as a statue. Elias felt chilled looking at the mantis head, the expressionless compound eyes, the huge wings—so like a mammoth roach's—that half cloaked the massive fighting arms. He felt a brief, unwanted empathy with Briana's revulsion for Chuddath. It was one thing to value in the abstract the intelligence—and perhaps the soul—that hid inside that grotesque body, and quite another to stand in the warrior's presence.

Elias thought of what lay beyond Chuddath inside that vault, and his chill deepened: a disembodied, living head. All that remained of the legendary Gregory Amerdath, former Imperator of Earth and the nine planets. Elias closed his eyes, remembering the awful images of Amerdath being struck down by an assassin, Martha surgically sawing his head from its blackened, dying body and putting it on a cushion of medical surgifoam.

He felt a twinge of nausea, resisting the images that

were even worse: Beth Tyson, sprawled on the next table over from Amerdath, her life draining away beyond reclamation. He felt a sharp stab of pain; then the cushioning of time and distance rebounded inside him, driving out all but a small, lingering ache. He focused again on the vault, on the spark of life preserved inside it.

It was as close as Amerdath could come to having a body.

In a way, it was very close indeed. In his memories, augmented by the incredible technology of the sliver implants, he possessed again the body of his younger self—and all the past that body had lived through.

What was Amerdath doing now? Elias wondered. Planning strategy in the great unification war? Fighting side by side with his viceroy, Richard DuMorgan, against the alien Andinaz raiders?

Or perhaps making love to a woman, climbing a mountain, drinking whiskey and dashing the glass into the fire.

And now we drag him back to hell, Elias thought, sickened. He felt Martha's hand slip into his and gave it a squeeze, trying to convey a reassurance he did not feel.

He watched Briana try to stare the Ornyl warrior down, waiting for it to respond, acknowledge her. Chuddath's huge, muscular legs remained planted apart. The mantis head looked out from the vault doors, the target of the blank, compound eyes a mystery. It was the absolute stillness of the insect which, lacking a purpose, does not move.

Watching Briana stubbornly await the Ornyl warrior's acknowledgment, Elias felt a sudden rush of insight: This was not about finding who had sabotaged the *Wager.* It was about power, love and *loyalty.* Within Amerdath's brain was embedded more than the sterile, memory-charged slivers of metal. Long before those slivers were in place, while Amerdath was still a whole man, he had taken into his own brain a piece of Chuddath's; the macabre S'edhite ritual, giving man and alien total insight into each other's minds. Amerdath could, indeed, see whether Chuddath had played any part in sabotaging the *Wager*.

But that's not why Briana wants to revive her father, Elias thought.

*She wants to destroy Chuddath.*

He felt a sudden sadness for her. How she must resent the alien's S'edhite closeness to her father—an intimacy she had never had and could never hope for. Now she had the perfect pretext for Chuddath's undoing. Because of the S'edhite link, Chuddath could not disobey his lord's last command: *Do not awaken me, not ever, unless it is to give me back the body.*

Briana, on the other hand, *could* disobey that command. In some perverse way she *had* to, to prove that she was truly Imperator and—in the same calculated stroke—to make Chuddath fail her father.

Elias saw her stamp one booted foot, and knew with a sinking feeling that she was through waiting.

"Chuddath, I order you to stand aside from the door," she said.

The alien stirred at last. The chubby vocal hands emerged from their protection under the massive fighting arms. With rapid, cricket-like motions, they stroked the contoured patch on the abdomen, producing the eerie, violinlike voice. "For what purpose?"

"Because I am your Imperator," Briana snapped.

"Do you wish . . . merely to look?" Chuddath persisted, pausing in the characteristic way to rest the hands between words.

"That is none of your concern."

"My orders were clear."

"I give you your orders. Stand aside."

"You mean to . . . awaken him?"

"Yes," Briana said, and Elias knew he was correct. All she need have done was lie to Chuddath. Once inside the vault with her father, she could have revived him before Chuddath could stop her.

But in that scenario, Chuddath would not have failed.

Do something, Elias thought. He stepped forward, then paused, hearing the disciplined quick-step of boots rounding the curving corridor to the vault. A cohort of praetorians in full battle gear ran into the chamber and formed up. To one side paced Alvar Sabin, himself, commander of the guard and old comrade of Gregory Amerdath.

Elias suppressed a groan. Any chance of averting this catastrophe had just shrunk almost to nothing. Sabin hated Chuddath, always had, and his reasons were as simple as Briana's were complex: Sabin had never accepted that his praetorians might not be enough to guard his old comrade—that he should be forced to share that honor with a loathsome alien. When they had *both* failed Amerdath, it had only inflamed Sabin's hatred of Chuddath.

Elias took Briana's arm. She turned, eyes glittering, and patted his hand. With an effort he kept himself from recoiling. "Let me talk to Alvar," he murmured.

"Why?"

"Because he is going to want to kill Chuddath, and we have to be sure he doesn't."

"I realize that," she said impatiently. "I'm going to order him not to."

" 'Accidents' can happen in the heat of battle. With a stubborn old bulldog like Alvar, orders *and* persuasion are better than just orders. You are Imperator, and can't be seen stooping to persuasion before your own men. But they won't think anything of it if I talk to him."

Briana looked uncomfortable. "What do you plan to say?"

"That a Chuddath humiliated is better than a Chuddath dead—a Chuddath incapable of appreciating who defeated him."

A look of shock crossed Briana's face, and he knew he had hit the mark, not just for Alvar Sabin, but for her.

She gave him a chill smile. "Sometimes you are almost too clever for your own good. Go ahead."

Elias hurried to Sabin and held out his hand. Sabin hesitated a fraction, then shook it, keeping an eye on the Ornyl warrior.

"You know that the Imperator wants Chuddath unharmed," Elias said.

"Yes."

"I want something too."

Sabin gave him a hard look. "What? Be quick."

"If you can take Chuddath—"

"Oh, I'll take him, all right."

"Try to persuade Briana not to revive her father. It should be enough for her—and for you—to put Chuddath in a cell."

Sabin's face reddened. "You presume, Kane."

"Let's not try to fool each other, there isn't time. You were his oldest and best comrade. You know his last orders."

"I don't need you to remind me," Sabin snapped. "And I know something else, too. He was half insane when he gave those orders."

Elias looked at the commander with dismay. What was this?

"Since Amerdath went in there," Alvar said, "I've had time to think. I should never have let it happen. The man who ordered that vault closed on himself was not the man I knew for fifty years, the man I fought beside. He's trapped, Kane. Trapped in an endless nightmare. At night, when I lie in my bed, I can hear his spirit screaming, pleading with me to get him out." A sudden sweat appeared on Sabin's forehead. He looked sick around the eyes.

He really believes it, Elias thought. He felt a surge of desperation. "Alvar, listen to me: What has been done for Gregory Amerdath is the best that *can* be done at this point. He is safe in his past. He does not even *know* it's his past. He thinks it's happening now. It is in every way real."

"You can't know that."

Elias heard a shuffle of feet, the restless clink of body armor among the praetorians. He had the panicky feeling of time slipping away. A sudden, irrational doubt struck him. *What if Alvar's right?*

Elias shook off the doubt. "I know that, if you allow Amerdath to be awakened, then he *will* be in nightmare."

Alvar stared back at him, stonefaced. "It's not my decision."

"You have influence. . . ."

"We've talked enough. Stand aside. And keep your pacifist Cephantine friend out of this. I bear him no malice, but if he tries to interfere, I'll do what I have to do."

Elias felt a hot, quick fury burn through him. He moved closer to Alvar, speaking barely above a whisper. "Harm a hair of Pendrake's head, and I'll see you broken."

He wheeled away before Sabin could answer. Behind him he heard the commander snap, "Form two squads."

Elias rejoined Martha and Pendrake. When he turned again, the praetorians had separated into two smaller groups, each partially flanking Chuddath. Pendrake stirred behind him, and dread settled in the pit of Elias' stomach. "They're not going to kill Chuddath," he murmured. "They're going to try not even to hurt him."

"Elias, I hope you are right."

"Whatever happens, *don't* interfere."

Pendrake did not answer and Elias' dread grew, spreading through him in a sickening wave.

"Sidearms!" Sabin commanded.

"Belay," Briana said.

Sabin paled, turned to her stiffly. "Imperator, this is an *Ornyl*. We need sidearm fire to subdue him. It can be done without killing him."

"I don't want it injured. Wrestle it down and bind it."

Chuddath made a derisive, keening sound, and bent forward, spreading the immense fighting arms in contemptuous invitation.

Sabin reddened and saluted Briana. "Take him," he shouted.

The two squads rushed Chuddath at the same time, a disciplined mass of black-clad bodies, hurling themselves on the alien. Chuddath braced his feet wider. The massive fighting arms blurred into motion. Men began to fly back from him. Elias watched in horror as the Ornyl flung praetorians against the walls, bashed them on the vault doors, crushed them together and dropped them. Blood spattered the walls and ran in darkly gleaming rivulets on the marble floor. Elias heard the terrible crunch of bones shattering and clenched his teeth against a surge of nausea. Dimly, he felt Martha's face pressing into his shoulder. He felt dizzy with disbelief. How could this be happening, in this unearthly near silence, the maimed praetorians too disciplined even to scream?

He saw Sabin turn beseechingly to Briana, whose face had gone white.

"Sidearms," Sabin hissed. "I *beg* you!"

She gave a slight, stiff nod.

"Blasters!" Sabin shouted.

Elias groped behind him for Pendrake, realized too late that he wasn't there. He watched, frozen in horror, as Pendrake raced between the praetorians. Those who were still standing were falling back and drawing blasters. Pendrake leapt between them and turned in front of Chuddath, spreading his arms in protection of the other alien.

The praetorians hesitated, turning back to their commander with confused looks.

Feeling paralyzed in nightmare, Elias saw Sabin raise his ruptor, aim it at Pendrake's head. *God, NOOO!*

Before Elias could move, Sabin fired.

**3**

PENDRAKE TOPPLED TO THE FLOOR.

Elias felt rage swelling, bursting inside him *bastard
I'll kill you smash your face.* Blankness, a dim pain in
his fist, then he saw Sabin's face at the end of a red
tunnel. He pressed after the face, hating it, feeling a
savage, tearing release in his pumping fists as he threw
his whole body into it. His legs tangled and he pitched
forward—a body squirming under him, then Sabin's
face again, now close, his nose spurting blood, eyes incredulous. Elias shouted something, feeling spikes of
fury behind his eyes, *control yourself no kill you, you
snake*—

Hands crushed down on his biceps, jerking him up
and off Sabin. He bucked and twisted in a frenzy *I'm not
through, let me go!* He saw black uniforms closing
around him, then the floor rearing up, slapping him in
the side. Pain penetrated for a second then puffed
away. Something slamming into his buttock, pain again
but it didn't matter—yes it did *a boot, the bastards,
kicking him.* He rolled, tried to spring up, but slipped
on the hard, gritty marble, banging a knee.

". . . stop, stop, *Stop!*"

His vision cleared and he stopped, disoriented.
Who—?

Briana, screaming at them to stop.

He realized he was sitting. Dimly, he was aware of praetorians standing frozen around him. Rage rebounded inside him. He did not want to stop, where was Sabin? There—sitting up, blotting at his nose with the meat of his thumb. Sabin gazed at him with a mixture of sheepishness and respect. "Not bad for a skinny civilian."

"Son of a whore," Elias choked. His rage began to mix with grief; a terrible ache rose through his chest and throat. *Beth and now Pendrake. Am I death to everyone I love?*

"I'm not done with you," he spat at Sabin.

"I warned you to keep him out of it—"

"Shut up, both of you," Briana snapped.

Elias felt his fury spilling over onto her. *Shut your face, damn you, if you hadn't, I'll—*

His rage burned itself out. He twisted around on the seat of his pants, feeling a startling jab of pain in his rear, dismissing it. He must get up, find Pendrake's body—

He saw Pendrake standing beside Chuddath.

For a second he could not believe—no one could outjump a blaster beam—and then he realized with dawning elation that Pendrake had not jumped, he'd been pushed.

Relief flooded Elias. He sprang up and shouted, "You're not dead!"

Pendrake gave him a reassuring wave. "I shouted at you, Elias, but you did not seem to hear me." Pendrake turned hurriedly back to Chuddath, and Elias saw that the warrior was hunched down on one side. His left fighting arm dangled limply, ribbons of greenish-black sludge pouring down from the shoulder. Elias felt a quick shock of sympathy, seeing suddenly the human part of Chuddath—a grotesquely deformed man, wounded and in pain.

Pendrake said something to Chuddath that Elias could not hear. Chuddath's vocal hands, unharmed, rubbed furiously at the contoured abdomen. "Keep your thanks. I care . . . nothing for your life. You . . . interfered. I need no . . . help from a grass eater."

Elias felt a laugh pushing up his throat. What ingratitude—so outrageous it was funny. A grass eater—no, worse: not just a nonfighter, an avowed pacifist—saving the fierce warrior. And Chuddath was so insulted that he unwittingly saved Pendrake right back, flinging him away just as Sabin fired.

Elias felt a rush of gratitude to Chuddath. Maybe his shove wasn't unwitting. Maybe he cared more for his fellow alien than he cared to admit. . . .

And maybe pigs could fly.

Elias realized his face was split in a stupid grin. Waves of euphoria rolled through him. With an effort, he forced the smile from his face. Pendrake was all right, but the ugly confrontation between Chuddath and Briana wasn't over. Chuddath had taken a bad wound, one fighting arm immobilized. He'd be completely vulnerable on that side.

Now he could be beaten.

Elias gazed at Chuddath, feeling a sudden, fierce resolve: *I won't let her destroy you.*

Sabin was still blotting at his nose. He glared at the hunched Chuddath with malevolent pleasure, then gestured to his praetorians. "What are you waiting for? Take the stinking bug!"

"Wait!" Elias snapped. "You don't give the orders here. Your Imperator does."

Sabin reddened. A corner of Briana's mouth twitched in a fleeting smile. "Your Highness," Elias said, "may I have a word with you?"

"Alvar, hold." She walked a few steps to the side.

Elias followed, feeling a throb in his buttock and shooting pains from his knee. The hand that had punched Alvar ached savagely across the knuckles. He remembered what Martha had said about endlessly repairing the shattered fists of brash young praetorians. He suppressed a groan. *I'm getting too old for this.*

"Well?" Briana said.

"This is the perfect point to stop."

"Out of the question." Her voice was mild, indulgent.

"You said you . . . valued me. I value you, too." He paused, surprised to realize that part of him meant it. He saw surprise in her face too, and then a wistful hope. He hurried on, flustered. "You've beaten Chuddath. Everyone here knows that you could take him now. If you don't, it will be seen as mercy, not weakness."

"Lovely," she said sarcastically. "And if we *don't* take Chuddath, just how do we get past him into the vault? He'll go on fighting until he's dead or chained, you know that."

"Not necessarily. He's a warrior, but not a fool. I think I can get him to step aside."

"How?"

Elias braced himself. "By giving him my word—and yours—that you won't awaken your father."

Briana gave an incredulous laugh. "What have you been sniffing?"

"It's the only way you can win," Elias said. "If you hadn't wounded Chuddath, you could have gone ahead, but the way it stands now, if you awaken your father, he'll be furious at what you've done to his bodyguard."

"I'm not afraid of Father. I am Imperator now."

"No question. You have the power. But your father has one power left to him, too: he can defy you."

Briana's mouth tightened into a grim line. "You think I can't force him to mindlink with Chuddath? Wrong. If I have to, I'll threaten to keep him awake. I can do it—just order stimulants and dream-blockers into his blood supply."

Elias looked at her, revolted and trying to hide it. *How could he feel anything for someone so ruthless?* "Yes, you can do that. But there's no way in hell you can make him tell you what he sees in Chuddath's mind."

"You're overlooking something. My father will

*want* to find whoever's responsible for the sabotage. He cares for you, considers you one of his most trusted friends and advisors."

"But not closer than Chuddath. No one is—no one could be."

Briana looked stung. He cursed inwardly. You went too far, he thought, but then he saw uncertainty in Briana's face. He turned with her to look at the vault. Chuddath had sunk to one knee, clasping his right fighting hand over the wound in his shoulder. Pendrake was fussing over him; Chuddath kept trying to shoulder him away. Elias looked for Martha, found her on her knees among the fallen praetorians. Her tunic was streaked with blood, and there was a red smear on her cheek. He felt touched, almost shaken, by the sight of her. There was something inexpressibly noble about her at this moment.

Briana cleared her throat, and he realized she'd caught him gazing at Martha. Her eyes were dark with clairvoyance, her expression stony. A chill went through him.

"Let me go to Chuddath," he pleaded. "Give him your word you won't awaken Amerdath. He'll stand aside for you, and the moment he does, you win. You'll be able to dismiss the guard and let Dr. Reik get the wounded evacuated."

Briana drew a deep breath. Her jaw muscles twitched, and he realized she was seething with fury and frustration. "You think I did all this to humiliate Chuddath," she said. "Clever, clever Elias. Maybe you're not *all* wrong, but you're wrong. Damn it, *I want to know who tried to kill you.*"

All of a sudden, the anger seemed to drain from her. Her eyes looked luminous, and he realized with amazement that she was close to tears.

"So do I," he said quickly. "And I'll find out, don't worry. Finding out is what I do best."

Her eyes cleared, and with startling quickness she looked composed again. She gave him a suggestive smile. "Oh, I don't know. You do some other things well, too."

He forced himself to smile back at the innuendo. A shudder of disgust went through him. But he knew he'd won.

"All right," Briana said. "Just go over like you're checking out Pendrake. When you turn back to me, I'll order him to stand aside. He'd damned well better do it, with none of his bug impudence. Be sure he understands that."

Elias worked his way through the sprawled praetorians, pausing to give Martha's shoulder a squeeze. She looked up with a wan smile, and he felt another uncomfortable stab of awareness: *Briana behind, watching us.*

He hurried on, picking his way through the much larger number of wounded concentrated around Chuddath's feet. Pendrake offered a hand, and he took it, savoring the grip, the final proof of Pendrake's aliveness. Pendrake helped him step over a fallen praetorian sergeant, whose skull was crushed into a sickening new shape. Elias felt a wave of revulsion at Chuddath, then caught himself. *The praetorians attacked him, not the other way around. He risked his life to do his duty to Amerdath.*

Elias released Pendrake's hand with a hard squeeze and turned to Chuddath. "I've come to—"

"Yes." The warrior flipped the word off negligently.

Pendrake leaned close to Elias as if to share a confidence. "He heard everything you and the Imperator said."

Elias was amazed, then remembered the intelligence reports on the Ornyl warrior caste he'd read while in the navy. One section detailed their incredible hearing. *But Briana and I were thirty meters away,* he thought, practically whispering. He felt suddenly small and inferior standing between the two huge aliens. *How do we humans have any power at all over beings like this?*

"Obviously you heard everything, too," he said to Pendrake.

"You may rely on my discretion, as always." Pendrake gave him a humble smile that half irritated, half amused him.

Elias turned back to Chuddath. "Will you stand aside?" he whispered.

The warrior barely touched his abdomen, producing a smooth, chilling parody of a whisper. "I accept the word of Kane."

Elias felt himself sagging with relief. "Do you need medical attention?"

"None that is available . . . here. I will mend. I've lost this . . . arm before. You were witness."

Elias remembered the pitched battle only a few months past, the rebel laser that had cleanly sliced off one of Chuddath's fighting arms. The left? He could not recall; only that it had grown back with incredible speed. "Fine," he said. "I may want to talk to you soon—a small matter of some s'uniphs in a breeding frenzy."

Chuddath made no comment. Elias searched the featureless compound eyes. They gazed everywhere and nowhere, as impenetrable as a fly's.

He signaled Briana by turning back to her, as she'd ordered. Beside her, he saw Alvar Sabin, talking urgently in her ear. She cut Sabin off with a sharp hand gesture.

"Chuddath, I command you to stand aside."

"Yes, *Imperator*."

Elias thought he heard the slightest touch of derision, but then the Ornyl warrior hunched away from the vault door, opening the way to Gregory Amerdath, fallen Imperator.

"I wonder if Father can hear us," Briana said in a hushed whisper.

Elias stared at the head of her father, feeling a mixture of sadness and a horror that was old now, but impossible to suppress. The surgifoam looked like a pillow around the base of his neck. Amerdath's eyes were closed, his facial muscles totally relaxed. His skin had a healthy, pink flush, and his hair, thick and white as it had been in his youth, was neatly combed.

"No, he can't hear us," Elias said.

"But I still get the feeling he's aware," Briana persisted. "Maybe subliminally. Maybe he smells us. He could be flashing on a dream of us right now. God, it makes my skin crawl."

"Then let's get out of here," Elias suggested. He was tired of her; weary with adrenaline withdrawal. He ached with bruised muscles, flogged nerves, and he could feel the interior of the vault closing in on him. Amerdath could not be awake, not in any way, or he'd have gone screaming mad in this womblike place, just as Alvar Sabin believed.

Elias felt a sudden bitter sadness at the irony of Amerdath's fate. Outside this vault, thousands of people loved and schemed and walked amid royal splendor, while the architect of that splendor sucked existence through tubes in his neck and lived out the half-lives of metal slivers. Amerdath's palace was a wonder of the world—shell upon shell of beta-steel expanding outward from this silent vault, honeycombed with a hundred thousand rooms and the ever-curving corridors. It could be seen for hundreds of miles in every direction, sitting like a many-tiered crown atop its desert mesa. Even that towering rock had been shaped to Amerdath's will, carved and blasted by his engineers into a smooth column, thrusting up two hundred and thirty meters from the Earth like a mailed fist taunting the gods.

And now the gods taunted Amerdath back.

Elias remembered the words on the note of warning, sent to Amerdath before the first assassination attempt. *Mene mene tekel upharsin:* Thou art weighed in the balances and found wanting.

"Elias?"

He realized she'd been talking to him. "What?"

"I said we can't leave yet. It would look suspicious —we worked too hard to get in here. Besides, I need to talk to you, and this place is as good as any."

Resigning himself, Elias found a chair, used by one of the people who maintained Amerdath's medical equipment. He sat, not caring about the breach of royal etiquette. If Briana minded, she did not show it. She turned her back on her father's head and toyed with the array of medical equipment on a rolling cart. Elias became aware of the measured, metronomic click of Amerdath's heart-lung module. At first the mechanical parody of a heartbeat chilled him. Then it became hypnotic, lulling him further into fatigue. He closed his eyes to rest them.

Briana said, "I called you back from space for a reason." He heard her take a deep breath. "I've lost three imperial inspectors on Cassiodorus."

Elias opened his eyes and looked up at her, forcing his brain back to work: Cassiodorus. The colony planet where the ore for beta-steel was mined. The only place the ore could be found, and thus of vital importance to Earth. Imperial inspectors went there quarterly, conducting detailed inspections to make sure the mining was up to quota—and that none of the precious ore was being diverted from the imperial monopoly.

He began to feel interested. "Lost them?"

Briana made an irritated throwaway gesture with her hand. "Two heart attacks and a stroke. All fatal. All before they could file their reports. Cassiodorus is a heavy-G planet, as I'm sure you know. Almost 1.5 G's, to be more precise. People not used to the extra weight could certainly keel over. In fact, it's happened once or twice before, in the past. But I think three inspectors in a row—and all fatal—is damned suspicious."

"So do I," Elias said.

"You understand what it might mean?"

"The Cassiodorans are trying to break the monopoly."

"Exactly. I'm pretty sure my viceroy there—Cay

Endor—is loyal. But if there's a covert rebel faction, they could be siphoning off ore. They might even have a beta-steel factory, probably not there, but underground on some other colony. If they do, and if they've been stealing ore, you know the first thing they'd do with it."

Elias felt her suspicions infecting him, dark and frightening, driving out the last of his fatigue. "They'd build dreadnoughts."

She looked grim. "Exactly. If they succeed, it would mean war. Think what that renegade, DuMorgan, could do against us with a couple of dreadnoughts. We wouldn't be dealing with an underground anymore, little bands of hit and run terrorists. They'd bring it to us, right here—they'd try to take Earth."

Elias detected an undercurrent of excitement in her voice and was both repelled and amazed. Clearly she knew the dangers, but just as clearly, she relished the thought of a face-to-face war with the rebels. The dreaming remnant of a man behind her would have fought such a war if he had to, and fought it well. But it would have appalled him. Briana would fight the same war with savage relish, and probably even more brilliantly than he. But she was too much the general, thinking she would defeat any attack. The sheer mass of numbers would, indeed, favor her.

But if DuMorgan *did* have dreadnoughts—even one of them . . .

"I need you to go there, Elias. Investigate the deaths of those inspectors. Do the work they were supposed to do, and bring me a report."

Elias felt his spirits lift. He would escape the palace after all. Space, a distant planet, a puzzle to solve. His blood began to sing in his ears. He thought of the dreadnoughts again, the brilliant and dashing Richard DuMorgan, so very dangerous. Yes, Imperator, he thought, you need me—more than you realize.

But what about the *Wager?* Someone tried to kill Martha and Pendrake and him, and he couldn't just . . .

*Damn!* A dark excitement filled Elias: Yes, someone had tried to kill him, and Briana had just told him *why!*

". . . a sizable renumeration, of course," Briana was saying. "And you would take Pendrake with—"

"Who else knows you plan to send me to Cassiodorus?"

She looked startled and he realized he'd snapped at her. "No one," she said. "I ran the odds on the inspector deaths through my compusayer, of course . . ." Realization dawned in her face. "You think that's why your ship was sabotaged!"

"What better motive does anyone have?"

"But, but, it's preposterous," she sputtered. "The compusayer is keyed to my own voiceprint only. It's a machine. It can't turn traitor. And there are dozens of safeguards on the data banks."

"Maybe someone with a dozen and one tricks got in," Elias said. "Then tried to stop me before I even got started."

Briana paled. "A traitor. He—or she—would have to be very close to me. Damn! Damn it to hell!"

"It's only a possibility," Elias reminded her. "Call in an outside expert to run a sweep on your compusayer. Don't let your present staff know about it."

She nodded. "I'm sorry, Elias. But you'll have to go anyway, even though this makes it all the riskier."

He saw the gloss in her eyes again, tears close to spilling, and felt a sharp foreboding. As if reading his mind, she reached for him, trying to pull him close. He resisted, and she dropped his hands, spun around, hiding her face.

All the dread of the past few days rose up to overwhelm him. He heard his voice, a bare whisper. "It's true, isn't it."

She turned back to him. "What's true?"

"You're pregnant."

She gave him a brittle smile. "Yes, it's true." Her voice was small, betraying the fear and vulnerability behind the smile. He was stricken suddenly with a feeling of tenderness for her. He held his hands out and she took them again. He squeezed her fingers wordlessly, shocked at how cold they were. Her smile faded and she gave him a searching look.

"Are you glad?" he asked gently.

"Yes, I am," she answered.

"Then I'm glad for you."

"But not for yourself?"

He looked at her, feeling a curious mixture of dread and eagerness. "I don't know how to feel for myself," he said. "Are you saying that I *am* the father?"

"If I said yes, would you take my word?" She bit her lip. "No, don't answer that. You have a right to the truth —there's no other way. There were other men, right around the same time. You were the last. I wish now that you had been the only one." She gave a convulsive laugh. "I was only a dumb princess then, not an all-wise Imperator."

He smiled, feeling a strange dislocation. It was so tempting to see only the woman that stood before him now—the surprising maturity, the humanity—and forget the cold, bloodthirsty woman she had been only an hour ago. But they were one and the same.

"We can know for sure if I'm the father," he said. "There should be a biopsy punch on that cart—they monitor your father's neck tissue for necrosis."

"A punch?"

"Looks something like a syringe."

"Oh, this thing."

"Yes, that's it." He showed her how to use it, then rolled up his sleeve. A feeling of fatalism swept over him. Either way, there would be emotional pain, but he must know—they both must. He felt first the pinprick, then a slight burn as she twisted the punch and withdrew the cells. He counted back in his mind, trying to fix the approximate day that she seduced him—that he'd *let* her seduce him.

"It should be several weeks yet," he told her, "before the fetus is big enough for a safe genetic cross match. But take the punch to the lab right away."

She nodded. Beyond her, he saw the silent, impassive face of her father and suddenly felt, as she had earlier, that Amerdath was somehow aware of them, aware that the father of his grandchild might be standing a few feet away. He wished now that Amerdath *could* be awakened. I need you, he thought. Your wisdom, your experience.

"Will you want to take Dr. Reik with you to Cassiodorus?" Briana asked.

He felt a warning twinge. "Why would I want to do that?"

"Don't pretend, Elias. I see the way you look at her." Suddenly, Briana was the cold, dangerous woman again.

He felt afraid for Martha. "She's just a friend. Pendrake invited her to Cephan." Technically true, he thought. But only technically. He suppressed a groan, feeling disloyal, slimy.

Briana gave him a cool half smile. "Shall we go? I believe you have some packing to do."

He followed her from the vault.

"So Dr. Reik is just a 'friend.' I'm glad, Elias."

She did not look at him, and he knew, with a sinking feeling, that she was not convinced.

CAREFUL TO USE HIS LEFT HAND ONLY, ELIAS PULLED
himself along the docking tube toward the battleship,
letting his legs trail out behind. The weightlessness felt
good after the buffeting crush of the shuttle. But he
could not shake a simmering anger at himself.

*Martha, I'm sorry.*

I really hurt her, he thought miserably.

Her embrace clung to him in memory. Over and
over, he felt himself breaking it, pulling away quickly,
because Briana had been watching *and you had no
choice, damn it!* Elias was filled with hopeless despair.
God, bad enough if he could have explained a few minutes later, apologized the next day, but he was gone
now. They were cut off, maybe forever, and if it *was*
forever, the final image searing his mind would be
Martha, standing there on the apron of the pad, lips
pressed together bravely, her nose just that little bit
red.

*Damn you, Briana!*

With savage concentration, he imagined the palace
receding over the rim of Earth, now nearly five hundred klicks behind and below him. He could almost feel
Briana's hold on him stretching thin over the yawning
chasm of space. It gave him a small relief, easing the

tension in his neck and shoulders a little. *Sayonara, Briana. I'm rid of you, at least for a while. And this time you won't be jerking me back before I can get past Luna.*

He tried to enjoy the sense of liberation. Instead he felt a vague sense of loss.

Regret at leaving the child in Briana's belly?

No. He'd not know for some time yet if it was his. And anyway, it was barely into the fetal stage. He'd be back before it was born—unless he discorped like the three men sent to Cassiodorus before him. The morbid thought sent a chill along his neck. He shrugged it off, projecting a twisted grin into the dim, swaying cylinder ahead of him. *Forget dying. You're not that anxious to escape Briana.*

Forgetting, he stretched his right hand ahead and grabbed the line. Pain flared in his bruised knuckles and shot up his arm. He was aware, suddenly, of a throbbing in his neck—must've twisted it in the fight yesterday without knowing. He yanked himself along to the end of the docking tube, relishing the punishing stabs of pain in his hand. He punched the glowing entry button, biting back a yelp and ignoring Pendrake's inquiring cough behind him. After a second, the hatch cycled open. He released the line and grabbed the rim of the hole above him, conscious for a dizzying second of his legs dangling at a crazy angle behind him. Then he reoriented, imagining himself in a manhole, levering himself up and through. He straightened and found himself facing a tall man in the working whites of the Imperial Navy: thinning hair, slight paunch, but the four gold stripes circled his wrist with all the authority a man in space could ever need. Behind him Elias saw an honor guard of marines drawn up in a rigid row along the curving floor of the corridor.

"Captain Streetham," said the naval officer, holding out his hand. "Welcome aboard the I.S. *Seraphim*, Mr. Kane."

"Thank you." Elias offered his left hand, shaking

awkwardly. The corner of Streetham's mouth twitched, as if he knew the reason, and Elias flushed with embarrassment.

"And this must be the legendary Pendrake," Streetham said.

Pendrake levered himself smoothly up from the hatch and gave a slight bow. "You are most kind, Captain. But I would hardly consider myself the stuff of legend."

Streetham smiled. "You're too modest. The whole planet knows how you saved the Palace from those rebels. Punching through half a meter of granite with your bare fist."

Elias watched Pendrake turn a deeper orange and felt a touch of pity at his discomfort.

"Actually," Pendrake said gravely, "I kicked it. And it was probably more like fifteen centimeters, though I did not stop to measure it—"

Streetham laughed. "Well, try not to do too much kicking in your sleep. We've quartered you here in the outermost ring of the ship as Mr. Kane requested. And our hull is simple steel—the *Seraphim*'s no dreadnought, I'm afraid."

Elias detected an odd note in Streetham's voice. Resentment? Was Streetham less than thrilled at diverting his ship into what everyone hoped would be mere taxi service? Small wonder if he was. The *Seraphim* was the next biggest thing in space to a dreadnought. Half a kilometer long, a crew of five thousand—plus a light legion of marines—and awesome firepower, including the new implosion missiles.

Don't blame me, Elias thought sourly. He wished again that he'd been able to talk Briana into a corvette. Hell, a scout ship would have been plenty. She didn't seem to understand that an imperial show of force would only inflame whatever anti-Earth sentiment might be harbored on Cassiodorus. Besides, mysteries were not solved by dreadnoughts, but by careful and unobtrusive investigation.

"You were navy yourself, weren't you, Mr. Kane?"

"A long time ago."

"The Andinaz raids, I believe. You made it from ensign to lieutenant in six months. Rammed one of the bastards' dragonships, if I recall correctly, and blew it up."

"A mistake," Elias said. "I was trying to get the hell out of there, and turned the wrong way."

Streetham gave him a knowing smile. "Perhaps you'd like to review the honor guard?"

Elias walked down the rigid row of marines. The faces seemed absurdly young to him. Their eyes tried with fierce pride to gaze through him, but many of the faces unbraced when he looked into them, letting slip awe and admiration. Their breathless regard depressed him. Were these nice young people hoping to follow the "famous" Elias Kane into battle, to win some of the glory that fate had sent his way? He wished he could give them whatever they thought he had, here and now, painlessly. Because, if the colonists on Cassiodorus *were* diverting beta-steel ore, and if they managed to build dreadnoughts, some of these proud, eager young faces would not get much older.

Elias reached the end of the line, an older face—the sergeant—scarred on both cheeks in the telltale pattern of an Andinaz pincer. No awe in this face. The scars made Elias think of Richard DuMorgan. Only a few men had ever gotten that close to an Andinaz and lived; DuMorgan was one of them. Elias felt a pang of sorrow thinking of the terrible loss: DuMorgan had been the empire's brilliant and stalwart ally. As its foe, he would be the very devil to defeat.

"Thank you, Sergeant. *Usmet danaar.*"

The man's eyes focused on him with surprise and a new respect. "*Usmet gheraal,* sir," he responded, promising in the Andinaz dialect, to "keep his charges well."

Elias turned and found Streetham right behind him, his face unreadable. "Very good, Mr. Kane. A bos'n's gone after your gear in the shuttle. If you'll follow me, I'll show you your quarters, then get us under way."

Streetham led them along the corridor. Elias fought the tendency to lean into the continual, slight upgrade. At the same time, ahead, the bulkheads and doors rose straight off the curvature, seeming to lean into *him.* He knew there was no escape—wherever you stood in any ship's corridor, it would rise behind and ahead of you. He was aware suddenly that he was spinning, head to the core of the ship, feet pressed outward, only the hull between him and a long, tumbling fall into eternity. His stomach lurched and he swallowed. *Relax. It's just like gravity, except it's always straight down through your body. Meanwhile, just keep your eyes on your feet until you acclimate.*

He said, "How long do you plan to take getting to Cassiodorus, if I may ask."

"Mr. Kane, you may ask almost anything," Streetham said in a neutral voice. "My orders make that quite plain. A week would be most economical on the Opperman drives. But I presume you'd like to get there faster."

"Yes," Elias said shortly, tired of Streetham's bland coyness.

"Two jumps minimum," Streetham said. "I could have us there in eighteen hours, but—"

"That's not necessary. I imagine you'd want to go subspace around the Freytag Anomaly and again around the yC-238 farther out. That would still get us there in less than forty-eight."

Streetham cast a surprised look over his shoulder, and Elias felt a small gratification, then was annoyed at himself for showing off. Briana's orders gave him virtually the powers of an onboard admiral. But—even for an attending admiral—on all matters concerning the ship in space, the captain ruled. Though Streetham would risk the Imperator's wrath later, he could still refuse or countermand any order Elias might give. It would be best to avoid all appearance of baiting him.

"Whatever you think best, Captain," Elias said.

"Thank you, Mr. Kane. Here we are." Streetham ducked through an oval bulkhead, leading the way into a two-room suite with head between. There was a bunk, a desk and two chairs in each half of the duplex. The rooms were spacious even for a battleship. Though bare of personal items, they held a lingering aura of warmth, an indefinable lived-in feel. Elias realized with a twinge of guilt that he had probably displaced two lieutenant commanders. A simple closet with bunks would have been more to his liking, but it would have been a serious breach of manners to protest.

"And here is the G-dial," Streetham said, fingering a knob on the wall. "This suite doubles as one of our acclimatization berths. You can get up to 1.5 max. Of course, if you like, I can get you beyond that with increased spin." There was an undertone of reluctance in Streetham's voice, and Elias understood—and approved. The outer shells of a warship were, in general, like the belowdecks of ships of old. Only a scattering of officers quartered there; the vast majority were bottom rankers. It wouldn't inconvenience Streetham or his circle of officers that dwelled in the weightless hub to throw on extra spin. But he cared enough for his men not to want them put under extra physical stress just for two passengers.

"I'm sure that won't be necessary, Captain," Elias said. "Temporary extra weight won't help us that much. When we hit planetside, our knees are going to buckle, one way or the other."

Streetham looked relieved. "As you wish. If you need anything, don't hesitate to hail me on the box. The legion's under Colonel Teegarten. I'm sure he'll be by to pay his respects. If there's nothing else, I'll get us under way."

"Thank you, Captain."

The moment Streetham was gone, a bosun appeared with their gear. Elias stashed his quickly under his bunk and paced while Pendrake, with his customary butler-like care, put away his own things. Elias watched the acceleration warning light over the door with growing impatience. The shuttle must have cast off by now. What was Streetham waiting for? Was this a little lesson to his VIP passengers? *I'm captain, and this ship moves when I say.*

Elias realized he was chafing and tried to put Streetham out of his mind. The man seemed decent and solid enough. Obsessing over him was just a pathetic attempt to bury unsafe worries with safe ones. He felt the weight of depression settling in again. Even the unimaginable, sundering span of a paraspace jump wasn't going to wipe from his heart his last act with Martha. He settled heavily onto the cot, then forced his back straight, determined to throw off his oppressive gloom. What he had done, he had done for Martha. The last thing she needed was a jealous Imperator, thirsting for her blood. It would be so easy for Briana to arrange an accident for her while he was away. He did not want to return to Earth to find Martha dead in a flitter accident or a plunge down a "malfunctioning" dropchute. He thought of the baboons in her lab, brought in for experiments in the grisly new science of maintaining Amerdath's head apart from his body. He was struck by a horrible image of Martha lying on the floor in a pool of blood, one of the cages standing open. A sad-faced Briana: *So sorry, Elias, but she must have neglected to latch the cage. We've had the animal destroyed, of course.* He shuddered.

"Are you all right, Elias? You look ill."

He looked up at Pendrake and forced a grin. "I'm fine, oh legendary one."

Pendrake gave him a vexed grimace which quickly faded to a look of concern. "I think you are not fine, Elias. I saw what happened at the launch pad, and understand why you did it. It was a noble, unselfish act—and it must pain you a great deal."

Elias felt embarrassed—and better. He waved Pendrake off. "I promise not to call you legendary if you won't call me noble."

Pendrake remained sober. "Perhaps it would be best to let yourself experience the pain now."

With a twinge of irritation, Elias realized what he was saying. *Get it out of your system, because once you hit Cassiodorus, you can't afford to have it messing up your mind.* "I'm all right," he said. "Don't worry, I plan to keep my mind on our work."

Pendrake looked dismayed. "I did not mean it so crassly."

Elias softened, touched by his concern. "I know you didn't, my friend."

"Just what *is* our work on Cassiodorus to be, Elias? This has arisen so suddenly, I am not entirely sure what we hope to accomplish."

Elias explained about the three imperial inspectors, all dying of heart failure before they could file their reports; Briana's suspicions that a rebel faction might be siphoning off ore.

Pendrake nodded thoughtfully. "We have discussed this issue of dreadnoughts before," he said.

"Yes, and if I recall, you seemed sympathetic to the colonists." Elias was stricken suddenly with concern. In all the rush and his inner turmoil about Briana's pregnancy—and then his misery at hurting Martha—he had not considered how the mission would affect Pendrake. He'd just assumed Pendrake would be with him emotionally as well as physically. But Pendrake was no man's lackey. The realization that he had come close to treating him as one filled Elias with dismay. He rose, putting a hand on Pendrake's shoulder. "Is this going to cause you problems?"

Pendrake gave him a melancholy smile. "The whole issue of dreadnoughts causes me problems, Elias. I do not wish that the colonists had them, but rather, that no one did."

"I understand. But Earth does—and has for several

decades. And in all that time, she has never used them against the colonies."

"Only, I think, because she has not needed to."

"Exactly. But if the rebel factions get a few dreadnoughts, I can promise you that Earth *will* need to."

"What makes you so certain? Do the colonists not say that they want the dreadnoughts only to defend themselves against attacks such as the Andinaz raids?"

"The 'viceroy' governments, yes, all of whom are—at least in theory—still imperials. But those same viceroys have no way to guarantee that any dreadnoughts given them could be kept from rebel hands. The planetary defense navies are no doubt infiltrated with rebels biding their time. Make no mistake, my friend. No matter what the viceroys say, if the rebels get dreadnoughts, they'll attack Earth."

"But why should they?"

Elias remained patient. He's smart, he reminded himself. In some ways, smarter than you. But for centuries, his entire race has had a horrified aversion to violence in any form. So don't expect him to understand the fine points of modern naval warfare. Elias said, "It's a matter of strategy. Three things have happened in recent history to revolutionize modern interstellar warfare. The first two were the synthesis of beta-steel, and the discovery of paradoxical space which was inferred from it. The third was the discovery that, because of its size, a dreadnought armored in beta-steel goes an order of magnitude faster through a paraspace jump than any other ship.

"The way this has revolutionized warfare is in breaking down the distinctions between offense and defense. The blinding speed of a dreadnought in paraspace means that, if a hostile ship appears off a colony planet, an imperial one can strike it and return to a defensive posture off Earth in hours. Which means that most of the imperial fleet can remain near Earth at any given time. It has taken us decades to mine enough beta-steel ore on Cassiodorus to make our fleet of ten dreadnoughts. So even if the colonists *have* diverted ore, they couldn't have enough for more than two dreadnoughts at the most. Even so, each one of them would be a potential planet killer—and that planet is Earth: It would do the colonists no good to have those dreadnoughts, then spend all their time in deep space trying to avoid contact. As long as the imperial government exists, they will not think themselves free. Their best—and only—chance for victory would be to try to jump in close enough to strike Earth before the surrounding fleet could stop them. Their chances would be better than I like to think about."

Pendrake looked grim. "So much pointless savagery. And you are all brothers. Couldn't this be resolved if Earth simply relinquished her governance of the colonies?"

Elias became exasperated. "Damn it, now you sound like a rebel propagandist. Understand this: The empire is culturally the direct descendant of the old United States, which finally imposed world government in 2041. U.S. history prevails—in the thinking of Earthmen and colonists alike—all the way back to the founding of the nation, when the U.S. colonies defeated Great Britain in *the* revolutionary war. Thereafter, U.S. government was never overthrown by internal revolution, but rather changed by gradual evolution.

"So, to portray themselves as heroic revolutionaries, the colonists see only one model—that first 'glorious' revolution against the English. They consider themselves the new Nathan Hales, Paul Reveres, Thomas Paines. Give me liberty or give me death.

"But there are two problems with this: First, Earth has not denied personal liberty, human rights or any other democratic privilege to the colonists. Colonists live under exactly the same laws as Earth citizens—who also, incidentally, are not allowed to have their own personal dreadnoughts. Earthers and colonists are taxed at the same rate and enjoy all the same privileges of movement, assembly and economic self-determination. Gregory Amerdath, who until a few months ago *was* the empire, can in no way be compared to the old tyrant King George III."

Elias realized he was working himself into a high dudgeon but was unable to stop. It felt good to raise his voice, get steamed up. "Second, there *wasn't* just one revolution in U.S. history, there were two. The colonists have conveniently forgotten the other one—the U.S. 'Civil War.' It was, in fact, an attempted revolution that failed. And it was a damned good thing for U.S. civilization that it did."

"I have read somewhat on that part of your history," Pendrake mused. "And I would certainly agree it was a good thing that the revolution—or rebellion of the slavers—failed. Slavery was a terrible moral wrong, and its defeat was necessary to the advancement of civilization. But the colonists do not advocate slavery."

Elias gave him a look of mock surprise. "Interesting that you, of all people, should say that."

Pendrake looked sheepish. "Very well, it is true that the slavers who abducted me from Cephan and sold me to Spencer Hogate were colonists, but it was not lawful."

"Slavery is not the issue now, and it was actually not the predominant issue then. The real issue is the same in both cases. The rebels—then and now—don't want the central government telling them what they can and can't do.

"Likewise, we must resist the rebels now for the same reasons we did then: the obligation of a fair and evenhanded government to keep all its people moving forward together. If the Unionists had failed, the United States would have broken into fragments. The principle of secession, once established, would in all probability have been reenacted over and over until the former nation consisted of dozens of splinter fiefdoms ripe for plucking by hostile powers."

Pendrake looked thoughtful. "And now you see the

alien cultures your species has encountered in space as the current hostile powers."

"Some of them, yes. If the whole universe except for us were peopled by Cephantines, there would be no problem—"

"Except, perhaps, for the Cephantines," Pendrake said drily.

Elias felt himself flushing. "All right, smart ass, you zinged me that time. If it's any comfort, I'd be on the Cephantines' side."

"I know that, Elias."

"But in our universe, Cephantines are—sadly—the exception rather than the rule. You've seen what Ornyl warriors can do. The Moitan are contesting us on planet after planet—so far, with their slippery diplomacy, but who knows how long that will last? Remember, they supplied the rebels with the device that almost brought down the palace and toppled our government. And the Andinaz have already had a crack at us. Against them, Gregory Amerdath and Earth's dreadnoughts fought side by side with Richard DuMorgan's planetary navy— the colonists, mind you—to repel the Andinaz attack off Alpha Centauri IV. Together, we beat them. Alone, DuMorgan would have lost—and Earth itself might have been next. . . ."

Pendrake held up his hands. "I surrender. You are most persuasive."

Elias caught his breath and grinned ruefully. "Sorry. I didn't mean to get on my soapbox."

Pendrake gave him a baffled look and he laughed, feeling energized, almost good. Pendrake had made him forget Martha for a moment, his miserable leavetaking from Earth. . . .

"You fnip," he said, realization dawning. "You were just playing devil's advocate."

"No," Pendrake said gravely. "You told me things that I had not considered. I am grateful."

Elias gave an ironic bow, thinking, I'm the one who's grateful. His eye caught a flash of red—the acceleration warning. "Here we go," he said. "Looks like Streetham plans a little sublight maneuvering before we jump."

Pendrake sat beside him on the bunk and followed his example, leaning back into the cushioned bulkhead. "About time," Elias added, feeling a queasy jolt of anticipation in his stomach. He felt his back pressing into the cushion as the *Seraphim* accelerated in a long, smooth leap. He wished suddenly that he had opened the port at his feet—he might have been able to catch one last look at Earth—but then the acceleration stopped and the air crackled with a glitter of electron displacement. He had the familiar, brief sensation that everything around him had jumped a fraction out of kilter, and he knew that Earth was no longer outside his window.

Depression settled briefly back on him, but he shook it off, determined not to succumb again.

Pendrake stood. "I still have some things to put away. If you will excuse me—"

The signal above the door pinged. Pendrake gave him a questioning look.

"Probably the marine colonel," Elias said. "Teegarten. Would you mind?"

Pendrake pushed the release and the door slipped back. Elias got up to meet the colonel and stopped, dumbstruck, as Martha Reik stepped over the low sill into the cabin.

## 5

"I CAME UP FOR THE REST OF MY KISS." MARTHA GAVE him a rakish grin.

Elias felt a surge of exhilaration. He covered the deck between them in one step, sweeping her into his arms, wildly happy to see her. So this was why they'd taken so long to move out—Captain Streetham had had to wait for Martha heading up behind him in a second shuttle.

I get another chance! Elias thought.

*But why?*

He gave the kiss everything he had, tasting her minted lipstick, filling his head with her rose petal scent. Her tongue darted mischievously, causing his heart to lift and race. He flushed, aware suddenly of Pendrake. But he was damned if he'd pull away from her again. Instead he clutched her rump with exaggerated lust, making *her* push off with a little gasp.

"Sorry. I've been in space too long without a woman."

She gave an incredulous laugh. "Two hours?"

He sobered. "A very long time, when you know it will only grow longer. I didn't like the way we parted."

Her eyes misted. "I understood."

Elias glanced at Pendrake, but the dusky orange

face looked distant with daydream, offering privacy. Elias was grateful for the sham, but changed the subject anyway. "Briana sent you."

Martha nodded. "She had another shuttle waiting. The minute you took off, she ordered me into it. She'd even packed a bag for me. Probably two months' worth of praetorian underwear."

"Or a chastity belt."

Pendrake's pose of detachment broke with an embarrassed cough. "If you will excuse me, I believe I will finish unpacking."

Martha winced. "I'm sorry, Pendrake. We forgot there's a gentleman present."

Elias gave a wounded harrumph and Pendrake smiled. "It is good to have you with us, Dr. Reik."

She squeezed the huge, three-fingered hand; the alien gave a little bow, then slipped from the room.

Elias gazed at Martha, suddenly uneasy. "What reason did Briana give you?"

"A pretty good one, actually. The previous inspectors died of stroke or heart failure, supposedly because of the sudden exposure to the heavy-G environment. I'm being sent along to inquire further into the medical circumstances of the deaths and assess whether Cassiodorus is really so brutal to the unacclimated. After all, my background *is* in medical research."

"Makes sense," Elias said.

"Yes."

"But so would legs on a snake."

"Huh?"

"Briana's deliberately putting you in danger." He felt a growing, indignant anger.

"Briana said you'd be upset—that you wouldn't want me along. That's why she waited and popped it on us both like this."

Elias took her hands. "She was wrong. I do want you along. But I can't help remembering the old Bible story about King David: He wanted the wife of one of his soldiers, so he sent the poor devil to the front lines of a murderous battle, knowing he'd be killed by the enemy."

"So we'll be careful, look after each other."

He made an effort to put aside his paranoia. "That last part sounds rather pleasant," he said.

"Yes." Martha placed his hands on her waist, held them there. He squeezed gently, delighting in her smooth, lean flesh, his heart beginning to race, his breath shortening in anticipation. She gave him the lopsided smile he loved, her face warming with that familiar, unfathomable beauty that so beguiled him. "Is the door to Pendrake's quarters locked?" she whispered.

"No, but it might as well be." He pulled her to him, filling with a tender hope. *I want to love again,* he thought. *I want to love* you.

Her hands busied themselves with his clothes. He reached around, smiling as their hands and wrists brushed, until she stood before him as naked as he. Her skin was pale, lightly freckled along her forearms and above her breasts. Seeing this part of her for the first time enchanted him, the little mysteries of her flesh, making him wonder suddenly what *she* wanted—from him, from her life.

Then his ability to think vaporized in pleasure as he let his hands travel her body, drawing waves of excitement deep into him—*ah, that's nice!*

He pulled her onto the narrow cot with him, feeling enclosed and protected by the upper bunk overhead. The universe contracted to Martha, her heat, her dizzying, secret smells, her hands roaming his back and flanks, pulling, pressing. So warm, soft, wanting him as he tried to get deeper, reaching, feeling her wanting him, yes, *yes!*

Distantly he heard her little cries growing, filling with a rapture so greedy that it silvered her voice with an exquisite sheen. He felt her hands clawing his back, his rump, striking sparks of agonized pleasure where the praetorian had kicked him. He clung to the last scrap of control, clamping his teeth to keep from shouting as she goaded him to explosion.

He floated in well-being.

He realized that he was lying on top of her, the length of her body cushioning him. He made an effort to roll off, but she held him in place.

"You're not too heavy," she breathed into his ear, her moist breath sending an aftershock of pleasure down his spine. She ran fingers along his ribs. "In fact, you're not heavy enough. How much do you weigh these days?"

"Same as always, Doc," he mumbled.

"Then why are your clothes so loose?"

"It's the new look. Baggy." Thinking was still an effort, even to joke. He had not felt this viscerally content in a long time.

"New look, uh-huh. You've had that outfit I just took off you for as long as I've known you. How's it manage to keep up with current fashion?"

"Maybe Pendrake's trying on my clothes when I'm out."

She laughed and gave up, turning onto her side, inviting him to nestle, spoon fashion. He fitted his body against her without desire, enjoying instead the comforting softness and warmth of her. He thought about how he'd lost the weight going into a depression after Beth. Odd that it hadn't happened right away, not while he was still after her killer, but afterward, when there was nothing more to be done. Long time ago—or beginning to seem that way. Was that all right? Yes. Elias felt a drowsy sense of wonder.

Gotta get those pounds back. Eat, drink and be, if not merry, at least less morose. In fact, I'm hungry right now. Too nice to move. Lie here . . . few more minutes, then get up and . . . get? . . . g . . .

When he awoke, Martha was gone.

Elias stood in the shuttle bay with Captain Streetham, staring with fascination at the huge, red ball of Cassiodorus that nearly filled the launch controller's viewport. The sunside crescent of the planet gleamed like a gaping, bloody mouth, sending a shiver of foreboding through him.

"That's a pretty high albedo," he observed.

"Highest I've seen," Streetham agreed. "The soil is highly viscous—basically wet clay. But it's brighter even than most water planets because the terrain is pretty flat, no wave troughs to scatter reflection. Get used to that red color. The atmosphere down there's so thick it reflects the red back down too. They tell me that, most days, the sky looks like blood. I don't think I'll be needing my new K-scope on this planet."

Elias realized Streetham was talking about the new, homeotropic "bloodhound" devices developed by the navy to track down sailors who went AWOL on port planets.

"Nights are better," Streetham went on. "Especially when their green moon, Reseda, peeks through the overcast."

Elias's nose began to itch as the antigravs of the shuttle pitched up into the subaudible range, vibrating his nasal septum. The craft was ready, Pendrake and Martha were waiting inside, and yet he lingered, staring down at the grinning hemorrhage in space. It repelled him even as his psyche sensed the pull of its crushing gravity.

He did not want to go down. The journey on the *Seraphim* had been too brief after all. With the last barrier broken, he had made love to Martha, again and again, touring her body until he knew it better than his own. Pleasure, yes, rapture. And a startling truth dawning: that he *did* want a child, very badly. Briana's pregnancy had pushed that into the open.

But how impossibly complicated it all was.

With Martha it would not be. He *liked* Martha, and so the last two days had happened, as if he thought he could, by some fantastic alchemy, switch the new life growing in Briana's womb to Martha's. He kept seeing himself holding a baby in his arms, protecting it while it slept, kissing its round downy cheeks, aching with love and awe.

He found himself grimacing in exasperation. This is how he'd prepared himself for his mission, not with hard thought and planning, but with feverish coupling and endless reveries about babies.

Staring down at Cassiodorus he was stricken by a sudden, dread certainty. *I'm going to die down there.*

His mind focused with a sudden, painful clarity. Was that what wanting a child was all about? Just having someone with his genes to carry on after he was gone? If so, then he was unworthy of a child.

No, he thought firmly. I want it to love.

But he knew it was both.

Streetham coughed discreetly. Elias turned and offered his hand. "I appreciate your hospitality."

"I regret I couldn't do more, Mr. Kane. But the trip was a bit rushed, and we barely saw you."

Was Streetham being sly? His face was poker straight. "You were better off without me in your way."

"We'll try to stay out of your way too, Mr. Kane. But I'm sending a portable subspace radio along with you. Neues Eisen is near their equator, so we'll keep an easy geosynchronous orbit right above you. I'm sure you'll be fine—but we'll be up here if you need to hail us."

Elias gave Streetham a grim smile. "Very good, Captain. I believe we understand each other."

Martha took his hand after he'd strapped in beside her in the shuttle. He squeezed her fingers with a reassurance he could not feel. The shuttle burned quickly down the fierce gravity well, skipping and planing through the thick atmosphere before finally settling on the pad outside Neues Eisen with a barely perceptible bump. Elias led the way out the shuttle door and almost collapsed. Monstrous weight crushed through him, every cell dragging him down, bending his bones toward the center of the planet. He felt Pendrake's hand under his elbow and waved him off, wishing a second later that he hadn't. Even the damned air seemed heavy. He gasped, sucking it in with a huge effort, feeling it slide down to his lungs like warm sand.

The second step and the next breath were marginally less torturous. He strained to hold himself back from tumbling forward. If he stumbled in this gravity, his head would crack open like an egg on the concrete at the bottom of the ramp. At last he stepped down the last few centimeters onto the flat apron of the landing pad. A small delegation awaited them; beyond, he could see the squat skyline of Neues Eisen, rajinate of Cassiodorus. He forced himself forward, his feet scraping the pavement, feeling the heat penetrate the soles of his boots. His face was slimy with sweat. The man who stepped forward to meet him was squat and bearish, his legs slightly bowed. His grip was powerful.

"Welcome to Cassiodorus, Mr. Kane. I'm Granit Holz, special assistant to the viceroy."

Elias managed to mumble introductions to Pendrake and Martha. He could see the strain on Martha's face, but she was holding herself straight. Only Pendrake, with his immense reservoirs of strength, seemed unaffected. Of course—he was born on a heavy-G planet. But not like this. God, this heat, the weight. How could anyone doubt that men could die from heart failure here?

Elias stifled the thought. He could not be objective at this point.

"We try to keep welcoming ceremonies brief here on Cassiodorus," Holz boomed. "I hope you understand."

Elias gave a nod, forcing his head back up with an effort. Just let me lie down, he thought. And put a flower on my chest.

Holz ushered them to a ground car. The seat molded itself to him, supporting his weight. The relief almost brought tears to his eyes. Holz chattered with animation as the chauffer drove them along a ruler-straight road flanked by featureless, rust-colored flatlands. This close, the shine of trapped water was not visible; the soil looked like ordinary clay.

They entered the outskirts of the city and Elias forced his mind to work cataloging his impressions: There were other groundcars, but only a few people walked the sidewalks. He was struck by how straightbacked they all carried themselves, as though afraid the slightest hunch would allow the hideous gravity to snap them down onto their faces. The buildings were low, which was natural enough in such a crushing gravity. But the architecture was more severe than it needed to be—tan, boxlike buildings that offered no solace to the eye. The cross streets were equidistant, the city squared off into an unvarying grid. Functional, but without aesthetic value.

Neues Eisen—New Iron. Already he hated the place.

The groundcar emerged into an open square, the first break in the relentless monotony of the city. A squat, geodesic dome sat in the precise middle of the square. From its base, a dark semicircle beckoned them. The driver jockeyed their groundcar into it, plunging them into the welcome dimness of a long, igloo-type entry portal. They emerged into a soft-lit interior that arched gently above them. The car stopped at once. The doors popped up like bent wings and cool, air-conditioned air bathed Elias' face. He found he could push up easily from his seat. Thank God! The dome was gravity controlled.

Holz bounded out of the car with almost spastic spryness and Elias realized the man must spend little time in gravity suppression.

"This is the acclimatization center," the viceroy's assistant said. "I'll take you right to the water tank."

Elias' relief disappeared. "Water tank?"

"Total immersion for four hours. We've found it's the ideal way for off-worlders to adjust quickly. If you'll follow me, please."

He led them down an escalator, through a maze of

corridors. The walls and ceiling were composed of small ceramic tiles. But the opportunity to create mosaic patterns had been squandered. Every tile was the same color—a slick, gleaming yellow. Elias felt a sharp annoyance. How hard would it have been to set some pleasing pattern into the tiles? He felt like stopping Holz, demanding an explanation, then realized that his annoyance was really transmuted fear. *Water tanks, no one had told him, and he didn't want to. He was afraid, damn it!*

His brain swirled with agitation, imagining tons of water pressing down on him. The ocean, yes, crushing at the dome of Spencer Hogate's hopter, trapping him and Pendrake inside, and then the shark nosing around, waiting to tear at his suffocated body. . . .

Elias realized he was gulping air, turning lightheaded with panic. He forced the air from his lungs, made himself walk ten steps before breathing. His heart steadied a little. But he still didn't want to go into any water tank.

"Here we are," Holz said cheerily, ushering them into an anteroom. A technician in a white coat turned and nodded at them. Beyond him Elias could see a heavy door. A porthole in its center writhed with drifting, spiderwebby patterns of light. He could sense the tons of water beyond. His throat went dry with fear. The technician handed him a swimsuit and an oxyplex headmask with a built-in watermike and earphones, then passed out similar kits to Holz and the others. Elias wanted to drop his and run from the room.

"I'll go in with you the first half hour," Holz was saying. "I think you'll find the acclimatization tank quite ingenious. It gives your body a chance to work against extra resistance without having to simultaneously bear up under the added gravity of Cassiodorus."

"But aren't most of your buildings gravity controlled?" he asked Holz.

"Many, though not all. But I presume you'll not

want to spend your whole time inside. Not if you hope to inspect our mining operations."

"Of course not. It's just that . . ." Elias swallowed against the knot of fear in his throat. This was ridiculous. He hadn't even known he'd become afraid of water. Without consciously avoiding it, he'd managed never to go back into deep water—not since he and Pendrake had found themselves at the bottom of the Atlantic in that sabotaged hopter.

Elias followed Holz and Pendrake into a change room. He could feel his heart pounding as he put on the suit. Holz helped him pull on his oxyplex mask, cinching the chinstrap back around his neck beneath his earlobes. For a second Elias felt he was choking, then the strap self-adjusted to his jawbone, molding into the crevice of his neck to complete the seal. His sinuses cleared; he felt a heady lift and knew the oxyplex was filtering out everything but pure $O_2$. When he entered the tank, it would go on drawing oxygen from the water, blocking out the hydrogen atoms.

At least that was the way it was supposed to work.

Elias felt sweat building up between his face and the mask. Martha was already waiting in the anteroom. She gave him a questioning look. He bugged his eyes out and rowed his hands in front of his face like fish fins. She laughed and his terror eased a bit.

Holz led them through the door into the lock. "Here we go!" he said. The earphones mercifully reduced his booming voice to an insectile buzz. A dozen valves opened along the base of the chamber. Warm water gushed around their ankles, rising quickly to their knees. Elias stared at it in dread fascination as it climbed his chest. He felt himself straining up on tiptoe, angling his chin up, gasping as the water closed over his head. He realized that his watermike was broadcasting his panicked breathing to the others. Holz was gazing at him through the clear water, a trace of smile showing through the plastic of his rebreather.

Angrily Elias got hold of himself. He must not start

out this way, panicking in front of the people he'd come to investigate. They probably had little enough respect for Terran imperials as it was. They'd have none at all for him unless he pulled himself together now.

The inner door of the lock inched open and Holz stepped through, motioning them to follow. Elias noticed that he could walk with no tendency to drift up. The tank must be under planet-normal gravity, giving them sufficient weight to decrease the buoyancy water would give them on Earth. He followed Pendrake and Martha through the crystal water into the main chamber. It was walled in the same uniform yellow tiles as the corridor. Elias pulled himself along with sidestrokes of his arms. Each motion required extra effort from all of his muscles—but not as much as walking down that ramp from the shuttle. Elias began to feel a grudging respect for the idea of the tank.

"Why don't we sit for the first half hour," Holz said, motioning to benches sculpted into the sides of the tank. "I'll brief you a bit on Cassiodorus, then give you some exercises we've found helpful in preparing your muscles."

Elias settled onto the bench beside Holz, finding he could sit back comfortably. Martha sat across the tank with Pendrake. Her slim body stirred echoes of arousal in him.

". . . find that if you're careful," Holz was saying, "the planet will not present insurmountable dangers. But I must emphasize the word *careful*. Cassiodorus is *not* a hospitable planet. Besides the crushing gravity, the wastelands outside the cities offer many other nasty surprises to the unwary. The one most to be avoided is an indigenous life form we call sauroids. Very dangerous. They look like smaller versions of your *Tyrannosaurus rex* of ancient Earth. But they're quicker and more clever than the old dinosaurs were thought to be. Yes, immensely dangerous . . ."

"What do they eat?" Martha asked.

Holz grinned. "You—if they can."

Elias felt unreasonably annoyed, but held back an angry retort, realizing again that it was the fear. Why was anger so much more comfortable than fear? *Because, fnipbrain, you get a lot more credit in life from fighting than from running.*

"I imagine," Holz said, "your question is based on the fact that you didn't see a shred of vegetation on our way in. But farther out, there are rudimentary plants— enough to feed small herbivores. We have our own version of your rabbits and groundhogs, and the sauroids eat those. They *will* readily devour a man if they have the chance, but you shouldn't have to worry about them. I'm not going to take you that far out.

"Unfortunately, the main menace on this planet is far more prosaic. I refer to the air. Our continual effort to gouge beta-steel ore from the mines has adversely affected the air, I'm afraid. The old coal mines of Earth had coal dust. Here it is clay molecules. Cassiodoran 'clay' is not like any other clay in the universe. To be strictly accurate, it isn't really clay at all. The individual molecules are very small and have an affinity for water. Mining releases ground water laced with clay molecules into the lower air. Some of this brew joins the general humidity. Luckily, it's breathable—what isn't exhaled, the body excretes. We've no equivalent of black lung here. But the 'clay' continually settles out of the air into machinery, where it jams gears, shorts out circuits, and fouls up everything from antigrav units to groundcars. No one flies conventional aircraft on this planet. Even though the air at normal flight levels is fine, we haven't built a hangar yet that can keep the clay from building up in the engines when the planes are on the ground. That's why our planetary defense aircraft are all quartered on satellites."

Holz droned on. Elias lost track of what he was saying, noticing, instead, a slight itch around his nose. As he focused on it, it grew. The oxyplexed air he was breathing seemed suddenly damp, making him cough. In reflex, he covered his mouth. Despite the water, the material over his nose and mouth felt sticky, as if it were melting.

Acid?

The fear began to well up in him again. He tried to gulp a deep breath, felt a teaspoon of water go down his windpipe, lancing his lungs with fire. He rose, coughing, feeling the dilute sting of acid on his lips and nose. Pendrake started to get up across the tank. Then the oxyplex sloughed away entirely and Elias felt a blinding rush of panic as the water poured in around his nose and mouth.

ELIAS HELD HIS LAST, WATER-TAINTED BREATH, fighting the burning urge to cough, knowing if he gave in, he'd gasp more water and drown. *Hang on—the door, you can make it!* He struggled toward the tank entrance, half swimming, half running in the high gravity, his toes slipping on the tiles. The heavy water fought him, dragging at his arms and legs, seeming to mass in front of him and press him back. He clamped his jaws against the souring gas in his lungs and battled the water with desperate strength, fixing his gaze on the locking wheel of the door. *There—got it!* but his hands grabbed impotently at emptiness, his eye fooled by the lens effect of the water. He lunged forward again, grabbing the wheel at last, wrenching with everything he had.

It wouldn't budge.

He cried out in a fury of frustration, precious air springing loose in a bubbling croak. He saw Holz beside him punching a button marked EMERGENCY. Martha and Pendrake arrived a second later. Pendrake had his own mask off, holding it out like a bag, slipping it down over Elias' head, not realizing that the inner surface was now contaminated with hydrogen, the delicate filtering valence broken. Elias felt a stab of fear for Pendrake. Now he had no air either.

In agonized slow motion, Holz hammered the emergency button, but the door stayed locked. Black spots spun, gnatlike, around Elias' eyes. Air, please God, he had to have it! He could feel his lungs twisting from the grip of his brain, preparing to suck their fill of water. He saw Pendrake grab the wheel and twist, saw it break off in his hands, and knew they would both die.

A terrible rage swept over him. He used it to hang on a second longer. Through a red haze of bursting capillaries he saw Pendrake, cheeks puffed, tear away the rubber seal of the door and force his fingers into the gap; saw the huge, orange back bulge as Pendrake tore the door from the wall.

Dimly Elias felt himself tumbling on a flood of water into the lock, Pendrake's hands under his arms, lifting him up, his lungs unlocking at last, tearing at the sweet air.

*Ah, God, Ah God!*

The water rose almost at once over his head, but he had new air, pure and wonderful, clearing his mind, giving him strength. Pendrake tore the outer door loose.

This time the water tumbled through more sluggishly, leveling out at waist level in the anteroom then dropping further as it converged on the door and spilled out into the corridor beyond. Elias staggered forward in the wash, dropping to his knees, sucking at the glorious, clean air until he'd had his fill.

He became aware of Martha's hand soothing his back, Holz helping him up, babbling apologies. Elias raised a hand, cutting Holz short.

"No, no—your tank works great! After that, your gravity will feel like free fall."

Holz peered at him uncertainly then gave a thin, hysterical laugh.

"How you can almost die and then joke about it is completely beyond me," Pendrake grumbled.

Elias cackled, hearing the edge of hysteria in his own voice. He couldn't help it. It was fantastic to be alive. In a moment the euphoria would pass, so enjoy it now! He grabbed Pendrake's hands and waltzed him around in a clumsy dance. Pendrake smiled finally. "I see, Elias. Humans *joke* to celebrate staying alive."

"And just what d'you do on Cephan?"

"We give everything we own to the first pauper we meet."

Elias winced. "Yes, well, that was going to be my *next* thought."

"Damn!" Holz said.

Elias saw that he was bent over something in the water—not a thing, a man. The attendant's body, face down, sloshing gently to and fro in the knee-deep, ebbing water. Elias' manic relief evaporated in an instant. He pushed past Pendrake, who had paled at the sight of the body, and helped Holz turn the corpse over.

The face stared up at him with such utter vacuity that his flesh crawled. He remembered seeing the same utter absence of expression on the face of a severely brain-damaged infant. He had never seen it before on a man—even a dead one.

He made himself ignore the face and search the body for some sign of what had killed the man. There was no blaster wound, no characteristic soft spot in a bone that might have indicated a ruptor beam. No ligature on the neck, no stab wound, no bruise anywhere on the body. He sat back on his heels, baffled.

"Allow me," Martha said, kneeling beside him. She grimaced when she saw the man's face. Gently, she closed the eyes, then, with a shudder, the mindlessly gaping jaw. Elias watched her, admiring her quick thoroughness. She turned the head back and forth, looking in the ears, and he realized he should have done that—looked for a puncture, see if someone had rammed a wire pick into the brain.

"Look at this."

She was pointing at the external canal of the right ear. He saw no puncture or bleeding, only a slight redness. She rolled the head, exposing the other ear for comparison. He saw that the first one *was* redder, as if it had been mildly abraded. Martha looked up at Holz. "Do you have autopsy facilities nearby? I'll need to examine this man at once."

"I'm afraid that's not possible," Holz said stiffly.

Elias rose. "Why not?" He kept his voice mild.

"This falls under the jurisdiction of our chief coroner. I'm sure he'll want to make the exam himself."

"Is there any reason I can't assist?" Martha asked.

"You would have to ask him."

Elias battled a quick, hot anger. He tore the remains of his oxyplex hood from his head. "Mr. Holz, we're going to send this to your best criminology lab. When the report comes back, it's not going to say moths. It's going to say acid—a water-potentiated acid that was deliberately rubbed around the nose and mouth of the mask. The man who handed me the mask is dead. If he was murdered, it would suggest that he knew what he was handing me—and that someone else rewarded him by permanently pulling the plug on his voice box."

Pendrake gave an agonized grunt.

"You don't know that he was murdered," Holz said. "The water sheeting in here could have knocked his feet from under him, broken his neck."

"It could," Elias agreed. "But if he was alive before Pendrake broke out the door, why didn't he answer your emergency alarm?"

Holz's mouth opened, closed again.

"So, you see, we need to determine if he was murdered."

"I'll arrange an immediate autopsy," Holz said. "I promise you'll be told all results."

"Mr. Holz, on behalf of the Imperator, I ask that Dr. Reik be present at the autopsy. And she must be free to intervene if necessary."

Holz colored. "I'm aware of your imperial carte blanche, Mr. Kane. But you won't win any friends on this planet waving it around."

"I'm not here to win friends. Nor am I here to become the fourth imperial inspector to die on this planet."

"All right," Holz said stiffly. "I'll order the coroner to do as you want. Will you be present, too?"

"No. Dr. Reik is the expert." Elias eye-checked Martha, saw her nod her OK.

"Then while she's with the coroner, I'll escort you to your quarters and—"

"I want to see a mine."

"Of course. As soon as you've rested and had a chance to acclimate. . . ."

"Now."

Holz looked at him as if he were mad. "You can't be serious, Mr. Kane. The mines are no place for an off-worlder who's just landed. You can't imagine the harshness of that environment, the dangers every minute. As you know, the last inspector had his fatal heart attack in a mine, and he'd been through the tank and a week of careful acclimatization."

"Thank you for your concern," Elias said coldly. "Please arrange it."

"Elias—"

Martha cut herself off, and he gave her a slight, grateful nod. She could not hide the concern on her face, though. All right, he was being stubborn, perhaps foolhardy. But he was tired of Holz and mad as hell at almost being killed. He'd use that anger, keep the adrenaline flowing, let it power his legs until he'd shaken things up a little. Someone had tried to kill him almost the minute he hit the planet. Whoever it was must be afraid he'd find out something fast. So that's exactly what he'd try to do. And he couldn't do it resting in his quarters.

Holz looked to Martha for support, saw she wasn't going to interfere and gave a hopeless sigh. "Very well, Mr. Kane."

"My title is 'inspector.' Use it."

"*Inspector* Kane. I'll hail us a groundcar. Mine

number three is close to the city. We can be there in an hour. But I want Dr. Reik to note that this trip is taken over my protest. I won't be responsible."

Elias gazed at the entrance to the mine. The air was thick and heavy, making the elevator gantry shimmer, carrying the rubbery stink of corside, used to spray-wall the shafts down below. Slick, reddish clay formed a broad mound around the gantry. At the bottom of that slope, near the groundcar, barebacked men strained and pushed at an ore carrier. The engine of the carrier shrieked like a wounded animal and Elias could hear the men cursing. In the dump cradle of the carrier, huge lumps of beta-steel gleamed like chunks of raw meat torn from the ground. The sky glowered with massive reddish clouds.

*Dante's inferno*, Elias thought.

He levered himself from the groundcar and shuffled along the steel catwalk leading to the entrance, feeling the gravity like a huge fist pressing down on his neck and shoulders. Pendrake offered his hand under one elbow. "Would the inspector like some assistance?"

"No, he would not," Elias growled irritably. "And it's *Mr.* Inspector, to you."

Pendrake chuckled.

"Why do I get the impression you're enjoying this?"

"It *is* refreshing to be on a heavy-G planet again. My legs were beginning to go soft."

"Just like my head."

"Would you like to turn back?" Pendrake asked, his voice touched with concern.

"Nothing would please me more. But I'm not going to."

Holz made a show of waiting up for them at the elevator. Wordlessly, he offered an oxygen mask from a receptacle beside the elevator.

"No thanks," Elias said. "I've had enough of masks for today."

"The air is very heavy and somewhat depleted at the bottom of the shaft."

"Let's do it."

Holz nodded fatalistically. He spoke into a call box mounted beside the oxygen, and Elias was startled to hear the outback colonist dialect flowing easily from his lips: "Be the foreman about? Would'st send him up."

A moment later Elias heard a ratcheting growl from deep below and a clanking at ground level. He was surprised at the primitive quality of the equipment. This elevator looked like something out of a history book on the coal mines of pre-imperial Earth. Surely better stuff was available. He asked Holz about it.

"Yes, it's available, Inspector. But it doesn't work in our climate. Remember what I said about the clay fouling everything? The newer machinery, with its downsized power components, is especially vulnerable. Anything that runs on microchips is worse than useless. If even one clay molecule suspended in this humidity infiltrates the motherboard of a modern ore truck, the thing turns into an outdoor toilet. That's why we can't maintain gravity suppression in the mines, and we can't use mechanized diggers either."

The elevator doors creaked open and Elias found himself gazing at the largest human he had ever seen. The man was only a few centimeters shorter than Pendrake and almost as broad in the back and shoulders. His face was filthy. His clothes glistened with clay slime.

Holz held out his hand and the monster gripped it in a slick, bear-sized paw. Holz said, "Jost. I thank thee. These be imperials. Inspector Elias Kane and Pendrake."

Elias held out his hand. Jost looked at it with contempt. "Another inspector? Thou fool. Ye be not welcome here."

"Well, at least you're honest," Elias said. "I hate honesty."

Jost gave a braying laugh. "A good jest, Earthie, but I'll still not shake thy hand." He scowled and spat into the shaft. "And what be this aberration?" Jost poked a thumb at Pendrake.

"I am a Cephantine, sir."

"I could whip thy arse."

"No doubt."

"Could'st take us down, Jost?" Holz inquired. "Inspector Kane wishes to see thy men at work."

"And if he passes out, what then?"

"I don't need much air."

"Thou won't get much, either. There isn't to spare. But if gruesome agonies be what thou cravest, I can oblige thee."

Jost motioned them into the elevator. Elias felt a wave of soreness in his legs and realized they'd stiffened up during the brief moment he'd stood immobile. There'd be hell to pay tomorrow. The cage dropped sharply, easing the pressure on his legs, but spoiling any relief by rolling his stomach like a ball of lead up into his rib cage. He swallowed against a tide of nausea and saw Jost smiling at him, his dark eyes glittering in the mudbath of a face. Elias pretended to study his fingernails; Jost gave a derisive grunt.

Elias put Jost out of his mind and focused his thoughts: What do I hope to accomplish here?

One: Get a rough idea how much Jost and his men can mine in an hour. Tomorrow, do some multiplication by working hours and the number of mines and get a rough estimate of how much beta-steel ore *should* be coming out of Cassiodorus. *Extremely* rough, but at least it'll give you something to compare to the official figures.

Two: Look for anything closed off, any shafts Holz or Jost don't want you to see, any locked doors, sidelined piles of ore.

Three: *Stay alive!*

The elevator cage hit bottom and the doors ground open with a nerve-racking screech. Elias recoiled from a blast of foul heat. He followed the others from the cage into a glistening red corridor. Stooping, Jost led the way down a low tunnel, walking on a strip of steel half sunk into the soupy clay. Elias found himself straining to see. Flares were set regularly into the shieldwall, but they were too far apart, making the tunnel glow in a guttering, hellish light.

"Those walls you're looking at are applied by a spraygun," Holz said, misinterpreting his gaze. "As soon as a meter is excavated, it begins to sag. The miners spray on the support—a chemical called corside, which quickly hardens. Then we dig through it where sampling or direct sighting indicates ore fistulas."

Elias did not bother to say that he knew it. Jost had been right—there seemed to be too little air for each breath. Down here, talking was a luxury.

At least the damned place wasn't underwater.

They rounded a bend and came upon a knot of miners working at a find.

Jost stopped and bellowed a greeting. Three men stood away from the wall and nodded at Jost, then gaped curiously at Pendrake.

"That be a pumpkin man," Jost announced. "And the other's an Earthie imp with a death wish."

The other miners laughed raucously. Elias saw that Holz was watching him closely, his face impassive.

"That looks like a false plate you're working on," Elias observed.

The miners beside Jost looked incredulous. "And how would'st thou know that, imp," one of them said.

"Too flat. Don't the payload fistulas show more rounding on the ends?"

Jost cleared his throat. "Generally, yes. But there be always exceptions. Thy master craves every scrap she can muster, so we look them all over."

"Not very efficient," Elias observed.

Jost bristled. "Where didst thou learn about false plates?"

Elias ignored him. "And isn't that sample hole a little big?"

Jost stepped close, bumping him. "We know how to

avoid cave-ins. Don't need a snot-nosed Earthie inspec-tor to tell us that."

"Get your belly off me," Elias said quietly.

Jost laughed. "Or what?"

Elias could feel the hostility all around him like an extra, savage heat. He blocked it out, concentrating on Jost's face. "Or you won't be needing it. You'll be vein-sucking your food through tubes."

Jost glared at him in disbelief. "Think'st thou thy pumpkin-colored friend can save thee from my wrath?"

"Pendrake is too big for violence," Elias said qui-etly. He could feel his heart pounding in his chest. Jost had still not stepped back.

Suddenly a loud crack split the air, echoing down the tunnel. Jost whirled away from him and stared fear-fully at the wall. A second later, Elias saw it—a small, hairline crack in the clear shielding, growing as he watched, splitting, admitting first a trickle of clay, then a sheeting gout. Jost pushed him and he staggered back the way they'd come.

"Cave-in!" Jost bellowed. "Run for thy lives!"

ELIAS FOUGHT TO RECOVER FROM JOST'S SHOVE, STUM-
bling forward, arms windmilling, then losing it, sprawling onto his face. He lay there a second, numb with fear,
hearing the shieldwall pop as mud and clay hissed into
the tunnel.

*Damn it, got to get moving!*

He tried to push up, but the quagmire on either
side of the narrow walkway sank under his hands, then
held them in a sucking grip when he tried to tear loose.
Forcing his head up against the fierce gravity, he saw
Holz running in wild panic toward the elevator. Then
huge hands grabbed the back of his tunic and tore him
from the clay, setting him on his feet.

It was Pendrake, shouting at him to run.

He almost did, then forced himself to turn back to
the miners. All he could see was a head—Jost's. He went
cold with horror—then realized the head wasn't severed; Jost's body was pinned under a huge slide of clay
and mud. Where were the others? They'd been behind
him. Completely buried now, *God, smothering!* Elias
fell to his knees and began digging barehanded around
Jost's shoulders, frantic with the need to hurry.

"Run, fool!" Jost hissed. He jerked his head toward
the shieldwall but Elias had already glimpsed the crack,

inching jaggedly past him toward the entrance. He could hear the wall cracking and groaning under the immense, shearing forces of the clay. He dug harder. An alarm klaxon began to hoot from the direction of the elevator. With dim surprise, Elias realized that he was no longer afraid. His body was light and powerful, fired with a single purpose. He felt Pendrake beside him, nudging him to one side so they could dig together. Elias gulped the hot, heavy air, panting like a dog. Sweat poured down his forehead into his eyes, stinging, half blinding him. He clawed at the mixture of mud and clay. Thank God, the stuff was sticky—just enough cohesion to keep it from instantly filling in. He grunted in triumph as he cleared one of Jost's shoulders. A huge chunk of wall plopped out behind Elias; he felt it spatter his boots but ignored it, digging and pulling until Jost's arm came free.

With a low growl, Jost grabbed the edge of the walkway one-handed and pulled, his face contorting in effort. Pendrake freed the other arm and grasped Jost's hand, pulling. Elias followed suit. Jost aided them, flexing his arms, wriggling with furious strength. With a loud suction noise, his body slid free. He leapt up with a roar and threw himself back on the hill of clay behind him.

Elias tried to follow, but with Jost saved, his strength washed away in a crushing wave of exhaustion. Unable to control his legs, he staggered against the wall, sliding down in a stream of mud. He blinked furiously and wiped at his eyes. Through the clay on his fingers he saw blood. Must have torn off a fingernail. Couldn't hold his hands up. They dropped into his lap, leaving him gazing dully at Pendrake and Jost. They dug like madmen, gouging out hunks of clay, hurling them behind.

Three more men, Elias thought. Still trapped.

He pushed to his feet again and saw that Jost and Pendrake had uncovered a head and an arm. Elias grabbed the arm and pulled, but it refused to budge. He dug a wad of clay from the man's mouth and tried to force air in, knowing he was fighting the lung-flattening weight of the cave-in. The man's eyes remained closed, the mouth slack. *Too late—no, damn it, keep trying!*

Pendrake finished digging out the shoulders and Elias backed off as he pulled the man free. A large slab of clay and mud came with the man's feet, revealing another limp, slimy body. Jost dragged it out. All right, that's two, Elias thought. Where's the other?

The crack in the wall widened, spilling more clay and mud. Elias tried to scan the deepening red-brown mass, but his vision was too blurred, his eyes stinging badly now. Damn this sweat! He tore his tunic off, but the savage heat did not relent. He could feel it sapping the last of his strength—

—and there was still one man, and he was smothering, *drowning, damn it.*

Elias dropped to his knees to dig, then found his arms clawing at the air as someone pulled him off.

Jost. "Breathest thou for these two. Pumpkin and I will dig."

Elias sprawled between the two bodies, forcing air into one mouth, then the other, until he saw the chest of one of them begin to rise and fall on its own. He groped for a pulse in the other man. Damn, none! He straddled the chest and pumped the sternum, then slid off to breathe for him. He repeated, trying to keep up the pace, but feeling himself fall behind with each repetition. Dark spots danced before his eyes. He heard a gasp and knew the man was breathing on his own.

"Yes!" he croaked, and collapsed onto his side.

The tunnel dimmed, the shieldwall flares shrinking to stars winking in a distant galaxy. A rapturous feeling of well-being flooded him, so good to just lie here and rest, never move again. Sounds of cracking and splitting filtered dimly into his consciousness, but they did not seem important. Air tasted like honey now, sweet. Vision going away, *open your eyes.* Or were they open already? Couldn't tell.

And then he was walking and wondering how, trying to play along with the spastic movements of his body, swinging each foot forward in turn, wishing he could just fall down and rest.

". . . little further, Elias." Pendrake, but why was he talking from the next room?

Elias fought his way back to awareness and realized that Pendrake was supporting him with one hand and carrying one of the miners across the other arm. I'm slowing him down, Elias thought with alarm. Digging down to his last reserves of energy, he shook off Pendrake's hand. " 'M awright," he growled. To illustrate, he broke into a shambling run, gritting his teeth in determination, pulling ahead. He reached the elevator door, pressed the call button and looked back to see where Jost was. He was behind Pendrake, carrying the other two miners slung over his shoulders like sacks of flour.

A huge roar sounded back up the tunnel. A shock of terror passed through Elias as he saw a solid mass of clay filling the shaft behind Jost and Pendrake, rushing down on them like congealing blood.

"Hurry, damn it! It's going!"

He pounded the call button, heard the gears only now beginning to clank to life far up the elevator shaft. He swore with fright and frustration. Pendrake and Jost were running now; ten meters, five, *come on, come ON!*

The doors screeched open and he tried to prod Pendrake in first, but Pendrake snared him with his free arm and pulled him along. Jost followed, still carrying his two men on his shoulders. The doors ground back together with agonizing slowness. Hurry, damn it! Clay spilled in, and the doors shuddered to a stop, blocked. Jost swore and kicked at the intruding clay, clearing it just enough for the doors to pinch shut. "Go, virgin whore!" Jost shouted. "Rise, damn thy bleeding corns!"

Elias burst out laughing. Jost glared at him. "Thou find'st this funny?"

"Definitely not."

The elevator lurched and began to climb. Elias sank to his knees, trembling, but still laughing. He waved in apology to Jost, who at first looked outraged, then began to laugh too.

Pendrake snorted in disgust. "Humans."

The doors opened again and Elias pushed to his feet, stumbling out and sitting down heavily, basking in the wave of fresh, cooler air. God, exhausted, but they'd made it!

He saw that the slope was full of miners who'd already escaped up the main and other elevators in response to the klaxon. They milled around frantically, calling each other's names. Jost and Pendrake laid the three men out. Two were stirring feebly. The other was very still, and Elias knew with a sinking feeling that he was dead.

Jost walked to Elias' side and knelt, giving him a hard stare. Just then Holz hurried up. "I had to get out, sound the alarm," he said. "Someone had to do that, or we'd have lost others."

Jost glanced up at him and Holz backed away, melted into the crowd. Jost returned his gaze to Elias. "That was a brave thing thou didst. Thou art still a fool."

Elias sensed the immense effort Jost was making to be grateful and was troubled by it. "A fool. And what does that make you?"

"I was *born* a fool," Jost said.

Elias offered his hand again. It was caked with clay and blood. Jost stared at it. Then took it and pumped it. "I owe thee. And I fear I cannot repay. It be on my head. Be thou warned."

Elias tried to understand. A chilling dread gripped him. He wanted to grab the other man, shake him. *What do you mean, "warned?"* But he was too weary to speak. Jost sprang up and strode away.

"The body was absolutely normal," Martha said. "Except for one rather odd finding."

Elias bent over his sink, splashing cold water on his

face, trying to rouse himself. Twelve hours of sleep. Damn, hadn't his alarm gone off? Every muscle ached, even though the guest quarters were gravity controlled at .8 G. His head felt stuffed with cotton. He wanted nothing more than to totter back to his bed and collapse again. Instead he toweled off his face and shuffled from the bathroom. The sight of Martha roused him a little. She sat in the lounge chair beside his bed, one knee hitched across the arm, proving that the slit in her stunning lavender gown was as good for comfort as for looks. He felt a stir of arousal. You take the comfort, sweetheart, he thought, and I'll take the looks. She wriggled her toes at him and he realized she'd tossed off her shoes at the door to the suite.

He said, "You are gorgeous."

"Thank you."

"Don't tell me Briana packed that for you."

She laughed. "Fat chance. While you slept, I shopped."

"You were talking about the autopsy," he prompted.

"The sodium-potassium balance along the attendant's nerves was wrong."

"Are you saying the water electrocuted him?" Elias felt a sharp disappointment at the thought that the death might truly have been accidental. Then he realized that, if the water spilling from the tank into the attendant's room had shorted anything electrical, the jolt would have hit all of them. "No," he said. "Forget it. I'm still not awake."

Martha said, "The coroner thinks it *was* electrocution. That the control panel shocked him *before* the room flooded."

"And what do *you* think."

"Exactly the opposite."

"He shocked the control panel?"

She laughed. "I think you're starting to wake up. If you're through splashing your face, hadn't you better get into your uniform? The banquet call is in half an hour."

"Come on, come on," Elias growled. "What do you think killed him?"

"I think he was electro*depleted*. I can't think of any other word for it. I know it sounds crazy, and I've never seen anything like it before. But why else would his sodium/potassium balance be so screwed up?"

Elias grunted, not sure whether to be annoyed or flattered. "I know it's hard," he said, "but pretend I don't know what you're talking about."

"The ratio of sodium ions to potassium ions inside a neuron changes as an impulse passes along the nerve," she explained. "I got the coroner to sample nerve tissue in the attendant's arm, leg and brain. Based on the readings, I'd say that every nerve in the attendant's body—including the neurons of his brain—had fired just before death. In the neuroelectric sense, he was completely blown out."

With a chill, Elias remembered the face of the attendant, so empty, as though the life had been torn from his body before even the cells themselves could sense what was happening.

He pulled on his white tunic with the two gold circles on the cuffs, struggling to make sense of it. What kind of force could do that to a man?

"When I was working on ways to give Briana's father an artificial body," Martha went on, "I needed to know how to turn on a synthetic network of nerves. To learn that, I had to first study what happens when a network turns off—at death. I hoped I could work backward from that. As you know, it didn't work. But one thing sacrificing all those poor baboons drove home to me was how *slowly* a nerve network shuts down. It takes hours for the neuroelectricity of a fresh-killed body to diffuse.

"Elias, we got to that attendant within half an hour of his death. There should have been something left."

"Do you think it was done by some kind of new weapon?"

"I don't know. All I know is that the coroner insisted on putting electrocution on the death certificate. If you plan to claim the man was killed to shut his mouth, I'm afraid no one will put much store by it." She looked suddenly doubtful. "Hell, Elias. I can't swear it was not electrocution. Electricity is a strange phenomenon, and neuroelectricity is even stranger. I'm sure this coroner has seen many more cases of electrocution than I have."

"How'd he react to your being there?"

"Seemed glad to have me. A sweet old guy, actually."

"Then why would Holz put up such a stink?"

She shrugged. "Because Holz is a bureaucratic twit."

"What about the lab report on the oxyplex?"

"No help there, either. They claim there was no acid."

Elias felt a hot flush of anger. "They're lying."

"Maybe. But what if the killer used an oxygen acid? Wouldn't all that water convert most of the hydroxyls?"

"Damn! It could." Feeling stymied and angry, Elias yanked on his pants, groaning as he lifted each leg.

"Are you OK?"

"As long as I don't have to move."

"From what Pendrake tells me, you're quite a hero."

"I didn't think. If I had, I'd have run out of that mineshaft so fast Holz would've had footprints up his back."

"Give me a break, Elias. I adore you too much already without having to admire your modesty."

*Adore.* He savored the word, letting it warm him. He gave her a lewd smile. "You want immodest? I'll give you immodest." He started to unbutton his tunic again.

She held up a hand, smiling. "The banquet. Remember?"

He grimaced. He did not feel like going to a stuffy dinner, making small talk with a bunch of hostile, stiff-necked colonials. But he could not refuse. The affair was not exactly in his honor—they'd never unbend to that extent—but if he didn't go, he'd cause a nasty scandal: *Earthie Inspector Snubs Viceroy.*

With a sigh he pulled on his boots, trying to think if he'd covered the autopsy completely. He remembered the mild abrasion in the ear canal and asked Martha about it.

"Afraid I can't explain that either. Maybe he dug at a piece of wax with his finger just before he died. That's really all it would take. There was no penetration of the eardrum, nothing was rammed into his brain. You ready?"

Elias offered her his arm. She took it with a radiant smile. Up close he could smell her perfume, sense the fine coordination in her fingers. He felt proud to be with her. The dinner might be a bore, but walking over and back with Martha on his arm was no small compensation.

At the door, she slipped into her shoes. "I still think it was shabby of them not to invite Pendrake."

"The protocol officer knows he's a vegetarian. I don't think that's a real popular lifestyle on this planet."

A militia captain—Martha's dinner partner—was waiting outside the door. Elias greeted him politely but did not relinquish Martha's hand. The man seemed content to trail along behind them. But at the door, Elias had to surrender her with as much grace as he could muster.

He found his own seat, took up position behind it, and looked around with some curiosity at the banquet hall of Cay Endor III, Imperial Viceroy of Cassiodorus. It was almost as spartan as the rest of the city. Its only concessions to luxury were the gold place settings that gleamed against the linen on the long table, and the high ceiling of the hall, intricately buttressed with dark wood in the imperial style. The flags of the nine planets hung along the ceiling, providing bursts of color. The tricolor of imperial Earth occupied one end of the hall, as protocol dictated. It waved gently in some random eddy of the air conditioners, alternately revealing the top band of blue, with its rows of stars, the featureless white middle; the blazing red bottom third, with its gold hammer and sickle.

Elias felt a small stir of pride looking at it. What did Cay Endor and the other colonists here feel? Before he left Cassiodorus, he would know.

Granit Holz, resplendent in a crimson ceremonial uniform, joined him. "Ah, Mr.—*Inspector* Kane, may I convey the appreciation of the viceroy for your courageous acts in the mine."

The little speech had a forced air, and Holz did not quite meet his eye. Elias realized the man was ashamed of his own role in the disaster, of running out so quickly. Thinking of it, he felt a twinge of contempt for Holz, then remembered what he'd said to Martha. *I didn't think, or I might have run too.* She didn't realize it, but he hadn't been trying to sound modest. The barest difference existed between him and Holz. He had jumped one way and Holz the other. No matter how many times it happened that way, the next time could always be reversed. That was the fickle nature of bravery.

"Thank you, Mr. Holz," he said. "But you saved more men than I did with your quick alarm."

Holz met his gaze at last, first with suspicion, then gratitude. "I'm afraid I was badly scared."

"So was I."

"At least I kept my head enough to hit the klaxon."

Elias could see the man inwardly rebuilding himself before his eyes—rather too fast for his tastes. He turned away and felt a stab of pain in his calves. Damn it, when was Cay Endor going to make his grand entrance so they could all sit down? The banquet hall was controlled at what felt like slightly less than 1 G, but now that his muscles had been abused, only time and acclimatization could leach out the fatigue poisons.

"His Excellency, Cay Endor!" shouted a page. Elias turned respectfully with the others, feeling a genuine interest. But the first thing he noticed was not Endor, but the creature behind him. *An Ornyl!* Elias' heart began to race. Endor's bodyguard, an Ornyl. It made sense, especially on a heavy-G planet. Gregory Amerdath, Endor's mentor, had had one, so why not Endor, but what did it *really* mean? Ornyl warriors were a small, close-knit group. The foul s'uniph insects were among the more exotic biological weapons controlled by them. Might this Ornyl have some connection to the s'uniphs planted aboard his scout ship?

*File it for later.*

Elias made himself pay attention, as good manners dictated, to Cay Endor. The viceroy was short and bald. His blue militia uniform was almost ostentatiously plain, the tight breeches revealing spindly legs that could not have spent much time in the true gravity of Cassiodorus. Elias caught himself, realizing he was prejudging the man. Endor might look ineffectual, but Gregory Amerdath had trusted him to oversee Earth's most vital colony.

Endor sat, and Elias joined in with the general rustle of guests sitting around the table. In a surprisingly strong, basso growl, Endor began to welcome his "many distinguished guests." Elias tuned him out, arranging in his mind the significant things that had happened since he'd landed on Cassiodorus. The attack in the water tank, the attendant, dead of no discernible cause, and now an Ornyl, here on this planet.

". . . and Inspector Elias Kane from the Imperial Palace itself," Endor said.

Elias saw everyone looking at him. Holz nudged him and he stood. "Your Excellency." He sat again, flushing, hoping he had not been expected to say more. But everyone bent to their plates, and he realized that the first course had been served while Endor made his welcoming remarks. It was a cold salad of greens and legumes, doubtless from some hydroponics plant.

He picked at it without appetite. So damned tired. If he could just go back to his quarters and have some undisturbed time to think. But he knew what would happen if he had that luxury—he would fall asleep again, probably for another twelve hours.

He *needed* to think. Because it wasn't just the tank, the dead attendant, the Ornyl. There was something else, nagging at his unconscious, obscured by the strenuous pace, the physical emergencies.

Perhaps the most important thing, and he was missing it.

Somehow he must throw off his fatigue, think, root out the part he was missing.

Elias felt an arm brush his shoulder, a waiter, whisking away the salad and depositing a large steak, steaming hot in a lake of juice. Dutifully, he began to saw at it with one of the gold knives. The meat was tender, cutting easily. When the first piece hit his mouth, his tastebuds awoke with the exquisite taste. He wolfed the meat as rapidly as he dared, answering Holz's murmured pleasantries with equally automatic banalities. The unexpected pleasure of the steak buoyed him, loosening the deadening grip of fatigue a little—

—and just like that he knew what he had been missing!

He'd been sent here to unravel a mystery: Were the deaths of the last three imperial inspectors truly accidental, or were they deliberate murder, committed to cover up a diversion of beta-steel to the rebels?

But he now saw that that was the wrong question.

The question was not whether three off-worlders, unaccustomed to the brutal conditions on Cassiodorus, might drop over of stroke or heart attack.

The real mystery was why the Cassiodorans didn't do the same.

Those men in the mines today, four of them pushing a stalled, six-ton hauler, others milling around the mine entrance after the cave-in, the spring in Jost's step, even after he'd been pinned under half a ton of mud—then dug out two of his buddies. Big men, and he'd slung them over his shoulders and carried them out of the mine. All right, there was adrenaline, and Jost and his men were all powerfully built, and if it had been Earth, their behavior would have been within the bounds of normality.

But this wasn't Earth. This was a planet where a two-hundred-pound man suddenly weighed three hundred. And never stopped weighing that. Three-hundred-pound men existed on Earth. Some of them had been heavy all their lives, years and years of building up the leg muscles, lugging the weight around. But such men did not work in mines or sling other three-hundred-pounders over their shoulders.

There were limits to what the human body could endure.

And somehow, on Cassiodorus, those limits were being broken.

A cold chill ran up Elias' spine. He stared down at his plate, his appetite gone again.

## 8

ELIAS LAY ON HIS BACK IN THE WARM WATER, FLOAT-ing downstream. A fat, phosphorescent moon beamed down on him from its bed of clouds. He was filled with a drowsy contentment, tinged with curiosity: What river was this? Why didn't he sink down farther? Somehow he was able to rest right on top of the water as though it were a mattress. Maybe the river was very salty. Not important.

He rolled his head to either side, making out distant shorelines, trees, glowing with a pearly radiance. Beautiful, but vaguely troubling.

*What am I doing out here at night?*

He became aware of a slight weight on his chest. Straining his neck, he tried to raise his head for a look, but the water clung to him like flypaper. At last he pulled free and saw: a baby!

Joy filled him. Tears coursed down his cheeks mingling with the water's salt, buoying him up even higher. He could feel against his chin the soft, pudgy touch of the baby's toes; its head was pillowed on his belly. He gazed raptly at the moon-bathed, sleeping face and wept for joy.

He became aware of a thumping sound—*thok, thok, THOK,* like an oil derrick. It grew louder, signaling the sudden nearness of the shore. Anxious, he looked to the side, and saw the derrick's looming shape. Then it blurred into something he could not recognize—

—a clock. Glowing red numerals, 1:07 A.M.

Someone knocking at the door. He groped his chest and stomach, regret swelling in him as he realized the baby—and the dream—were gone. His cheeks were wet. His throat hurt.

Knocking, knocking.

"Damn it, who?" he snapped, then remembered he was not in Briana's palace, but Cay Endor's modest guest quarters, where there was no compusayer to answer him.

"All right, coming!" Fuming, Elias slid his ruptor from under his pillow and thumbed off the safety. When he rose from the bed, the stiffness of his legs panged him. Muttering curses, he limped to the door and opened it, keeping the weapon hidden behind it.

Jost grinned down at him. Elias stared at him in surprise, hardly recognizing him with his mask of clay and mud scrubbed away. But no one else was that big.

"Dost plan to sleep the night away, Earthie?"

"Jost, it's one o'clock. I've only been asleep since ten."

"That be six whole hours."

Elias realized it was true. A day on Cassiodorus equaled about thirty Earth-standard hours. He'd got back from the banquet around ten, but midnight came at fifteen o'clock, not twelve. Some of his indignation at being wakened seeped away.

"I thought thou might like to see the *real* Neues Eisen."

Pendrake, still tying his bathrobe, materialized in the hall behind Jost. The big man whirled into a crouch, arms and fingers splaying into a combat stance.

"I beg your pardon," Pendrake said mildly.

Jost blew out a breath and straightened, looking sheepish. "Don't ever do that again, Pumpkindrake."

Elias suppressed a smile. At least Jost was getting closer to Pendrake's name. *The real town.* This opportunity might not come again. His legs would warm up once he started walking.

"So what sa'st thou, Earthie? Be game for some amusement? See how we miners play?"

Behind Jost, Pendrake frowned his opinion.

"Does your invitation extend to Pendrake?"

Jost looked nonplussed. "Ah . . . the next time, perhaps. 'Tis my treat, and I be too short for two tonight."

Elias flushed. "Sorry."

Jost waved him off with a huge paw and shot an apologetic look at Pendrake. "My pardon. We two big ones will ditch this Earthie the next time."

"No apologies are necessary," Pendrake said. "Elias, will you still wish to be awakened at eight?"

Elias recognized the hidden message, *Don't go.* Pendrake was worried about his safety. But nothing on Cassiodorus could be accomplished without risk. "We'll only be a few hours—right, Jost?"

"If that be all you can take."

"What's the gravity where we're going?"

Jost looked amused, condescending. "Normal, Earthie. Can't afford much suppression on this planet."

The hell with it, Elias thought. I'll take a stim. "See you at eight," he said to Pendrake.

While Jost waited outside, Elias pulled on a jump suit with padded sleeves that hid a special flat pocket. He made sure the needler inside was loaded and charged, then went to the sink and washed down a two-hour stimtab.

As he hurried after Jost down the hall of the guest quarters, the stiffness in his legs subsided. He felt a rush of optimism and knew it was only the chemical energy of the stimulant. But some pleasure *was* warranted. It appeared that Jost had decided to be friendly after all, shaking off whatever conflicts he had felt earlier. Elias savored the breakthrough—having a mining foreman in his corner could be a very big help when it came to penetrating secrets or, at the least, estimating how much beta-steel ore Cassiodorus *should* be producing—

Elias realized suddenly the full significance of where Jost was taking him: the nightlife of Neues Eisen.

But there shouldn't *be* any nightlife for men like Jost.

Elias felt a mixture of excitement and vexation with himself. He kept slipping into the same seductive trap, damn it. *This wasn't Earth.* He must move that fact to the forefront of his thinking and keep it there. He would "see how we miners play," when those same miners should be lying in their beds exhausted, gathering themselves for the superhuman demands of the next day.

Elias' excitement grew. Maybe tonight he would find the answer to the real mystery of Cassiodorus!

Jost halted at an elevator marked SERVICE. He punched a code into the access panel and the doors slid back. "Here we go, Earthie. This way to the escapes of the flesh." His grin was hard, giving Elias a chill, dampening his enthusiasm.

*Why won't you use my name, Jost?*

Elias offered no conversation as the elevator descended, waiting to see if Jost would speak. Jost said nothing, did not even look at him. His earlier jocularity was gone, replaced by a tense, preoccupied aura. Elias remembered Jost's warning after the mine rescue and thought, Escapes of the flesh? Or escape *from* the flesh? Was Jost taking him down to some deserted subbasement to kill him? He felt the nerves of his neck and shoulders tense with alarm and battled the upsurge of paranoia. Surely there was more honor in Jost than to kill the man who'd helped save his life.

*But if he means me no harm, why didn't he want Pendrake along?*

Jost's excuse of not having enough money to treat both suddenly seemed transparently false. Jost had something on his mind other than entertainment. Elias became aware of the needler along his right wrist and was glad for it.

The elevator opened on noise, laughter and light; Elias felt himself sag in relief. Jost gave him a knowing smile and nodded toward the door. Elias stepped out—

—into carnival.

The air was warm and smoky, alive with wonderful smells—hot rolls, peppered meat, the malt of spilled beer, the nasal bite of tobacco smoke. He drew it all into his lungs, savoring it as he looked up and down the wide, vaulted concourse. It stretched in either direction as far as he could see, alive with people, movement, noise and color. Elias felt himself surrounded by powerful, half-naked flesh—brawny men and muscular women, dressed in leather shorts, knee-length boots and little else. Some of the women wore halters, but most displayed their chests as casually as the men. He watched in wonder as they strode from stall to stall, jostling each other, moving with manic energy. His own legs ached—despite the stim—in the heavy gravity. He was damp with sweat. How could these people, strong as they were, work in the mines all day, then party in 1.5 G's? Elias looked above the milling crowd at the blazing marquees. The dozen or so open stalls he could see from where he stood advertised everything from food to booze, to sex.

Jost punched his shoulder. "Don't stand with thy mouth agape. Choose one and participate!"

Elias barely heard him. His gaze was captured by two men, ringed by onlookers, in a stall across the concourse. The men clenched each other's throats in a death grip. Elias watched, shocked, as they circled, backs straining, biceps and forearms bulging with effort. Both their faces were turning a dark, congested red. Their eyes swelled wide and the tongue of one of them started to protrude. His opponent, seeing this, kicked out, trying to trip him, but his feet were braced too far back.

Elias was appalled. "Why doesn't someone stop them?"

"And spoil the fun?"

The crowd of onlookers shifted, parting a little, and Elias saw a pile of bills on the ground. Last-minute bets fluttered down as he watched. The man whose tongue was out buckled at the knees. His eyes rolled up and the other man released his throat, flinging his arms wide and stepping back as his opponent crashed forward face down and lay twitching. The crowd yelled and jeered. A smaller man in black scurried forward at once and slapped an oxygen mask over the fallen fighter's face.

"See?" Jost said. "Just a game."

Elias controlled his outrage. "A game. It would be very easy to die from that game. A crushed windpipe, collapsed carotids—"

"On thy world, yes," Jost said. "But not here. Behold the muscles on those necks, Earthie. The frailties of anatomy thou namest are deeply armored in those men." Jost looked at him closely. "Thou be offended. I want thee to have fun tonight. Come, I'll find something to thy tastes."

Jost led him farther into the concourse, through the crowd, past stall after stall. Elias kept seeing shops that offered back rooms supplied with ropes. Gaudy ads invited colonists to pair off and tie each other up. He paused at one of the bondage shops, drawn with a mixture of revulsion and fascination to the animated holo advertisements. Men binding women and women binding men; so much rope that only slivers of flesh were visible. Total immobilization. The looks on the faces were neither pain nor ecstasy, but a sort of contrite acceptance, as though they were performing a religious ritual rather than an erotic game.

"Be that to thy liking?" Jost asked.

Elias flushed, embarrassed, though there was no scorn in Jost's voice. "No thanks. I wouldn't want some woman coming unraveled over me."

Jost did not smile. "Then this, perhaps," he said,

leading Elias on to the next stall. It was a porno shop, filled with both men and women, poring over racks of magazines and holos.

The predominant theme was bondage.

"Doesn't anyone do normal sex around here?"

"Sex?" Jost asked, as if it were a completely new topic.

"Yes. Sex. You know, what people do for fun and babies."

"Why didst thou not say so? Thou be Earthie, but if I ask it, the finest woman here would take thee in."

"No thanks. Just asking." With a pang, Elias remembered the dream Jost had interrupted to bring him here. "Speaking of babies, do you have any kids?"

"No." Jost bit off the word.

*Did I offend him?* Quickly, Elias tried to soften his question. "Now that I think of it, I haven't seen any kids since I arrived."

"There be few children here."

Elias looked at him, surprised. Cassiodorus was a harsh planet, capable of snatching away life in a second. In such environments, humans usually bred like rabbits, obeying the strong survival instinct programmed into their genes.

As if reading his mind, Jost said, "This world be no place for little ones."

His voice was full of suppressed pain and loss; Elias felt a sudden bond of warmth for him. "I agree. But how do you keep the population up?"

"Immigration. Each year there be enough new fools willing to come here."

Elias sensed an immense pride that Jost was trying to hide. Substitute the word *heroes* for *fools* and the sentence would ring true.

Sudden shouts and cheers in the stall ahead distracted Elias. He saw that it was another of the grotesque choking matches, two women this time, circling, their faces horribly reddened and contorted above each other's strangling hands. He turned away sickened.

"It be time for a drink, Earthie." This time there *was* scorn in Jost's voice. He led the way across the concourse under an archway of carved, intertwined snakes into a low, dim-lit stall. Two huge men sat slumped over a bar. Jost grabbed the shoulders of both and yanked them backward, spilling them to the floor. They struggled up drunkenly, fierce-eyed until they saw who it was. "Ye be finished anyway, lads," Jost said coldly. They wandered off and Jost took one of the stools, motioning Elias to the other and bellowing an order for two whiskeys.

Elias gazed at him, feeling unsettled, dislocated. He tried to see the man who had just talked about little ones with such tenderness, who'd fought like a maniac to save the lives of his friends in the mine.

The drinks came and Elias touched his glass to Jost's. "Can I ask you a question?"

Jost downed half of his drink in one swallow. "Why not?"

"What are all of you trying to escape here?"

Jost gave him a dull look. "I don't understand."

"Don't try to run a 'big-and-dumb' game down on me, Jost. You're too smart a man to do a gig like this without at least once in a while asking yourself why."

"Maybe we don't know each other well enough to talk about that," Jost said in a low voice.

"Maybe I didn't know you well enough to save your oversized carcass yesterday, either."

Jost grimaced, as if in pain. "Thy mistake, Earthie."

"What does all this mean, Jost?"

"What dost thou think it means?"

"That you hate yourselves."

"Saurcrap. This is a frontier planet, Earthie. What'd thou expect? Prayer meetings?"

Elias shook his head, vexed. "I don't want to shock you, Jost, but I've been around a bit. I can tell my pant-legs from my fly, and I know which end of a blaster to stand on. I've seen port on five of the eight colonies. Before I learned better, I'd had enough gambling, rowdy sex and boozing to break an organ bank. So don't try to tell me that choking each other into oblivion, or chaining each other to chairs, is normal just because thou be'est a bunch of slap-happy colonists."

Jost's face darkened. "Be thou mocking me?"

"No, damn it. I'm trying to get some answers."

"I don't like thy questions."

Elias sighed, frustrated. He leaned back on the stool and sipped his whiskey. It was raw and biting, bringing tears to his eyes and a welcome heat to his stomach. Jost downed the rest of his in another gulp and ordered two more.

"Were *you* born on this planet?" Elias asked.

Jost shook his head. "Cerulyx."

"Then how in God's name did you acclimate to this?"

Jost hesitated. "No one ever acclimates to Cassi."

Elias gestured around him. "How many of these people spent the day working the mines?"

"Most of them."

"One point five G's, and yet they have the energy for a night on the town. What is it, Jost? Some kind of wonder drug? A new stimulant that somehow doesn't crash you after a few days flying?"

Jost did not answer for a long time. The two whiskeys came and he downed both of them, a gulp for each, and warning bells went off in Elias' mind.

"We become strong," Jost said softly. "Then we stay strong."

"What does that mean? There are limits—"

Jost stood and stalked from the bar. Elias took out his card, looking for someone to accept payment. The barman glanced contemptuously at it and turned away, polishing glasses. The warnings in Elias' head grew louder. *Jost had said he couldn't pay for two, but he wasn't even having to pay for one.*

Elias hurried out to the concourse, then saw Jost waiting for him. "There be more to see, Earthie," he said with an amiable smile.

"I'm sure there is. And most of it, you're not going to show me."

"Dost want to go home?" Jost asked with mock solicitousness.

"I guess I'm not like you and your comrades. I need rest. Nasty habit, but I can't seem to break it. I have the feeling it might be healthier than more of this."

Jost shrugged with elaborate unconcern. "Follow me then."

Elias could see the tension in the huge body, the abnormal, stiff drop of the arms, the set of the shoulders. *You're a very bad faker, Jost.* "I think I can find my own way back."

Jost shrugged again.

"Thanks for the whiskey." Elias turned, feeling a warning itch swell along his spine. He got two steps before Jost grabbed him. Adrenaline slammed through him. *Bastard, I knew it!* He bucked hard but Jost had his arms pinned. Elias tried to kick, but Jost bent forward instead of lifting him, and the floor stopped his heels.

Elias shouted for help.

No one looked at him. He glared at the crowd around him with a mixture of fury and fear. *"Damn it, somebody help me!"*

"Don't lose thy dignity," Jost murmured.

Elias struggled but Jost kept his grip easily, dragging him backward through a door into darkness, cutting him off from the noise, people, laughter—from his last hope of help. Elias' fury fled, leaving only the fear—and a bitter regret at his own stupidity.

THE NEEDLER, ELIAS THOUGHT. HOPE ROSE IN HIM, spurring him to an extra, furious strength. He fought Jost's grip in the darkness, trying to squirm down inside the crushing bearhug. Big bastard had him pinned right across the elbows. But if he could just slip down enough to bend his left arm up and across, he'd be able to trigger the holster release below his right elbow. The needler would slap down into his palm.

*Damn—so strong! Grip like steel—*

Lights came on, and Elias saw two more men. His heart sank and he stopped struggling, knowing they'd realize what he was trying to do. With a start he recognized the men—the same two Jost had unseated in the bar. One looked about forty. He had a red weal across his forehead. The other was younger, his boyish face incongruous atop his muscular, bullnecked body.

Elias looked beyond the two men and realized they were in a service alley—probably for a power substation. The alley dead-ended in a wall with control boxes and a narrow exit door that must lead to the machinery. The door was shut, but maybe it wasn't locked. Elias tried to goad his body into another effort, *break free and get out that door—or smash a box and black out the concourse, that'd bring people running.*

But why should anyone help him in here, when they hadn't outside?

Stymied, he tried desperately to think, but it was too late—the men were stepping forward. He saw that Bullneck was carrying what looked like a set of earphones.

"Am I glad to see you," Elias said. "Are you going to let this big lummox get away with yanking you off your stools?"

Elias felt Jost's body flinch with an anguished laugh. "Thou art truly a Mensch," Jost murmured. "I would this did not have to be."

Bullneck stepped closer, raising the earphones, and Elias saw that there was an earpiece only on one side—a slim cone, shaped to fit into his ear. He remembered the mild abrasion in the ear canal of the dead tank attendant, and panic flooded him. He fought it with a fierce effort of will. "Oh, are we going to listen to music?"

"*Thou* art, Earthie," Weal said. "A funeral march."

"Shut thy face," Jost snarled. "This man saved my life."

"That's all right," Elias said. "You don't have to thank me. If you'll just set me down in the concourse out there—"

"Quickly," Jost hissed. "Elias, I be sorry."

*Now* he says my name.

Elias went limp, sagging in Jost's grip, but Jost didn't go for it, so Elias kicked off the floor with both legs, shifting up just enough to jam the holster release against the underside of Jost's arm. With a muted click, the needler dropped into his hand, *don't drop it!* and he groped the trigger, swinging his legs to the side, aiming for Jost's foot, squeezing.

*Whup-p-p.*

Jost gasped; the iron grip broke and Elias twisted free as Jost fell behind him. Elias saw Bullneck and Weal springing forward, grabbing for him. Bullneck slapped his wrist up just as he fired; the flechettes clanged off the ceiling and rattled around the alley as Elias jumped over Jost's writhing body toward the door. Jost caught his ankle. He twisted in a terrified rage and fired the needler into Jost's arm, riddling it. Jost let loose, but then the two colonists had him, one grabbing either arm. He went down, cursing, his fingers stinging as the needler was torn from his grasp.

They rolled him over, slamming his back to the floor, knocking the wind out of him. From the corner of his eye, he saw Jost squirming across the floor. He was awed by Jost's strength. How could the man stay conscious and not scream?

A hand twisted into Elias' hair and jerked his head straight, sending sparks of pain down through his eyes. They held his head still, and he knew with an icy shock of fright that they could now easily put the earphone on him. He bucked and writhed, trying to tear free. Pain spiked into his eye sockets with each jerk, until tears blurred his vision. Then he saw the needler and stopped struggling, cold with dread. Its ugly muzzle was inches from his eyes. Beyond it, Weal's face blurred to insignificance.

"I ought to jam this down thy throat."

"No," Jost gasped.

Elias caught movement above his head, felt a rubbery thing go into his ear. It melded perfectly with his skin, clammy and cold as dead flesh. He bit back a panicked yell, knowing he must hang on and fight, break free, or he was lost. He gathered himself for a desperate lunge. *Now!*

His body would not respond.

He tried again. Nothing. He could feel his arms and legs draining of strength, his muscles trembling spastically. His mind remained brutally clear. He could sense and feel, but he could not act. The muzzle of the needler receded and he felt Weal get off him. *Roll away,* he thought. *Jump up!* But he could not. Bullneck was still squatting at his head, holding the earphone securely to his head. The cone was warming to the heat of his ear. He could feel its deadening touch inching through him, slowing his heart to a leaden booming. He knew that this thing had killed the attendant and possibly the three imperial inspectors. The Cassiodorans had developed a new weapon, deadly and untraceable.

Elias was sick with despair. His strength was all but gone now. He could barely twitch his hands. Stupid, so incredibly stupid. Jost warned you, but you had to ignore him. He was too honorable, you thought. But this is bigger than honor, more vital than a blood debt. The rebels are here, they're operating on this planet. How? Where? You don't know, fool. You *do* know they're stealing ore to build dreadnoughts—only something that important could make Jost do this to you.

Terrific. You know it, and it's too late.

Elias felt someone take his hand and squeeze and realized that Jost had crawled to his side. He could feel with perfect clarity the sticky blood on Jost's hand. He wanted to jerk away, but he could not.

"Thou . . . nailed me good, Elias. Fought well. Take . . . that thought with thee."

"I'd rather take you."

Jost gave a pained, bubbling chuckle. "Thou might at that. Maybe we'll find each other in hell."

We already have, Elias thought. He felt the room receding from him, the ceiling soaring away to a dizzying height. He no longer had the strength to talk. With distant horror he felt himself dwindling down to a spark inside his own brain.

Something crashed. He saw Bullneck leap forward across his body as if shoved, then felt a horrible pain in his ear, the fleshy cone tearing loose. He screamed.

Reality rushed back. He felt a draft sweep his face and knew that the door from the concourse was open. He struggled with all his might to get up, but succeeded only in lifting his head. Peering down along his body, he could see Bullneck and Weal scrambling back from him, their faces contorted in fear. A boot swung past his shoulder, then another. Elias let his head drop back, his gaze rising up along the towering figure. . . .

Pendrake!

*God, no!*

With a fierce effort, Elias twisted onto his side. He saw Jost lying on the other side of Pendrake's feet in a pool of his own blood, his face contorted with pain.

"Take him," Jost croaked. "Thou *canst!*"

Weal halted, but Bullneck kicked open the back door of the alley. Weal grabbed Bullneck before he could run out, holding him in place. Elias saw Weal swallow, and knew the man was gathering his courage to lunge at Pendrake, and Pendrake would do nothing, because Cephantines did not injure or take life.

*"Take him, Beelzebub curse your chickenhead bones!"*

Weal started forward.

"Tear his head off, Pendrake," Elias shouted, knowing it was hopeless.

With a deafening, animal roar, Pendrake sprang to meet Weal. The sound was vicious, striking fear into Elias, raising the hackles on his neck.

*Pendrake? God!*

Weal fell backward, spun to his knees and scrambled out the rear exit behind Bullneck as the terrifying roar came again. Elias looked at Jost, trying to pin down the nerve-shredding sound, still not believing Pendrake could have made it. Jost's face was white with fear. He gazed wide-eyed at Pendrake's back. Pendrake whirled back, teeth bared in a feral snarl, his face distorted with murderous savagery. Jost held his palms up in surrender.

Elias stared at Pendrake, stunned.

The horrible snarl vanished from Pendrake's face and he bent over Jost. Jost shrank back. "Don't touch me!"

"But you are bleeding," Pendrake said. "You have been injured. I must get help." He turned to Elias. "Are you all right?"

Elias stared at him, disoriented by Pendrake's sudden change back to the peaceful Cephantine. Then relief flooded him—followed by fury. He glared over at Jost. *Bastard, you almost killed me.* "You're falling behind on that bleeding," Elias said. "Why don't you lie there awhile and practice? Pendrake, get us out of here."

"But Jost—"

"We'll send someone after him."

Jost grunted bitterly. "I'm sure thou will'st. Someone in an imp lackey uniform."

"It's more than you deserve."

Elias felt Pendrake's arms cradle his back and knees. As he was lifted up, an ugly thought occurred to him: Jost might have a backup on the concourse, in case he botched the kill. "I'm going to play dead out there," he told Pendrake. "Don't worry about it. Just act sorry, like you're carrying the corpse of your dear friend."

Pendrake put on an expression of exaggerated mourning, as though the great tragedy of the ages had stricken him. "Like this?"

"No, sadder," Elias advised.

Elias lay in his bed back in the guest quarters, practicing moving his toes and trying to look down Martha's nightgown as she bent over him. She ran her biopotentiometer over his arm and clucked in distress. "It's the same effect I found at the attendant's autopsy. Fortunately for you, it's not as severe, or you'd be dead too. Can you lift your arms now?"

Elias raised first one, then the other off his bed, then lifted his legs, too. "It's coming back," he said with relief.

"I still think you should be in a hospital."

"I'm safer right here in my room. There isn't a better physician than you within four parsecs. And besides, I've got Godzilla over there to protect me."

Pendrake paced back to his bed and gave him an injured look. "Please, Elias. What I did is troubling enough to me already."

Elias tried to keep a straight face. "How did you

roar like that? I wish you could have heard it, Martha. Like a lion in an echo chamber. If my hair turns white, I'm going to blame you, Pendrake."

"Leave him alone, Elias."

Her mild rebuke pricked him with shame. She was right. This was the closest Pendrake had ever come to doing something violent, and he needed reassurance, understanding. "I'm sorry, friend. You saved my life. And I know that if your bluff hadn't worked, you'd never have hurt those men. You'd have let them kill you first."

"Thank you, Elias. I do not doubt that either. But what if my roar, as you call it, had caused one of the men to die of a heart attack?

"And another thing: However did I manage to make such a vicious sound?"

"Maybe way back in your history, Cephantines weren't pacifists. Or maybe it's just a prehistoric mating call—" Elias saw Martha's warning frown and fell silent.

"I must research the matter," Pendrake said gravely, "if we ever get that vacation on Cephan."

Elias gripped Pendrake's hand. "Right after we leave this miserable hellhole of a planet. I promise you."

Pendrake smiled. "Maybe we should not visit Cephan. If we do, you will not need to worry about someone trying to murder you. The boredom of that might kill you instead."

"He zinged me again," Elias complained to Martha.

She nodded with an air of distraction and walked to Elias' closet, rummaging until she found a robe. As she wrapped herself in it, he gave her a disappointed look. "You would deny a dying man his last peek?"

"If you're well enough to peek," she said with mock severity, "I think you're off the critical list."

"Oh, I wasn't being critical, believe me."

Martha blushed. "I think you should shut up now and rest."

Pendrake rolled his eyes, as if disgusted with both

of them. Elias felt his relief at escaping death again fading. He began to think about the earphone weapon, and realized that trying to kill him with it did not make sense. He could understand why Jost might want him dead—to keep him from uncovering a rebel conspiracy in the mines. But why not just bash him on the head with a rock? The earphone weapon would leave less sign, true, but it was still detectable. Martha's autopsy on the attendant—and the exam she'd just done on him —proved that.

"You look pretty grim all of a sudden," Martha observed.

"I wish we'd been able to grab that earphone."

"You mean this?" Pendrake pulled the earphone weapon from his vest.

Elias looked at it astonished. " 'You mean this,' " he mimicked. "Get him."

"I took it as soon as I entered the alley," Pendrake explained. "I saw that the colonist was holding it on your head and assumed it was what had felled you. So I gave him a little push and removed it. It seemed wise to keep it."

Martha took it from Pendrake and inspected it. Elias tried to see too, then realized with pleasure that he'd sat up. "Looks like I'm mending fast."

Martha groped his wrist for his pulse. "Heart rate's almost back to normal," she agreed, looking relieved. He took advantage of her distraction to pluck the earphone from her other hand. He examined it. The rubbery, fleshlike cone that had been pushed into his ear was mounted on a standard plastic earphone base at one end of the curving headset band. He prodded the cone gingerly. His first impression from the alley grew stronger. "This isn't synthetic," he said. "It's real flesh." He felt a queasy revulsion. Flipping the cone over, he looked at the reverse side of the earphone disk. Set into it was an unlabeled switch. Probably activated the damned thing. He turned it back and forth. Nothing seemed to happen.

Martha took the earphone weapon back, laid it on the bedtable and opened her medical case, removing a small cylinder that looked to Elias like an outsized jeweler's loupe, or a small opera glass. Martha studied the cone through it, then looked at him, her face grim. "It's real flesh, all right. But nothing human."

His unease deepened. "If it's biological, how is it preserved?"

"It's not. It's alive."

"You mean it's some kind of small animal?"

"No. It's *part* of an animal—or more precisely, a biological being. My spectral readings indicate that the base of the cone is sheared flesh. The cut surface is embedded in a wafer of solid nutrient base, which must feed the severed tissue and keep it alive."

Elias shuddered. "And somehow the thing can shut down your neuroelectric energy. But *why?* What's the advantage of this damned thing? You've got to get close, hold the victim still."

"Maybe it's just a prototype," Martha said. "Maybe they've been using their enemies as guinea pigs to assess the effects. If so, you can be sure they're working on ways to beam it at people from a distance."

Elias imagined the thing being built into a broadcaster, hidden aboard a battleship; men and women slumping over at their posts, dying with no sound or flash of light to track back to what was killing them. He felt chilled and sickened. "I hope you're wrong."

"We've got to get this back to Earth," Martha said, "where our weapons people can really study it."

"That might not be so simple. This nasty little gizmo is like nothing the Imperium has seen. Jost will know we took it. We've got at least several more days before we're finished here. Jost can't afford to let us keep it."

"If he's still alive," Martha pointed out.

"Even if he's not, those two bully boys with him can't have run off too far. They probably got over their panic pretty fast and went back for Jost—and the earphone. One way or the other, they know we've got it. I think they'll do almost anything to get it back."

Someone rapped at the door.

Elias felt a surge of alarm, and then annoyance that his body was still so close to panic. He picked his needler up from the nightstand and pulled the ruptor from under his pillow, ignoring Pendrake's grimace of disapproval. Shoving the earphone weapon under his sheets, he called, "Who is it?"

"Krevvy."

The cop who'd gone looking, along with the medical team, for Jost. Elias relaxed a little, then realized it might be someone trying to sound like Krevvy.

He nodded at Pendrake, tossing his needler to Martha and motioning her to stand behind the door. But when Pendrake opened up, it was indeed Detective Lieutenant Krevvy. He looked more awake than when he'd answered their call, but an air of deep weariness still clung to him. Elias saw something in Krevvy's eyes that he'd missed in all the rush earlier: an extra gravity of untold violence; choke matches that had gone too far, perhaps; bondage games that ended in blood and death.

Elias lowered his ruptor.

Krevvy stepped into the room and Elias saw two uniformed police behind him. Krevvy said, "We went where you said and found a lot of blood but no Jost. We're searching the concourse, stall by stall, and we've issued holo alerts with his pic. If he's still in Neues Eisen, we'll find him."

Elias glanced at the clock on his bedtable. Only four thirty-five. It seemed impossible that only three and a half hours ago, he'd been peacefully dreaming of rivers and babies. "Very efficient, Lieutenant. If you find him, what will you do?"

"Arrest him, of course." Krevvy advanced into the room and looked around with casual nonchalance, but Elias could see that his eyes were sharp. "Ma'am."

Krevvy nodded at Martha, who had her hands clasped behind her back, hiding the needler.

"Lieutenant."

"That ruptor," Krevvy said to Elias. "Did you register it when you came planetside?"

"No, Lieutenant."

"Then I'm afraid I'll have to ask you for it."

"And I'm afraid I'll have to say no."

Krevvy stiffened and Elias felt a weary annoyance. The man was getting his back up, and Elias didn't want to deal with it, but he'd have to anyway. "Lieutenant, if I could speak to you alone for a minute." Elias nodded toward Krevvy's two men.

"Give me the ruptor," Krevvy said, ignoring him. "And I'll have to search your quarters for any other illegal weapons."

*Or for a headset, Lieutenant?*

Time to step down hard. "I remind you, Lieutenant Krevvy, that I have full powers as the direct representative of the Imperator on this planet. That makes me your superior officer. So back off, or I'll have your badge for insubordination."

Krevvy's face went white. He reached into his V-coat.

"I wouldn't do that, Lieutenant," Martha said coolly.

Krevvy looked at her with surprise, saw the needler she pointed at his stomach, and eased his hand away from his shoulder holster. Good move, Martha, Elias thought with admiration.

"You're making a big mistake," Krevvy said.

"You should thank her," Elias said. "If you'd pointed a weapon at me, I'd have slapped you into one of your own cells on an assault rap. Now, can you accept your position, or do I have to get Cay Endor out of bed and have you removed from the case?"

Krevvy's expression did not change, but his shoulders sagged fractionally. Elias almost felt pity, but his acute awareness of the headset under the sheets stopped him. *You want that headset, don't you, you bastard? Not stray weapons. And I never mentioned the headset. I just told you that Jost and two other men attacked us. So how could you know about the headset, unless you've found Jost, or knew he meant to kill me— and how—ahead of time?*

"You're dismissed, Lieutenant," Elias said coldly.

With a last look at Martha's needler, Krevvy turned and stalked out.

When Pendrake had bolted the door, Martha clicked the safety on the needler and dropped it on the bed. Elias saw that her hand was shaking. He felt a surge of warmth and gratitude for her. "Nice work," he said.

She gave him a wan smile. "You should have that man arrested."

"You think he was after the headset, too."

She nodded.

"But it's only that—*thinking.* We don't have any proof. And I can't see us getting any."

"But if Krevvy *is* what we think—a rebel sympathizer—he'll be dangerous to you running loose. You could have him arrested on suspicion of treason and held for forty-eight hours. . . ."

"Yes, and if we're wrong about him, the Imperium will have jailed an innocent colonist—a public servant, no less—and given all rebel sympathizers on Cassiodorus a nasty little rallying point. And even if he *is* guilty, jailing him won't make us safe. What we have to do now is put that headset where no one's going to find it." Elias looked around the room, knowing even as he did that there could be no adequate hiding place here. The minute they were out, someone could toss the place so completely that a cockroach wouldn't escape. But there had to be some way. . . .

His gaze fell on Martha's medkit and the idea hit him. He laughed, delighted. It would be simple—and foolproof.

"What?" Martha said.

"You still think I'm too thin?"

She looked blank, then her face lit with understanding. "Just a couple of centimeters," she said. She gave him a raunchy grin. "Do I get to decide where?"

# 10

ELIAS' CHEST ITCHED. HE FOUGHT THE URGE TO scratch it as he waited in the anteroom of Cay Endor's viceregal office. He could almost feel the earphone pressing now against his heart. The cone of severed flesh—*God, was it really alive?*—and what if it could function in more than the ear canal? What if it somehow activated and went to work through its encasing layers of plastiflesh, striking at the nerves of his heart? He shuddered with revulsion.

And was annoyed with himself: What's done is done, he told himself. And it's the perfect hiding place.

Damn it, how much longer did Endor plan to keep him waiting?

He got up and paced across the anteroom, past the militia sergeant who stood at ease before the huge, gothic doors to Endor's throne room. Elias studied the doors. They were at least six meters tall at their rounded apex. Each door was Terran oak inlaid with gleaming, gold bas-reliefs. Their luxury annoyed him. After the stark austerity the colonists lived in, the doors were ostentatious.

The guard pulled one of the great doors open, straining against the weight of wood and gold. "Inspector Kane, the viceroy will see you now."

Elias entered, feeling the plushness of deep blue carpet under his feet. Endor sat behind a huge, ornate desk in a high-backed swivel chair. He wore a white imperial uniform, pure silk, trimmed in gold braid. Around him, the vast room gleamed in the brilliance of crystal chandeliers. Priceless paintings hung along the walls, separated by tall, narrow windows which were shuttered against the meager, reddish daylight of Cassiodorus.

Elias was struck by the contrast from the banquet. Evidently, the plain banquet hall and Endor's humble militia uniform were concessions to his subjects' sensibilities. Here in this office sat the true man, surrounded by the wealth of his power.

Behind Endor, his Ornyl bodyguard stood with characteristic stillness.

"Your Excellency. Thank you for seeing me."

Endor nodded, motioned over his shoulder. "This is Subrath."

Elias tried vainly for contact with the Ornyl's blank, compound eyes, feeling the usual uncomfortable slippage of nerve in his retinas. He thought of the s'uniph attack and felt a stab of paranoia. Had this creature had anything to do with the attack? As Endor's bodyguard, Subrath would hear most of what Endor heard, know almost everything he knew. Subrath would have known Briana was sending another inspector.

With an effort, Elias regained his perspective. He was here to get a feel for Endor's loyalties, not Subrath's. If Subrath *had* arranged for the s'uniph attack, he could only have done it if Cay Endor wanted it—if the treachery on Cassiodorus started at the top.

"How is the Imperator?" Endor asked.

"She's well."

Endor flushed and Elias knew with a flash of intuition that Endor had meant Gregory Amerdath, not his daughter.

"And her father?" Endor said.

"As well as can be expected."

"A rotten, sickening business," Endor said. "We were comrades. I was his navigator on the *Scaramouche,* back in the war. God, that man could lead. We'd have followed him into hell. You've seen him, Kane, you know his condition firsthand. D'you think there's any chance he'll rule again?"

Elias realized at once the importance of the question—and of his answer: Amerdath had ruled through bonds of loyalty forged in fire and sealed with blood. Each of his viceroys were old comrades. Even Richard DuMorgan had not turned against Amerdath while he was on the throne.

If Gregory Amerdath were still in power, even DuMorgan might have been brought back into the fold. If Gregory Amerdath were dead, DuMorgan might by now have been openly joined by many of the other viceroys.

But Amerdath was neither in power nor dead.

That left Endor in a sort of limbo. Should he transfer his loyalty to Briana to honor her still living father? Or should he consider his loyalty to the Imperium ended? On the answer, everything might depend.

"He could rule again," Elias said. "If he can be restored to a body."

Endor's gaze was intense. "Subrath tells me that he wanted only to die."

"And how does Subrath know this?" Elias said, sensing the danger, putting scorn into his voice.

Endor lifted a hand in the Ornyl's direction, freeing him to speak. The chubby speech hands twirled into motion across Subrath's abdomen. "All Ornyl know of . . . the noble Chuddath. And of how you . . . thwarted his loyalty."

Elias felt his cheeks grow hot, as if Subrath had slapped him physically instead of verbally. He controlled his anger, realizing Endor was watching him closely. Coldly he said, "Then all Ornyl should know this, too. The only thing the 'noble' Chuddath proved is that Ornyl aren't fit to judge the human mind." Elias looked pointedly at Cay Endor. "With respect, sir: I assume you've bonded Subrath to you with the S'edhite link. That's fine. You can depend on his absolute loyalty. But may I advise you never to mindmeld with him. As men, we all have thoughts and wishes we don't really want carried out."

Endor looked at him with a mixture of fear and fascination.

"May I speak further," Subrath said.

"No," Endor said, and Elias knew he'd won a small victory.

He decided to press it. "Amerdath may rule again, and in the meantime, his daughter has his full trust."

"Is that so? And tell me, Kane. Do I have hers?"

"Yes," Elias said without hesitation, even as he knew that it was not true.

Endor gazed at him a moment, as if assessing him. "Why did you want to see me?"

Elias told Endor about the earphone weapon, watching for any reaction. He described the autopsy findings for the dead attendant and his tangle with Jost —the terrible draining of strength he'd experienced firsthand. As he talked, Endor sat up straighter, clenching the armrests of his throne, his face dark with anger.

If he was faking, he was doing it well.

Elias asked, "What do you know about this weapon, sir?"

"Only what you've just told me. Damn! It's a shame you couldn't have grabbed that one away from the men who attacked you."

"Yes," Elias said uncomfortably. "But one of Jost's men ran out with it when Pendrake caught them by surprise." He hoped the lie sounded convincing. Even if Endor was clean, there was still no benefit from handing the exotic weapon over and risking it disappearing into the hands of a rebel mole in Endor's camp.

And if Endor wasn't clean, he'd pass on the lie and it might spread some confusion among the rebels—take some of the steam out of any effort to reclaim the weapon.

"By God, Lieutenant Krevvy better catch this Jost character."

"Maybe he could use some help, say an independent investigation by your own intelligence people."

Endor looked at him with narrowed eyes, as if trying to gauge whether he was overstepping his bounds. "Not a bad idea, Inspector Kane. I'll do it—if for no other reason than to demonstrate how deeply I regret these attacks on you."

Endor gave a heavy sigh. "I know what's really on your mind, Kane. You're asking yourself: Who can I trust here? Who can Briana trust? I know you have doubts, and I know damned well those doubts include me. It'd be naïve of me to deny that there could be rebel elements stirring up trouble on my planet, the way they are on all the others. The fact is, I keep a careful lookout for any such sign. I do my best to run a tight ship.

"But this is a rough planet. The kind of people it takes to survive and work here need to feel that they are, as much as possible, in charge of their own affairs. A good many of them *do* resent off-worlders in general, and officials from Earth in particular. That by no means makes them rebels in the political sense. But it *does* make some of the rougher types among them dangerous to men like you. Frankly, if Briana was as trustful as she claims to be, none of this would have happened to you."

"The three previous inspectors—"

"Yes, yes," Endor said irritably. "I understand. Still, I cannot help but feel questioned, despite her protestations of trust. I'm in a delicate position here. I must represent the Imperium, *be* the Imperium to these people—but do it in such a way that they do not resent it or feel governed from outside. *That* is the best way to keep the Imperium together. Increased imperial presence—like your battleship orbiting up there—is the worst way.

"I think I've done a good job the last two decades, and so, obviously, did Briana's father. The people of this planet are loyal to me, and I am loyal to the Imperator, so by extension, the people of this planet are loyal to the Imperium. We don't need imperial inspectors tromping around here with carte blanche papers from Briana, if you'll excuse my bluntness. Trust us and we'll continue to get as much ore to you as we possibly can, just as we have always done in the past."

Elias was impressed despite himself. Endor seemed sincere and he had stated his case well.

But "sincere" could also be "dead wrong."

Endor, himself, had put his finger on the problem: How did you tell a colonist loyal to the Imperium from a rebel thirsting to overthrow it? The rebels were not fools. They wore the same clothes as loyalists, worked in the same mines, probably even drank in the same bars. They also met in secret, plotting, planning; *killing.* It was not innocent colonists that had tried twice to murder him. There *are* rebels operating here, Elias thought. Whether you know it or not, Endor.

"I appreciate your position, sir. I hope you'll appreciate mine. From the moment Briana decided to send me here, there have been three attempts on my life. We're not talking heart failure now, we're talking murder."

Endor pinched the bridge of his nose between his fingers. "What do you want from me?"

To know if you're loyal, Elias thought. Just as you've said. But that's not going to be so easy, is it?

"Two things," he said. "First, I'm ready to see the mining books. I'll need to review man-hours, cave-ins, daily averages, projected goals and actual production for each mine."

"That information is compiled continuously by my compusayer. I'll give you access, but I'd prefer you not let that be known."

"Understood."

"What else?" Endor said.

"I'd like another tour of a mine—hopefully one that's not about to cave in on me. And while I'm at it, I might want to look around in general. Your permission ahead of time would make it a lot easier. Then I can stop waving that carte blanche you mentioned. Believe me, I don't like it any more than you do."

"All right," Endor said. "I'll have Holz drive you around today. I'll tell him to take you wherever you want to go. But I'm warning you: Tread lightly. Be careful how and where you poke your nose in. In your zeal to root out rebel spies and secrets, remember that the vast majority of my people are hardworking, proud men and women whose worst sin is a nasty chip on their shoulders.

"Don't try to knock that chip off. Men have died from that, too."

The fierce gravity pressed Elias deep into the back seat of Holz's groundcar. He was sweating profusely from the last little walking tour. Some company store or other that Holz was still babbling about. Elias was acutely aware of Martha beside him and hoped he did not smell as bad as he felt. His nose was too clogged with dust to tell.

But then again, hopefully, Martha's was too.

As Holz drove them back toward the guest quarters of the Rajinate, Elias tried to catalog what they had seen, sift it for meaning. Only one thing kept coming up: the children.

Or rather, the lack of them.

"Before Jost got around to trying to kill me," Elias said, "he told me you don't have many youngsters on the planet."

"That's true," Holz said.

"But you do have some."

Holz glanced back from the front seat of the groundcar. "Of course."

"Where are they? We've been all over Neues Eisen, and I haven't seen one yet."

"In school."

Elias began to feel a mild sense of wrongness. All through the tour, Holz had been loquacious, showing them this company store, that bank, the other cafeteria, answering all their questions with more than they wanted to know. He'd even indulged in a friendly, long-winded discussion with Pendrake on the feasibility of hiring Cephantines to help work the mines. Now, suddenly, he seemed to have a two-word limit on his answers.

Elias remembered something else Jost had said. *This world be no place for little ones.* Jost's voice had been full of sadness. Maybe kids were a sore point with Holz, too.

Elias decided to probe a little further. "I'd like to visit one of the schools."

Holz laughed. "Aren't you getting just a little tired?"

Elias felt the gravity again, flattening his muscles, bending his bones. He became aware of his weariness, the unnatural stillness his body had adopted. As long as you sat in these nice cushions, you were barely aware of it. But your body still felt it. You looked at Martha from the corner of your eye instead of turning your head, you kept your hands on the seat beside you instead of on your knees, you worked hard to find a comfortable position, and once you had it, you shifted only when your spinal cord began to feel like a hot steel rod turning inside your back.

"I was planning to drive us back to the guest quarters now," Holz went on. "A rest period, and then some drinks before dinner at the Sisyphus. It's really a grand restaurant—and controlled at point seven."

Elias felt Holz's suggestion enticing him. To shuffle back out in the thick heat of Cassiodorus when they could all go home to a bath and a drink? He wasn't being fair to the others.

"I would find a visit to one of your schools most

interesting," Pendrake said with apparent clairvoyance.

"So would I." Martha put a hand on Elias' knee. He felt a surge of gratitude to them both and realized how much he wanted this. It had nothing whatsoever to do with his mission on this planet. I want to see a child, Elias thought with longing. In something besides my dreams.

"I guess that makes it unanimous," he said to Holz.

"Perhaps I could arrange it for tomorrow."

Elias thought of the mining books Endor was having compiled for him. That is what he would be doing tomorrow. The prospect was deadening, sharpening his need. "What would be wrong with right now?"

Holz sighed. "I must clear it first."

"You have a phone right there," Elias pointed out.

One of Holz's hands left the wheel, inched toward the phone as if the air had petrified around it. "It may be difficult to arrange on such short notice."

"I'm sure you can persuade them," Elias said, tired of Holz's sudden foot dragging.

Holz made the call, muttering so low that it was difficult to understand him. "All right," he said as he hung up. "I'll drive you over now."

"Thank you," Elias said, feeling better at once.

The drive seemed to go on and on, through the outskirts of Neues Eisen and then a quarter of the way back around the city. As Holz drove, he talked. "You must understand, Inspector Kane. These children may not look and act like you expect. The heavy gravity in which they are born and raised affects them much more seriously than it does adults. Their muscles are small. It is very difficult. Often, they suffer developmentally."

Elias saw sweat rolling down Holz's face for the first time today. He began to feel a gnawing anxiety. Just what was Holz trying to tell him? Why was the man so afraid? Elias began to be afraid, too—that what he would see would tear at his heart instead of refresh it.

He felt Martha's hand close over his. He tried to give her a reassuring smile, but couldn't.

Holz pulled up outside two low, stone buildings. Both were windowless. The farther one was surrounded by a high, chain link fence with barbed wire at the top. The flag of Cassiodorus hung straight down on its pole outside the entrance to the nearer building. The pole beside it, which should have carried the flag of the Imperium, poked emptily at the sky.

Elias felt the more distant building drawing his gaze again. "What's the story with the fence?" He asked Holz. "Looks more like a prison than a school."

"That fence is to keep people out, Inspector Kane. Not in. That is the former school building. Twenty years ago there was an almost impossible freak accident with the power plant. Some radioactive dust was carried through the duct system. Several teachers and children were affected and later died. The building was sealed off. We don't use nuclear anymore, of course, and sealing prevents any danger to the external environment. We keep the building as a monument. The fence is to keep any curiosity seekers out—there are no doubt still some radioactive atoms firing off in there."

Elias looked away from the grim walls, the gleaming fence, chilled and sickened.

"How horrible," Martha said.

"Indeed. Now, if you'll follow me."

Every muscle in Elias' body protested when he climbed from the car, but he ignored the pain, pressing forward with a mixture of dread and anticipation. The minute they passed through the entrance, he felt the welcome lift of gravity suppression, the blissful sweep of cool air on his face. The director, Hol Brader, was there to meet them. Elias felt a mild shock at Brader's youth —the man couldn't be more than twenty-one. Though he was big, his handshake was curiously lifeless. His eyes had a hard, burned-out look.

Elias' dread deepened.

"Doctor, Inspector, Mr. Pendrake, we're honored

by your interest," Brader said without conviction. "If you'll follow me, I'll take you to the gym. The children are at recess now."

Brader led the way down a dim, empty hallway. The floor was thick with dust, as though it was seldom used. A low bank of lockers gleamed with an unblemished coat of green paint. Elias felt Martha's hand groping for his again and knew she felt it too: *what a grim, lifeless place!*

But when Brader opened the gym door, bright light and the happy cries of several dozen children spilled out. Elias stepped into the gym and stared at the children, transfixed with pleasure and relief. They were not playing any organized game, but running around the gym with wild, cheerful abandon, pushing each other, tumbling and clambering up, laughing. They're so awkward, Elias thought with a pang. He remembered what Holz had said about their development being hampered. His relief began to fade.

One of the children, a small, thin girl, spotted them at the door. She stared at them, blinking, as if uncertain what she was seeing.

"Hi!" Martha called out.

The little girl smiled and ran toward them. The other children saw them now and ran over, too. One tripped and others fell over him in a tumbling chain reaction, making Elias wince. But they scrambled up and were soon surrounding Martha and Pendrake. Elias watched, miffed and a little envious, as Pendrake marched around the gym with two children on each massive shoulder.

Martha brought him the little girl who'd seen them first. "Elias, this is Jun."

He bent down, smiling, and took her hands. "Hi, Jun."

The little girl said nothing but smiled back shyly. Her fingers felt soft and small in his. Something about her smile touched him deeply and he felt tears springing to his eyes. He blinked them back, embarrassed. "What's that game you kids were playing?"

She looked at him without understanding.

"Tag?" he prompted.

Still she said nothing. He realized suddenly that she was older than she looked. Something in her face gave it away—perhaps the length of her nose or a few extra millimeters of development along her jawline. She was on the verge of adolescence. And yet, her overall size made her look about eight. He looked beyond her to the other children. None of them were big. Not one showed the bullish robustness so routine among adults on the planet.

It was as though Cassiodorus had stolen the calcium, the very marrow from their developing bones.

Elias felt a spasm of hate for the planet. The Imperium ought to shut it down, he thought savagely. Bring all these people home. Forget the damned beta-steel and the dreadnoughts.

At the very least, the children ought to be evacuated, taken to Earth, where they'd have the same chance other kids had to grow up normally—

Elias felt a jolt of realization: That is exactly what Holz had been afraid of. Everyone on this planet must be afraid of it—that the wrong person would see, a person with the power to act against them.

*To take away their children.*

He watched Jun run back to her friends, his throat tight with emotion, his head swimming suddenly with questions: *Why* did the heavy gravity do this to the children?

And knowing that it did, how could anyone on this Godforsaken world ever let himself have a child?

## 11

ELIAS COULD NOT SLEEP. HE ROLLED ONTO HIS SIDE, staring at the wall. It glowed in the dim spray of light from the slitted bathroom door. Maybe he should shut the door completely. But he did not like sleeping in the dark. Needed to see, in case someone slipped in.

He felt under his pillow for the ruptor, then tossed restlessly back onto his other side, peering down past his feet to the room's entry door, knowing he'd locked it.

He felt uneasy anyway.

He checked his clock. Four-fifteen. The silence of his room oppressed him. He caught himself talking to himself—running an aimless inner chatter in his mind to block out the silence. He rolled onto his back and stared at the ceiling, remembering the two fairy tale days aboard the *Seraphim*. Martha in his cabin almost all the time. The wonderful warmth of her closeness, her touch. How deeply he'd slept when she was with him, never waking or looking at the door. Needing no light through the endless night of space.

In the empty silence now, he remembered how they'd talked. He could hear her voice rising and falling in its own natural music, full of life and intelligence and enthusiasm. How fascinating, the things she said, letting

120

him see her thoughts and feelings—what she wanted, hoped for and feared. Even her little cast-off remarks were full of interest—medicine, her lab, hiking. She liked to climb big rocks, inching up high and clinging; deliberately looking down to spook herself. He wanted to hear more. He wanted to keep listening to her, filling himself with her. I'd never get it all, he thought. There'd always be more. He felt a sharp yearning for her.

She's just down the hall.

After the *Seraphim*, why did I go right back to being alone?

Because I'm an idiot. He stared up at the ceiling, feeling his eyes widen with revelation. He'd been describing love to himself. *I love her!*

He felt a burgeoning excitement, realizing that something had changed inside him. Changed at some indeterminant time in the past few weeks, and at last he'd let it through and realized it. He sat up in bed. I've *been* loving her!

A flood of emotion broke through inside him like a dam bursting—the love, and a giddy, thrilling fear.

He grinned into the semidarkness. An idiot, yes. But not anymore. He got up and strode to the bathroom, his legs springy despite their aches and pains. Humming, he scrubbed his face, combed his hair, brushed his teeth—still humming around the toothbrush. He pulled on his robe, threw the bolt on his door with a flourish of his wrist.

He hurried down the hall to her room, eagerness bounding inside him. He knocked gently for almost a minute, until at last she opened the door, blinking sleepily, the pattern of her bedspread imprinted on one cheek. "I'm in love," he announced.

She closed the door in his face.

Inched it open again. "With whom?"

"You. I want to spend the rest of my life with you."

She looked wide awake now. "Don't beat around

the bush, Elias. If you've got something to tell me, just come right out and say it."

He grinned, trying to think of a reply, but before he could speak, she grabbed him around the neck and gave him a long, slow kiss, backing into her room, pulling him along. He felt the dissipating heat of sleep all along her body.

She drew her head back at last. "No fair. You brushed your teeth."

He ran his tongue along her lips and she gave in, flicking him back then admitting him. Her mouth tasted musty and sweet. He felt her even through the centimeters of plastiflesh, then thought of the buried, alien thing he was pressing against her and tried to pull away. She would not let him. Her kiss was hot and eager, rousing a rush of passion in him. Dizzy with pleasure, he pulled her back to the bed, falling over with her, laughing. She divided his robe, her warm hands sliding on around his ribs, electrifying his skin. "Elias, oh."

She raised her legs along his flanks, channeling him down until her ankles locked behind his waist, sealing him into her. He had the sudden overwhelming sense of her goodness, her perfectness for him. I love you, he thought with joy; without amazement, as though he had always known it.

She was smooth and firm, sliding around his hardness, moving to her own pleasure and increasing his until he had to shout, biting it back, exploding, soaring with her in molten, golden arcs.

He lay with her, feeling an idiotic grin stretch his face.

He went back to her with his hand, wanting desperately to please her. She took it greedily, making soft, joyous cries, grabbing him at last to make him stop, shuddering, crying out over and over. She gave a huge sigh and rolled tight to him, draping her arm and leg over him.

"I love you," he said.

"I believe you," she said with wonder.

She stroked his back. He held her smooth flank, moving his hand just enough to keep the warm, satiny sensation alive in his fingers. His mind floated back and forth. Martha. Me. Martha and me.

And children.

His mind leapt back to the children he had seen yesterday. He saw little Jun's face again in his mind. Her mute smile haunted him, repainted in his memory as a plea for help.

Elias looked at Martha, gazing into her face, entranced with its slightly lopsided beauty. She gave him the crooked little smile he loved. "What are you thinking about?"

"How I worship you—the pads of your feet, the little curls in your ears, and the way your top and bottom teeth don't quite match up."

She dug him in the ribs. "And what else?"

"Those kids we saw yesterday."

"I know. I can't get them out of my mind either."

"That other building," he said, "the one behind the fence: If there was really a nuclear accident there twenty years ago, why build the new school right next to it? OK, the building was sealed off, it was probably safe, but still it nags at me."

"Holz said they kept it as a memorial," she said, "but I wonder. If a bunch of their kids had been killed by a sauroid from the wastelands, would the colonists stuff the damn thing and display it as a memento?"

"Exactly. And yet they keep that building. Why not run a decon on it and raze it to the ground? And another thing: If the gravity is so harmful to the kids' development, why don't they just keep them in Earth-normal G until they grow up?"

Her hand came to rest on his back. "Mmm. Good point. Adults from off-planet seem able to acclimate. How, I can't imagine, but they do. So why not keep their kids inside under gravity suppression until they become adults, then acclimate 'em? Maybe it has something to do with expense. Suppression is too expensive for most regular homes. It would mean giving up their kids to separate dorms, visiting them there instead of having them at home."

"Wouldn't you do that, before you let a child of yours become like what we saw?"

"Yes I would," she said soberly. "Elias, what are you getting at?"

"I'm not sure." He felt a sudden exasperation. The paradoxes on this planet kept piling up: People who could work all day in 1.5 G's, and have enough strength left over to kick up their heels half the night. Then those same hyperstrong, hyperactive people having weak, dull children. Having them even though they must know what would happen to them.

Elias made up his mind suddenly. "I'm going back to that school. What time is it?" He raised himself to an elbow, looking over her to her bedtable clock. "My God, almost eight o'clock."

"Aren't you supposed to look at the mining books today?"

"I can still do that."

"Holz won't want to take you back there."

"I'm not going with Holz. Have you got something in that medical bag of yours that will detect radiation?"

She turned on the light beside her bed, making him squint. "Elias, not *that* building. You can't go there." Her voice was frightened.

"I don't think they had a radiation accident there. I think that building is in use."

"Why? How?"

"I don't know, damn it. But too many things don't add up right. Has it occurred to you that all those kids we saw yesterday were at least nine years old? They looked younger, but I'm betting they weren't. So where are the five- and six-year-olds? I think they might be in that building. And for some reason Holz didn't want us to see them."

"But how are you going to get in there? Even if you're right, they'll stick to their story."

"I'll sneak in."

"It's light by now. Someone'll see you."

"I've got to go in during the day. That's when the kids would be there. I'll wear clay-colored clothes and dart from bush to bush." He gave her a weak grin.

"There aren't any bushes. And there isn't any darting, either, not on this planet."

"So I'll crawl."

She shook her head. "Elias, maybe there *is* something strange going on with the kids on this planet. But even if there is, what could it have to do with the mines? With rebels siphoning off beta-steel ore?"

Elias felt frustrated, knowing she was right, irritated that he could not refute her. "Does it have to be connected? If these people aren't taking proper care of their kids, I want to know it. I want to do something about it." He realized with embarrassment that he was almost shouting.

But Martha only smiled. "I love you, too, Elias. And I'm coming with you."

Elias looked at her in alarm. "No, two of us slithering around would just make it twice as hard." *You can't come, because the place might really be radioactive, and I can't let anything happen to you.*

She took his hands. "Elias . . . OK, what you say makes sense. It'd probably be harder for two of us to get in. But you're thinking something else, too, and you and I both know why. You loved Beth and she was killed. You've been so afraid to risk it again, and now you're beating that fear. Don't slide back."

Elias brought her hands to his lips and kissed them, unable to speak, afraid, just as she said, and determined not to be. But it was so hard.

"You're not going to lose me," she said.

"No," he said with fierce determination. "I'm not."

Elias walked out through the empty lobby of the guest quarters onto the street, feeling the extra gravity drop like a huge pack onto his back. The air was already warm and soupy, the sun a miserable reddish glow over the tops of the squat buildings. The streets were empty except for a large airtruck, filled with big men heading for the penetrator road out of the city. Miners on the way to work, no doubt.

Elias waited several minutes for a cab. Sweat built up at his hairline, rolling down his face, as his calves began to work up to the familiar ache. Finally a cab cruised up. He gave the woman at the wheel an address several blocks from the school. If she recognized him and reported in, they'd no doubt guess where he'd gone, but no sense handing it to them straight out. As she drove, she kept giving him odd looks in her mirror, and his heart sank. I'm too thin, he thought. Everyone who's been on this damned planet any length of time is built like a landing pad.

"From what planet be you?" the woman asked.

He felt a small relief: she knew he was an off-worlder, but she didn't know he was from Earth.

"Cerulyx," he said, trying to give it the proper accent.

"Good," she said. "Ye be miners, too."

"But not like thee."

That did the trick. She held forth on the "devlish perils" of life on Cassiodorus. She pointed out each dead groundcar they passed and complained bitterly about the clay fouling everything. She was still talking when she pulled to a stop. He realized with sudden alarm that he had to pay her in cash and he had nothing but a few imperial credits. Damn! Now that he'd said he was from Cerulyx, he couldn't give her those. Might as well beg her to report him.

He broke into a sweat, patting his pockets.

Her face hardened. "Don't tell me thou hast no money."

"Will'st take this watch?" He slipped it off his arm and held it out to her.

Her eyes widened. "That be from Earth!"

"I didn't think the imp who wore it would miss it."

She laughed. "Rogue! 'Tis too valuable."

"Not if thou wilt come back for me too, say, in three hours, at this spot?"

"Done, stranger. But even then, I'll have to make thee some change." She peeled off twenty Cassi credits from her roll, looked at the watch again and gave him another ten, each bearing the image of Cay Endor in his plain uniform.

She drove off and Elias sighed with relief. He looked around him, trying to orient himself. This was Luxor Street, a narrow throughway lined by warehouses and maintenance depots. According to the map Martha had got on her shopping trip, the school should be two blocks down, to the west of the warehouses. He began to slog down the street, wondering at its emptiness at nine o'clock in the morning. Probably there were tunnels below the street connecting everything, like those Holz had taken them through yesterday. That way the colonists could walk between the buildings in relative coolness.

*Coolness.* He stopped to blot at his face with his sleeve. After the air-conditioning of the cab, the heat seemed even worse. He wished grumpily that he'd had the cabbie drive him closer. Setting out again, he felt his extra weight dragging him down, flattening the cartilage in his knees and ankles, pumping rivulets of sweat down his back. God, you could never get used to this—not in a year, not in ten years.

Two blocks brought him to a couple of hydroponics warehouses separated by a narrow alley. He sighted down the gap. Beyond lay open ground. That ought to be the school. He cut through the alley, pressing his hands against the walls, easing some of the weight off his aching feet. Looking out the end of the alley, he saw the two squat school buildings surrounded by several acres of flat, hard-looking clay. He could see no one around outside, just what he needed for his approach, and yet somehow the air of desertion touched him with foreboding. The high, chain link barrier gleamed redly into his eyes as the sun found a gap in the endless heavy clouds. He patted his pocket, feeling the reassuring, pencil-shaped outlines of Martha's laser scalpel and radiometer.

Elias set out for the fence, trying to just stroll calmly, thinking how he would use the laser scalpel and . . .

He caught movement shimmering through the corner of the fence and dropped flat, jarring his ribs and knocking his wind out. He sucked a hard breath and looked up. The moving thing winked through the fence to the corner, then emerged into the open. With a shock of dread, Elias recognized the massive, insect legs, the forward-leaning body with its double sets of arms, the vicious, mantis head.

An Ornyl!

An instinctive terror crawled along Elias' spine. He pressed himself flat. Damn it, why hadn't he seen the Ornyl yesterday?

Because Holz had called ahead.

What in God's name could an Ornyl warrior be doing here? A watchman he could understand—someone to warn away the ignorant or careless, but an Ornyl was born for one thing: to kill. Almost half again the size of a man, a keen sense of smell—and those eyes: multifaceted, insect eyes, the best in the universe for detecting movement. Elias thought of the times he'd seen an Ornyl in action, the fighting arms striking faster than his eye could follow, tearing a man into bloody meat within seconds.

If this thing caught him, he would have no hope against it. And it would show no mercy to him.

Forget it, he thought. Get out of here, now!

*But if they have an Ornyl here, they're hiding something important.*

Elias suppressed a groan. With infinite slowness, he raised his head and watched the thing prowl along the fence, its long, reverse-jointed legs stalking, the awful head swiveling in constant motion. *Has it already caught my scent?* Elias wondered. Fear stabbed through him. He had the overpowering urge to spring up and run back into the alley, keep running, find someplace to burrow and hide. He held himself still and watched. The Ornyl moved toward him along the fence, pausing at the near corner and continuing on around, beginning to recede.

It hadn't smelled him.

Elias watched the Ornyl until it rounded the next corner of the fence, winking along through the mesh then disappearing beyond the building itself. *God, I've got to do it, go, GO!*

Elias pushed to his feet and began to lumber forward. A fresh sweat sprang up on his face. His legs stabbed him with agony at each step. The fence crept closer at an agonizingly slow pace. How long before the Ornyl rounded the corner again and saw him?

*You're not going to make it.*

He sank to his knees and lowered himself flat, his heart booming with dread and exertion. He could feel the answering beat of the Ornyl's feet through the clay, growing, coming toward him. He had only one hope now: that those cold, insect eyes, so good at detecting movement, were poor at recognizing a static pattern.

Elias willed himself to absolute stillness. His cheek pressed against the ground, his gaze fixed on the Ornyl. It walked down the fence toward him.

Stopped.

Its head stilled and pointed at him. Suddenly the small speech hands tucked back into the protected position and the massive fighting arms extended toward him. A horrifying image flared in Elias' mind—of his own body, a reddish pattern of dots, registering now in the Ornyl's savage brain. He felt a thrill of pure terror in his stomach.

For a long time the Ornyl stood, looking toward him. Go away, Elias thought desperately.

The Ornyl's vocal hands reemerged, sawed across the contoured speech plate of the abdomen. "Man?"

Elias tried to empty his mind, to be a piece of clay. The Ornyl moved off.

Limp with relief, Elias watched the Ornyl until it disappeared again. He got up and scrambled forward, covering the ground to the fence with frantic, adrenaline speed. He settled on his side against the fence, saw that it continued down into the dirt. Damn! He pulled the laser scalpel from his pocket. Quick, now—hurry! He activated the laser and started cutting the mesh at ground level, snipping with horrid slowness through link after link. Beyond the mesh he could see a ladder going up the side of the building, steel rungs set into the block. Get under, get to that ladder, and he might make it.

Ten links. He cursed steadily under his breath. Fifteen. That should do it. He pushed under head first, wriggling forward on his belly. The cut ends of the fence raked his back, drawing fiery tracks of pain into his skin. There—through!

He pushed up and lumbered to the ladder set into the building. Climbing straight up made the gravity seem to redouble. His shoulder and leg muscles burned with the effort. He rolled onto the roof, pulling his legs out of sight just as he heard the measured tread of the Ornyl below him. When the steps had gone again, Elias crawled across the rooftop to the nearest air stack, a big, circular duct topped by a mushroom-shaped hood. It seemed to be sealed with black metal, but as he neared it, he saw that the "sealing" was really a porous, black screen. The interior of the school was open to the air! To make sure, he checked it with Martha's radiometer.

There was no sign whatsoever of radiation.

He felt a rush of excitement and vindication. *I knew it! What are you hiding in here?*

The laser sliced easily through the screen. He

wormed down inside the vent, clinging to a strut, his
legs dangling below him. At once he felt the blessed
relief of gravity suppression. Chilled air flowed past
him, clean and wonderful, drying his sweat and restor-
ing some of his strength. He hung a moment on the
strut until his eyes acclimated to the semidark of the
ventilation shaft. He saw that the large vertical stack he
was in turned at right angles under his feet. He eased
himself down to it, finding there was enough room to
crawl on all fours. Ahead he saw a grid of light thrown
up through a vent grille from a room below. He crawled
to it and peeked down through. Below him was a classroom, small desks lined around the walls. There was no
one in the room.

There was another grille ahead. As he crawled to it,
he heard the growing murmur of a voice. A mixture of
anticipation and unease filled him. He edged his eyes
over the grille and looked down into another classroom.
Children—seated in the desks around the walls! These
kids were much smaller than yesterday's lot. They were
looking down at what appeared to be alphabet primers
—Elias could see the large, single letters and colorful
illustrations. This must be the earliest grade.

A terrible sense of wrongness gripped Elias. The
children were so still. Each little head bowed unmoving
over its book. They almost looked asleep. But he knew
they were not asleep. He could detect just enough
movement to be sure of that—a hand twitching, a head
rolling sluggishly to the side.

No normal child was ever that still.

Were they drugged?

A woman's head and shoulders came into view just
below him and he froze. She walked up and down
slowly, looking from side to side at the children along
the walls. She walked over to a little girl who was moving feebly, fretting the edge of her page with one finger.

"And what letter is that, Marly?" The woman's
voice was kind.

The child did not reply.

"*K*. Can you say *K*, Marly?"

Elias heard the child say it, a voice so soft and weary that it tore at his heart.

"Excellent!" cooed the woman. "You see, you can do it. Everyone listen to Marly. Say it again, dear!"

But Marly didn't say it again. The teacher moved on.

Elias felt a wrenching distress. What's wrong with them? A disease? Dear God, they're all so tiny, so still.

He thought of the unborn child growing in Briana's womb. How it would burst into life, squalling, beating its little arms and legs almost from the first day, filled with the wonderful energy of new life, so necessary to learning and growing and developing. Tears came to his eyes.

And then he realized that the door to the room below had opened. He started to pull his head back, but he was too late. The Ornyl's long fighting arm snatched away the grille, the horrible compound eyes stared up at him.

A cold shock went through him.

"Man . . ." commanded the Ornyl. "Come down. *Now.*"

THE CHILDREN! ELIAS THOUGHT, TERRIFIED FOR
them. But they seemed unaffected. A few raised their
heads and stared dully at the Ornyl. The others did not
even look up.

Elias saw the Ornyl reaching up for him. He sprang
over the grille opening. Metal screeched; the duct
slanted suddenly, and Elias felt himself sliding backward toward the Ornyl's clutching hands. He scrambled with desperate energy, realizing that the warrior
was yanking the duct down through the ceiling. The
teacher screamed at it to stop, but it did not stop.

Elias caught a duct joint and pulled himself up the
slope, barely feeling the sharp, metal band tear at his
fingertips. He made it into the flat duct again and
scrambled over the next room. It's going to get you, he
thought, but he scrambled on anyway, until the duct
line grew completely dark.

He made himself stop and listen. All he could hear
was the rushing sound of the air. The Ornyl could be
below him this instant, and he wouldn't know it.

He heard a crash right behind him; the Ornyl
smashing up into the duct! Elias sprang forward. A second later he heard the Ornyl slithering along behind
him, *Christ, it was in the duct!* Its acid, oily odor washed
over him, striking him with terror.

Then he heard a loud crash behind him. The Ornyl was too heavy—it had fallen through the ceiling!

He laughed with savage glee and scuttled on.

He lost track of time, hurrying through the dark, small space. The children sprang back into his mind—their utter indifference to the Ornyl. Incredible! A gruesome, huge insect man bursting into their midst could not be an everyday occurrence for them. It should have triggered panic, or at least excitement.

Elias felt a sick apprehension for them, then put it from his mind. He had to get out of here. Next time the Ornyl might strike up directly into him.

Elias heard a distant crash. The ductwork shuddered. He realized the Ornyl was looking for him along the straight trunk line. He'd thrown it off. Elation filled him. He realized that the air was rushing with more force now; he could hear the low thrum of machinery. He must be near the school's power plant ahead—*Damn!*

His fingers jammed down through a grille and he fell forward, spreading his feet, catching the edges of the duct, swinging head down in the dark. Sweat burst from his face and he felt queasy. He extended his hands and let himself go, dropping down into the room. Shocks of pain shot up his wrists as he hit and rolled, sprawling onto his side. He smelled dust and oil, heard the tick of metal contracting. He got up and groped ahead, his eyes peeling wide, straining to see in the darkness.

He found a wall and quested along it until he found a switch. He hesitated. What if the switch shut down the air conditioner or the lights? The Ornyl would know instantly that he was here.

But he had to see. If he did not get some light, he might stumble around in here until he wasted his advantage and let the Ornyl get back on his trail.

He flipped the switch. The lights came on.

He blinked and squinted, his eyes adjusting slowly, making out the rest of a switch panel. Fresh sweat popped out on his face. He'd been lucky! There were rows and rows of rheostats only inches from the one he'd thrown. They controlled the gravity suppression for various sectors of the building. If he'd bumped the wrong one he could have dropped a huge, extra weight over a classroom of children.

Or brought the Ornyl running.

Elias looked for the door. There—through a forest of ducts and pipes, at the top of a short, cement staircase. As he headed for it, it opened. The Ornyl stared down at him.

Elias felt an overwhelming despair. Trapped! The Ornyl would show him no mercy. He ran back into the room, trying to find another door, but there was no other door. He heard the Ornyl's steps crashing behind him. *No chance, I'm dead,* but he turned anyway and braced himself, thrusting his hands out. "Come on!"

The Ornyl stopped and stared at him with its fixed, mantis face. No expression—and yet he could feel its mocking amusement. His fear turned to rage.

The chubby vocal hands slipped forward from their protected place under the fighting arms and caressed the contoured abdomen. "Do you think you . . . can fight me, human? You were dead . . . from the moment . . . I smelled—"

Now! Elias thought, lunging forward, seizing the Ornyl's whirling hand in midsentence and crushing down with all his might. The warrior arched back as though riven by a huge jolt of electricity. Its fighting arm swept around in agonized reflex, catching Elias at the hip, flinging him across the room. Elias hit on his side, feeling a burst of pain in his ribs as he slid into a cabinet, upending it, showering himself with tools. Pain raged in his chest. He couldn't breathe, had to breathe! He sucked at the air, knowing the Ornyl would recover and come after him. *Get up, God, hurry!*

Elias pushed to his knees, saw the Ornyl circling drunkenly, supporting its injured speech hand with the other one, its head still arched back to the ceiling. He knew he had only seconds. If he could rush around it—

He tried, but the warrior swatted him back against the wall. Pain rolled over him in waves, making the room go dim and spin around him. His legs felt paralyzed. He fought to stay upright against the wall, filled with fear as he saw the Ornyl's head come down. It stalked toward him and he could sense its rage.

I'm finished, Elias thought, despairing.

He realized his hand was on the master switchplate.

Gravity suppression!

He turned to the plate, scanned desperately for the rheostat marked POWER ROOM. There! From the corner of his eye he saw the Ornyl leap for the kill. He twisted the rheostat to zero.

The warrior's leap sent it crashing against the ceiling. Rebounding, it smashed into the floor, then drifted up more slowly toward the ceiling again. Despite the two tremendous blows, its fighting arms reached out for him in passing. He shrank back, hooking his foot under a low pipe to hold himself against the floor; waiting until the Ornyl touched ceiling again. It positioned its arms to fling itself down on him. As it pushed off, he reversed the rheostat, spinning it as far as it would go. The gravity struck him down, sprawling him on his side. The Ornyl rammed into the floor half a meter from him and lay still on its side, its head drooping over.

Elias felt a huge load of fear dropping from him. I got it! he thought. Fighting the gravity, he pushed himself along the floor, putting several meters between himself and the Ornyl. He stared at its huge body, afraid it would rise again. One of the huge fighting arms was bent at a crazy angle behind the body. The other arm was twisted and broken in several places, oozing green liquid. The Ornyl was helpless.

Elias sat up against the wall. "Yeah, bastard," he muttered. "I think I can fight you."

The Ornyl moved, sending a prickle along his

spine, but he saw that it was only the injured speech hand, waving feebly. No doubt it still pained the Ornyl, even through its graver wounds.

Elias remembered how Briana had taken Chuddath's hands after her father had been gunned down in Chuddath's presence. It had seemed like a consoling gesture. Later he'd learned she'd been inflicting excruciating pain on the Ornyl. He'd felt sickened at her cruelty.

Thank God he'd seen it, or he'd be dead now.

Elias realized it wasn't over—he had to get out of here. The teacher would have called for help. Police, or a rebel cadre, or maybe even more Ornyl might be arriving any minute.

He hesitated. The Ornyl was helpless and conscious. It knew things he needed to know. An opportunity like this would not come again.

"Who sent you to guard this school?" Elias asked.

The Ornyl gazed at him with its unnerving mantis eyes.

Elias thought of another question—important: "Do you know who I am?"

The Ornyl's uninjured speech hand struggled up to its abdomen. "Your speech . . . is different. An offworlder? Earth?"

Elias nodded, digesting the implications: The Ornyl did not know him, had not been stationed here specifically to stop him. That meant that what was going on in this building was a secret to at least some of the citizens of Cassiodorus, too. But how could that be? Surely the parents of these children knew their condition. So what was left to hide?

He worried at the conundrum, but no answer came. He felt a throbbing in his ribs and his back, where the Ornyl had flung him against the wall. The pain maddened him.

"Who put you on guard here?" he snapped.

Again the Ornyl did not answer.

"Why does this place need a guard?"

"That is not . . . my concern."

Elias swore. Time was passing. Help would be coming. If he was going to get the answers, he had to get them fast. He pulled Martha's laser scalpel from his pocket and slid across to the Ornyl. He took the injured speech hand gently in his, seeing the Ornyl's body shudder. "If you live," he said, "you'll get over this pain. But what if I lase out your eyes?" Hearing the words come from his mouth, he was revolted. But he kept his face impassive.

"You cannot threaten an . . . Ornyl."

"Tell me what I want to know, or spend the rest of your life in the dark. How would that feel? Your days as a warrior would be over. And what good are you for anything else?"

"I don't fear death," the Ornyl said, inflecting derision with a flip of its hand.

"I'm not talking death, I'm talking blindness." Elias felt sick to his stomach.

"You could not force . . . me to live."

"Who stationed you here? You have no S'edhite scar on your head, so I know you're not linked to anyone. You can answer me."

The Ornyl made another contemptuous sound. "You insult me. What have I done . . . to make you think . . . I have no honor?"

Elias activated the laser and brought it close to the Ornyl's eye. He felt sweat rolling down his face. His hand trembled before the gleaming, multifaceted eye, a thousand hands trembling in the Ornyl's brain, triggering its contempt, and yet he couldn't make it stop. His reluctance exasperated him. This creature would have killed him without an ounce of remorse, but he couldn't even take one of its eyes in cold blood, not even if it would solve the mystery of Cassiodorus.

And it would be futile anyway: You could see mankind in the Ornyl's body, but not in its soul. Where a human might have screamed for mercy, this Ornyl simply accepted, never even *thinking* it might have a choice.

With a curse, Elias withdrew the laser scalpel. A huge relief filled him.

"You are not like . . . other men," the Ornyl observed. "The men I serve are . . . Ornyl in their hearts. They would have blinded . . . me. Why do you not?" Its voice was subdued now.

"Don't push your luck," Elias growled. But he felt a coldness in his chest. *Ornyl in their hearts.* If this warrior is talking about rebels, he thought, then there is no hope for the empire. Elias Kane might unravel the dark conspiracies of this wretched planet, even defeat them. But in the end, Earth would lose to the colonists. Her own children. What had happened to those children, the adults of Cassiodorus? Had the cold of space, the brutality of their new worlds, somehow seeped into their souls and transformed them?

Elias struggled up, feeling weary to his bones. He had to get out of here. It was past time to leave.

"You fought well," the Ornyl said. "Even though your heart . . . is soft."

Elias walked out without answering.

The hallway outside the power plant was deserted. Gratefully he savored the physical lift of 1 G. He started down the hall, then realized that he had no idea how to get out of the building. Were there even any doors? He searched his memory: He'd seen the front of the building yesterday from a distance, and the back more closely as he'd crept in today. There was no door in back, and the fence around the building had no gate. If there was a front entrance, the fence—and distance—had kept him from seeing it yesterday.

A tunnel, he thought. The children must go into the unfenced building and then are taken here through an underground passage.

Should I try to find that passage?

He couldn't decide. Tired, too much pain. Think, damn it: The teacher called for help, if anyone did.

She'll assume I came in the usual way and hid in the duct. Only the Ornyl knows I cut through the fence. So any reinforcements will expect to head me off in the tunnels—or whatever's the usual way in.

I'll have to go back out through the roof.

Elias groaned. He broke into a weary trot, trying to estimate his way back to the room where the Ornyl had first exposed him. He pushed in two doors, finding deserted classrooms, their ceilings intact. The third room was the right one, deserted now, its ceiling half shredded by the Ornyl's furious attempts to get at him. He stood on one of the little desks, hoisted himself into the torn and bent duct and crawled back to the roof vent. His arms ached in protest as he grabbed the struts in the vertical shaft and pulled himself up. Protecting his bruised ribs as much as possible, he eased out from under the mushroom-shaped hood, back into the oppressive heat and weight of Cassiodorus.

*Sirens!*

Damn! He flattened himself on the hot roof and peered across at the unfenced building. A groundcar pulled up and spilled four men in blue uniforms. Militia! He felt a dim surprise. Somehow, he'd not really expected that. A colony's militia was always under the direct command of the viceroy. Cay Endor had seemed loyal to the empire. Maybe I should just give myself up, Elias thought. Wait for the soldiers to get over here, then surrender. Endor will give me a stiff lecture, but he'll have to turn me loose.

The idea lured him with almost irresistible force. To sit down, rest and wait passively until they took him someplace cool. His muscles cried out for it.

Instead, he waited until the blue figures had rushed into the school building, then pushed up and staggered to the ladder. Back on the ground, he hurried to the spot where he'd cut the fence and forced his way under. As he stood, he heard a shout and turned, his heart sinking. It was a militia man, heading over from the main building. They'd thought of the fence after all.

Elias cursed and broke into a lumbering run across the hard, red clay. He was much closer to the buildings along the border of the school grounds than the militiaman was to him. He should be able to get back into that alley with plenty to spare.

But if the man started shooting—

The thought sent extra speed into his legs. His lungs burned with exertion. Sweat soaked him, and his ankles stabbed him with each step. He could feel a small, round spot spreading on his back, an imaginary target, making his skin flinch and crawl.

But the man did not shoot.

Right! he thought. You don't mind if an alien warrior tears me to pieces, but you don't want a militia blaster wound to explain, do you?

As he entered the alley, Elias glanced back at the man. Only ten meters back. Damn it—how could anyone run that fast in this gravity? It was uncanny, inhuman!

Elias staggered into the shadow of the alley and tried to set himself, to find some last strength to fight. The militiaman plunged into the alley, too rash, not expecting him. Elias hit him in the face with all his strength, sending a rocket of pain back up his arm. The militiaman's eyes crossed and he rocked on his feet.

*Drop, damn you!*

Elias smashed his other fist into the stunned face. The man crashed over backward.

The fury of adrenaline drained from Elias. Exhausted, he limped down the alley to the street beyond. He realized he was panting, but could not stop. He had to sit down soon, or he'd fall down. How long had he been gone? Would the cab be waiting? He tried to check his watch, then realized he'd given it to the cabbie. A bitter laugh formed and died in his throat. *Be there, please!*

She was there.

Elias crawled into the cab without a word. She said

something as she started off and he grunted. Her head blurred. Just rest his eyes a minute.

Someone shaking him.

He struggled awake, feeling that a long time had passed. But no, he was still in the cab. They were stopped, back at the place where she'd picked him up. "Here we be, sir. And I thank thee for the fine watch."

Elias suppressed a groan at the thought of moving. Four blocks to the viceregal guest quarters. Couldn't he just have her take him there?

With an effort of will, he pulled himself from the cab. A terrible weariness gripped him as he walked back. Just a little farther, he kept telling himself. Then you can rest.

By the time he reached his hallway in the guest quarters, he was walking hunched over, supporting himself with a hand on the wall. He thought with longing of his bed, waiting for him.

Then saw that his door was standing open.

He felt dim alarm, wondering if he should turn back. A fierce resentment welled up in him. No, damn it. Enough was enough. They had to let him rest. He paused in the doorway, seeing Pendrake sitting on his bed, wrapping his white hair in a headband—no, a bandage. Elias stared at him, trying to comprehend. Pendrake saw him, got up, hurried to him. Pendrake's clothes were torn and there was blood on his arm and stomach, too.

A terrible dread seized Elias. "Martha?" he said.

Pendrake took him by the elbows, gripping him firmly. His black eyes shone with grief. "They have taken her, Elias."

## 13

ELIAS FELT DREAD FLOWING INTO HIM FROM PEN-
drake's clutching fingers. *They have taken Martha.*

No! he thought.

His room snapped into focus: Ransacked—his mattress ripped to shreds. All of the drawers torn open,
some of them strewn around the floor. His head spun
with the violence of it. He felt choked and breathless.
*Poor Martha—please, God, don't let them hurt her.*

They had wanted the earphone.

When they hadn't found it, they'd taken Martha.

God *damn* them!

A surge of fury burned away his fear, driving out his
weariness. But he knew the exhaustion would return
and drag him down as soon as his rage faltered. He
pried Pendrake's fingers from his elbows and walked to
the sink, taking two stims from the cabinet and down-
ing them with a glass of water. His heart began to hammer with furious, shocky speed. *Bastards!* He turned
back to Pendrake, and this time Pendrake's wounds
registered fully, panging him, fueling his fury. "You're
hurt."

"Not as much as I ought to be," Pendrake's voice
was heavy with self-contempt.

Elias looked for a place to sit Pendrake down. The

chair by the bed was strewn with clothes. Elias threw them to the floor and pulled Pendrake to the chair. He checked the bandage on Pendrake's head, prodding gently at the wound. A trickle of orange blood was still seeping into the bandage and a huge, lavender bruise was spreading to either side of it, but he could detect no fracture. He examined Pendrake's arm and stomach, finding shallow knife wounds, the kind made by slashing. Pendrake's clothes around the wounds were soaked with blood, but the bleeding from them had stopped.

Elias felt his rage blazing too hot, threatening to consume him. *They didn't need to hurt you.* He took a deep breath and let it out slowly. He said, "Tell me exactly what happened."

"I was in my room. I heard Martha screaming. I ran to her room, but she was not there. She was here, with the two men who helped Jost try to kill you the other night. They were trying to make Martha tell them where you had hidden the earphone. I tried to frighten them again, but someone must have been hiding behind the door. As I rushed in, I felt the knife stab me. Then something hit me, here." Pendrake pointed to his head wound. "I lost consciousness." His head sank down to his chest, and Elias saw that tears were trickling down his cheeks. "I failed her, Elias. And you."

Elias felt a rush of compassion for Pendrake. Those bastards had wounded him inside, too. "That's not true."

Pendrake raised his hands to his bowed face clenching them into fists. "All this strength," he said bitterly, "and what is it good for? In the world of men, nothing. Why was I cursed with it and then put among you?"

"To show us that strength doesn't have to turn into brutality."

Pendrake threw his head back. An agonized sound rasped from deep in his throat. "I let them take her."

Elias gripped Pendrake's arm, suddenly frightened for him. He had never seen him like this. "Listen to me,

Pendrake: Don't ever think that you should become like us."

With relief, Elias saw the orange face firming, reclaiming some of its calm strength. "We've both got to pull ourselves together, my friend. We're going after Martha. We're going to find her and take her from them. And then we're getting off this planet."

Pendrake shook his head. "I am with you, Elias, but is it not hopeless? They have a big start; we do not know—"

"It's *not* hopeless. Just before we left the *Seraphim*, I heard Captain Streetham mention his K-scope. It's a new device the navy uses to track down AWOLs—an imitation bloodhound, only much better. The pigs that kidnapped Martha left a trail and probably don't even know it." Elias felt a savage determination giving shape to his fury: *Find you, hunt you down, yes, and when I catch you, God help you all.*

Elias found the subspace radio Streetham had sent down with him lying on the floor, scratched but undamaged. He raised the *Seraphim* and asked Streetham to send a lander down with a K-scope. Then he hurried to Martha's room. Her things, the smell of her perfume, struck into his heart, making him want to weep. He found the nightgown she'd been wearing when he'd left her that morning. Picking it up, he touched it only with a thumb and forefinger, interfering as little as possible with its characteristic signature. He dropped it into a specimen bag from Martha's medkit.

He got Pendrake and hurried out to the street to catch a cab to the spaceport. The sun was high now; the street baked and shimmered with its heat. Groundcars and cabs flowed by steadily, and he flagged one almost at once. As he settled into the cab's thick cushions, Elias realized he'd barely felt the walk through outside gravity. The stims were working now. They'd keep him going for about three hours. By then he should know whether the rebels had taken Martha out of the city. If they had, it might mean a long haul in a groundcar, and he could rest while Pendrake drove. Otherwise, he'd take more stims, take them until he found Martha, or until the chemicals burned him into a twitching shell.

He peered at the squat city sliding by, hating its ugliness, impatient to get to the spaceport. Rage flared again in him. *They've gone too far.* Then he plunged into a cold fear for Martha that drove his stomach down inside him and made it hard to breathe.

*You're not going to lose me, Elias.*

And he'd believed her. Dear God, he'd had to, if he was ever going to love again. But she'd been wrong. He *had* lost her, and it might be for good.

And he should have seen it coming.

Elias felt a choking tightness in his throat. All right, kidnapped, and he had to stop feeling and *think:* try to understand why they'd done it.

Was it really to get back the earphone?

Elias prodded his chest, feeling the perfect skin, the false but lifelike mat of hair; wanting to tear the plastiflesh away, release the foul thing beneath, find the rebel bastards, fling it at them. . . .

But it couldn't just be the earphone. If that's all they'd wanted, they'd simply have waited for him with a gun to Martha's head. Give us our toy back or we kill her.

No, they wanted more than that.

They wanted to control his report to the Imperator.

His heart sank as he thought about it. If it was true, they'd keep Martha captive for weeks or months. He'd soon get a message warning him to go home and give a benign report on the mines. He'd also no doubt be instructed to claim that Martha had died in some accident, so that no one back on Earth could know they were holding her life over him. To make him do it, they'd promise that, after a certain amount of time, if he did nothing to contradict his false report, he'd see Martha again. Otherwise, they'd kill her. The amount of time they kept her would be the amount they needed to convert their ore to beta-steel, their beta-steel to dreadnoughts.

And after that, they'd either give her back or kill her.

We were doomed, he thought. From the moment we came to this planet. Somehow they learned I love Martha. It made us both vulnerable.

He felt the choking sensation again, realized he was slipping out of control. He had to get hold of himself.

The cab pulled to a stop and Elias realized they were at the spaceport. He paid with the Cassi credits the other cabbie had given him and got out. The two giant landing pads made empty white circles in the red clay. The control tower windows hemorrhaged red light from the sun. Elias was relieved at the spaceport's emptiness—probably a normal day for a planet no one visited unless they had to. He looked around, spotting only two colonial officers, one at the gate and the other visible through the glass of the control tower, reading a book. The man at the gate was old—at least sixty. A large potbelly stretched his uniform. He looked surprised, but opened up when Elias showed him the Imperial carte blanche. As Elias hurried through, he saw the man pick up his phone. Never mind. Too late for that to stop him. Elias searched the sky as he hurried toward the shuttle pad. After a minute, he located the orange, flaring burn of the *Seraphim*'s descending shuttle. He watched it with fierce impatience.

"Elias," Pendrake said. "The colonist from the gate is following us. He appears to be quite agitated. And a groundcar is pulling up outside the gate. It looks like a police vehicle."

Damn! Elias thought. He checked the needler release below his elbow, hoping he wouldn't have to use it, readying himself with grim determination.

The spaceport officer lumbered up, breathless and sweating in the heavy gravity. "Sir, sir, what be that ship? We've given no clearance to any ship to land."

"Don't worry about it," Elias said shortly. "It's an imperial ship."

"But *all* ships must be cleared to land. They must go through normal procedures. . . ."

"A pox on your normal procedures," Elias snarled.

The man's jaw gaped. Behind him, Lieutenant Krevvy of the Neues Eisen police trotted up, leading three uniformed cops. Krevvy's coarse features were alight with anticipation. "Mr. Kane, I have orders from Cay Endor to bring you in for questioning on a breaking and entering charge. The school—"

"I countermand those orders."

Krevvy smirked. "Do you now?"

A sonic boom rolled over the spaceport, followed by the swelling roar of the shuttle. Elias glanced over his shoulder and located the craft. It looked much bigger now, and he could see its frontal shields shimmering in a corona of fire. *Hurry!*

Krevvy said, "I don't recognize your authority to countermand the viceroy. I answer only to him."

"And what will the viceroy do to you if you shoot me?"

Krevvy looked suddenly uncertain. "No one said anything about shooting you, Mr. Kane."

"That's the only way you'll get me away from here."

Krevvy gestured to his men. "Arrest him."

Elias popped the release on the needler. It dropped into his palm. "The first man who takes a step is going to have porcupines for eyeballs."

Krevvy's face hardened. "This is a very serious matter, Mr. Kane." He raised his voice, shouting above the descending roar of the shuttle. Then, as if noticing it for the first time, he turned toward it with a shocked expression. It was settling on the pad now, retros blasting up a storm of grit and dust. Krevvy turned back to Elias with an almost comic look of betrayal.

"I ought to gun you down right now."

"But you won't. How long ago did you immigrate

from Earth? You still speak like one of us. That might help you survive in prison."

"You are directly defying the orders of the duly constituted government of this planet," Krevvy yelled.

The shuttle engines idled down and the sideport cycled open. Elias said, "Duly constituted by the Imperator. Why do you keep forgetting that, Krevvy?"

The sergeant who'd presented his troops when Elias had first boarded the *Seraphim* brought his marines down the ramp of the shuttle at a trot and formed them up in two rows of ten between Elias and Krevvy. Elias could see the strain on the determined young faces of the squad and winced inwardly, knowing exactly what they were suffering to look so tough and efficient thirty seconds after stepping into 1.5 G's. No doubt Captain Streetham had ordered high-G drills during his orbits, but this was still a rude shock, even to their strong, young bodies.

The sergeant cast a deadpan glance at Elias' needler, then stepped forward, ignoring Krevvy's dark look of fury, handing Elias a package. "Here is the item you wanted, sir."

"Thank you, Sergeant."

"Will there be anything else?"

"Yes. Arrest these men."

The sergeant barked an order. The squad broke ranks and scrambled around Krevvy and his men. Before the colonials could react, they found themselves looking into twenty ruptors.

"You can't do this!" Krevvy protested.

"You know I can. You may have forgotten that's an imperial uniform you're wearing and imperial laws you're sworn to uphold, but don't expect me to."

"What's the charge?"

"Repeated obstruction of another imperial officer in performance of his duties. Sergeant, take their weapons."

For a second Krevvy looked about to resist, then something—perhaps the Andinaz scars on the sergeant's cheeks—changed his mind. He and his men handed over their weapons and Elias felt a small relief. He realized that Krevvy's presence here had presented him with an opportunity. "I'll need the key to your groundcar," he said to Krevvy.

With a black look, Krevvy handed over the thin plastic tab.

"Sergeant, take them up to the *Seraphim* and confine them in the ship's brig," Elias said. "After a few hours, you can radio the viceroy and let him know."

"Understood."

"Don't give him any trouble, Krevvy, and you may get out of this all right yet."

The sergeant said, "Sir, my marines here know what happened. We'd be honored to accompany you at your command."

Elias considered the offer, tempted. If and when he caught up with Martha's kidnappers, he might need all the firepower he could get.

But it was more likely that firepower would be useless; that only stealth and guile would get her back. These young men and women were totally unacclimated to the planet. And if the colonists learned that a full squad of imperial marines were running loose on the planet, even those who had no sympathy for the rebels would consider it a provocation. Elias felt hot frustration at his limitations, wanting to care about nothing but Martha, just get her—and those poor kids and any others like them—off this bloody planet.

But no, he must still do his duty—

*Or as much of it as he could.*

"Thank you, Sergeant. I'd prefer you stay ready on the ship. I'll hail if I need you. But I *will* take one of those ruptors."

"Sir." The sergeant motioned and a young woman stepped forward, her face proud, shrugging out of her pack and handing it and the ruptor to him. The sergeant made another motion to his troops, and they moved off with Krevvy and his men. Elias turned and brushed past the potbellied attendant, who was still standing with his mouth agape. Should I do something about him and the other man, too? Elias wondered. No. The guy in the tower's already called out about the unauthorized landing. So just get out of here, before the next wave rolls in.

He inspected Krevvy's groundcar, making sure it had a survival kit and a radio. The survival kit was even better than he'd hoped, containing rations for a week. That would be vital if they had to follow Martha's trail into the wilderness of Cassiodorus.

Elias drove the long, straight road back to the vice-regal compound with the air conditioner on full, glad to be out of the merciless sun. He explained the K-scope to Pendrake: "This thing has just been developed on Earth, as an outgrowth of research in a number of fields, including Kirlian auras. As I said before, it's basically a mechanical bloodhound, only better than any bloodhound ever was. Every person produces a unique and complex field, or 'signature,' composed of his smell, a neuroelectric charge or aura, characteristic heat patterns and a number of other things. A steadily decaying remnant of this signature lingers wherever that person has been. The K-scope can be tuned to track any signature trail for as long as twelve hours after a person has left an area. Though the navy uses it on AWOLs, it was really developed for prison breaks. One pass over a sailor's bunk, and this thing would track him through the rawest cathouse on Centauri."

"Even if he were, say, inside a groundcar?"

"Yes. Groundcars have to exchange air with the outside. This thing will pick a signature out of a car's vents."

"And you have brought Martha's nightgown to give your machine her signature."

Elias nodded. He found he had to pay more attention to his driving now. As he neared the center of Neues Eisen, the traffic picked up steadily. He rounded the last corner before the viceregal compound and slowed the groundcar to a crawl, looking ahead, feeling a knot of anxiety in his stomach. Sure enough, there were several police and militia groundcars drawn up within and outside the gate to the compound. He swore under his breath and circled back around until he was several blocks from the compound. Then he took the K-scope from its case, opened the specimen bag and pointed the scope into it. He watched the scope's screen until the word *ready* signaled that the tuning process was over. He handed the scope to Pendrake.

"I'm going to drive a perimeter around the compound from a couple of blocks out," he said. "Somewhere in that 360 degrees this thing should flash on her."

Pendrake held the scope to the open window. Elias drove, keeping his attention on the inside of the perimeter, ready to evade if he saw a militia or police car. Halfway around, Pendrake said, "I have it, Elias!" His voice was high with excitement.

"Good!" Relief and hope filled Elias. He wheeled the groundcar to the right, away from the palace. "Still picking it up?"

"It is weakening. You need to drive right."

Elias centered the K-scope, finding the exact street the kidnappers had taken. It was the penetrator road, leading directly in and out of Neues Eisen. Some of Elias' relief vanished. If the scope held to this bearing, they might be in for a long chase.

He thought about his subspace radio back in his room, and was annoyed with himself. He should have lugged it along in the cab, but he'd been thinking only of Martha, and getting to the spaceport. Now his room was crawling with militia and police and the radio was out of reach. Without it, he'd be cut off from the *Seraphim*. He'd be taking an immense risk to follow the kidnappers very far into the wilderness.

He checked the groundcar's radio and saw that it had a subspace channel. *Thank you, Lieutenant Krevvy!*

Elias gripped the wheel, his spirits lifting. There

was nothing to stop him now, nothing to slow him down. *Hang on, Martha, I'm coming.*

He pressed the accelerator down, speeding through Neues Eisen, confident that no one would interfere with a police car. In minutes they'd left the city behind. The road became rougher and narrower. When they were several kilometers into the Cassiodoran wilderness, the K-scope signal departed from what was left of the road and arrowed straight across the desertlike terrain. The groundcar slid easily from the road onto the flat ground, its aircushion drive leaving no impression in the hard clay. The groundcar of the kidnappers had left none either, as it might have done in softer terrain. That worried Elias. He'd have preferred not to depend entirely on the scope. *Keep working, baby!* he thought.

He drove another few kilometers, then began to feel weak and slightly nauseous. The stims, fading from his system. He stopped the car and drank some water to help flush his system. "Think you can drive and keep the K-scope centered?" he said to Pendrake. "Gotta have a little rest and food."

"Of course."

Elias crawled into the back seat and opened the ration kit, chewing on some tasteless protein bars. He sprawled out on the seat and, instantly, was asleep.

He awoke to darkness. He suffered a moment's disorientation before realizing where they were. And why.

The knowledge sprang back on him with vicious force. He felt a despair so hopeless and deep that he could not move for a moment. He lay on the seat and said to himself, *You'll get her back.*

He gazed out of the clear dome of the groundcar at the few stars visible through the murky atmosphere, feeling something nagging at the edge of his consciousness. A dream he'd had while he was asleep. Something about Briana.

*That Briana had done this.*

Absurd, of course.

He pushed up in the seat. Pendrake glanced back at him from the front seat, started to say something, then saw his face.

"Are you all right, Elias?"

He waved a hand, still thinking about Briana, too horrified to speak. Pendrake turned back to his driving.

*Dear God, could it be?*

Briana wanted him. And she could be both ruthless and devious. She'd be too smart to think she could ever win his affections if she herself got rid of Martha. But if she could get the rebels to kill Martha, she could even go through the charade of grieving for her.

Hadn't he feared something like it from the moment Martha had stepped into his quarters on the *Seraphim?*

Elias stopped, realizing the paranoid madness of it. Briana was desperate to find out what was going on here. The Imperium might stand or fall on the answers he was sent to find. Briana would never jeopardize his mission by giving the rebels a way to control him, even if it meant getting Martha out of the way.

Elias put the idea from his mind.

Suddenly, he became aware of a whining sound and realized it had been going on for some minutes. The groundcar began to vibrate, and then he felt it settling, bumping against the ground, slewing halfway around before it came to rest.

"Why are you stopping?" he asked Pendrake.

Pendrake looked back, his face eerily lit by flashing red telltales on the instrument panel. "I fear it was not my idea, Elias. According to this message, our power supply has just become inoperative."

Elias felt dread building in the pit of his stomach. "The radio—does it still work?"

Pendrake flipped the switch. There was no burst of static, no life on any of the bands. The radio was dead too. Elias felt a cold flush of alarm. Damn it, what could be wrong? The powerpack of this groundcar should be able to take them around the planet several times. He remembered with a sinking feeling what Holz had said when they'd first landed—about the clay molecules fouling machinery. "How long have I been asleep?" he asked, fearing the answer.

"Nearly eight hours, Elias. We've come almost a thousand kilometers, if that is what you want to know. Too far to walk back, even in normal gravity. But we do have some food. Perhaps someone will come looking for us. Or there may be a city or outpost nearby. . . ."

Pendrake didn't finish the sentence, but it spun to its ugly conclusion in Elias' mind: If not, he thought, we're dead.

## 14

"ELIAS, YOU CANNOT KEEP PUSHING YOURSELF THIS way," Pendrake said with deep concern.

"Sorry. I don't know any other way to push myself." Elias' voice trickled out in a hoarse whisper, sandpaper mouth grating on his parched tongue. He felt a torpid indignation at the heat for sucking even his voice away. He would give anything to be cool again. With each step, he could feel his sweat-soaked clothes clinging to him like a feverish extra skin. He glanced over his shoulder at the sinking red ball of the sun, trying to calculate how long till dark. Turning his head threw his body out of sync, making him stagger drunkenly to the side several steps before he could get control again. An hour more, he thought. Then the sun'll be gone and it'll cool off. We'll stop a few minutes, eat, take some more water. Four swallows for me, eight for Pendrake.

He did not want to stop, even for a few minutes. As much as his body craved rest, his mind dreaded it. In the past hour, his legs had gone past pain to numbness. He had almost managed to blank out the shooting pains in his ankles. But he knew that as soon as he let himself rest, the anesthetic numbness would dissipate and stiffness would set in. Trying to stand again would be agony; to walk, pure torture.

And stopping would mean that Martha was fading farther away from him. Elias felt a dry spasm of anxiety, followed by dull spots of pain in the small of his back. With no adrenaline left to draw on, the emotion faded.

"I have always enjoyed your jokes, Elias, even though I do not laugh. I hope you know that."

"Why are you telling me this now? We're not dead yet."

"I wonder what is taking us so long?"

Elias laughed brokenly, his lips cracking, sending little slivers of pain through his face. "You've been hanging around me too long," he rasped. "No question about it."

"There is another rise up ahead," Pendrake said. "Some hills. Maybe there will be another cave."

Elias saw where he was leading and felt an instant resistance. "We can't stop long. Night is when we should be walking."

"That is what I told you this morning, when you insisted on leaving the cave after only a few hours and pressing on in the heat of the day."

Elias refused to be chided. "Yeah, and by leaving when we did, we picked up an hour on them." He felt a savage satisfaction remembering the spots where Martha's signature had freshened suddenly, the K-scope signaling the change with a triumphant beep. Elias felt a grim pride in Martha's resourcefulness. The first stop had been only ten kilometers beyond the kidnappers' abandoned groundcar, and she'd forced her abductors to a halt twice more after that. She runs and climbs rocks, Elias thought. She'd be stronger out here than I am, but she's got them convinced she's weak—she's doing her best to slow them down.

*Or maybe she's hurt.*

His stomach went hollow with fright. He suppressed the thought, knowing it would drive him out of control.

*You're all right, I know you are. Keep it up, my love. Make them rest; I'll keep walking.*

He steadied the K-scope on the end of its neck strap to take another reading. The numbers looked blurred. He had to stop and hold the scope up close to his eyes. He could feel his body weaving wearily beneath him. "We're still gaining on them," he said, feeling a lift of hope. "We're only two hours behind now. If we push on—"

"You will drop," Pendrake said. "Listen, Elias: I am just as determined as you are not to let them escape us. But they have been on foot almost as long as us and are probably just as tired as you."

Pendrake's voice was strong and confident. His gait showed no weariness. Elias felt a twinge of envy, and depression at his own weakness. "We've got to keep going while the K-scope's still working. Sooner or later, it'll jam up, just like the groundcars."

"I do not think that would matter at this point. As you have no doubt noticed, Neues Eisen, their abandoned car and our present position form a perfectly straight line. Martha's kidnappers do not know about the K-scope and have no reason to think we are behind them, so I think we can safely assume they are taking a straight course toward their objective, whatever it is. All we have to do is keep to the same bearing."

He's right, Elias thought with relief. And I *didn't* notice it. Has the heat weakened my thinking, too? He realized with dismay that it had.

"You *must* rest now," Pendrake said.

"I can take another stim."

"You have taken too many already." Pendrake's voice was maddeningly logical and patient.

Elias tried to muster another argument. None would come. Abruptly, he felt his resistance crumbling. "All right, but only for a couple of hours." He could feel the last dregs of the noon stim draining out of him, as though the idea of stopping had pulled a plug inside him. Tears welled up in his eyes and rolled down his cheeks, startling him, driving home how drained he was. He felt a dull hate for the endless, empty plains of

Cassiodorus, the murderous sun, the hard clay baking and flattening your feet, the gravity dragging you, not just physically downward, but mentally and emotionally backward, until your mind was as blurred and your feelings as tender as a baby's.

The tears continued to ooze from his eyes. *Cut it out, you can't spare the water.* He swept his cheek with a finger and wet the tip of his tongue with a salty droplet. He concentrated with grim determination on the nearest hill. He could make out patches of blue on the hillsides now. Must be more of those ropy plants they'd been seeing lately. Where there were plants, there should be water. Probably underground, but they could look around to be sure. If they found some, they could top off the water sacks and increase the ration.

Eight swallows!

The thought made him almost dizzy with longing.

His legs gave out, dropping him hard to his knees. He struggled to rise, determined not to show Pendrake his weakness. He could not make his legs work. He battled a wave of despair. Pendrake's arm slid under his shoulders, lifting him to his feet, half carrying him up the hill. Elias could feel his legs stretching, feet tapping against ground that seemed a hundred meters down. "I'm all right," he mumbled.

Dark rock swung over Elias' vision, cutting off the brassy sky. Shade! He savored its delicious coolness, the relief to his seared eyes. He blinked and looked around; the dim, rocky irregularities of cave walls firmed up as his eyes adjusted. The air was moist, delicious. He could feel his skin drinking it in greedily. Pendrake eased him down. The chill of the clay floor penetrated his seat with a mild, pleasant shock. He peered back into the cave. It was a big one, meandering back and down, shrinking into an irregular black oval that promised unseen depths beyond.

A lot could be hidden in here. Were Martha's kidnappers heading for a place like this?

Before he could pursue the idea, Pendrake bent

over him and pressed the water sack to his lips. The warm, stale water filled his mouth with a fountaining pleasure. He had never tasted anything so good. *One, two, three, four—that's all.*

He pushed Pendrake's hand and the water sack away, filled with a sharp regret. "No, damn it, get it out of my sight!"

Pendrake started to put it away.

"No, wait—you drink too."

"I already did."

"I want to see you. Eight swallows." He raised his fists with mock ferocity. "Don't make me fight you."

Pendrake put the water sack to his mouth, but it was impossible to tell if he was really swallowing. Elias felt an overpowering urge to lie back and rest, but fought it off, knowing he'd not have the energy to rouse himself again and eat. He rummaged in the survival pack, finding four protein bars, handing three to Pendrake.

Pendrake gave him an exasperated look. "You must stop this, Elias. I will eat and drink what you do. Nothing more."

"But you're twice as big."

"And twice as strong."

"Modest, too."

Pendrake smiled. "Remember, Elias, I was *born* in heavy gravity."

Elias tipped his head back, resting it against the rocky wall. He could feel himself reviving in the cool, damp atmosphere of the cave. With it came the pain he'd expected, his calves knotting up, his feet burning as the tissue he'd pounded flat decompressed around the capillaries and nerves.

Mentally, he pushed the pain aside and thought about what Pendrake had just said. "Born in heavy gravity. Just like the kids on this planet. But you weren't small and weak as a child, were you?"

Pendrake's gaze went distant. "When I was four,

my father and I were walking. There was a rock slide. I lifted a hundred-kilo rock off my father's leg."

Elias nodded, feeling his mind butting up against the problem: What was it about the gravity of Cassiodorus that was specifically so hard on children? If the young on Cephan were hardy and strong, why not here, too?

"But it might not be correct to generalize," Pendrake said, as though reading his mind. "Even though Cephantines look similar to humans, we are also different in many ways. Perhaps I was not only born in heavy gravity, but born *for* heavy gravity."

"That's a very good point," Elias said. He chewed his protein bar in silence, his mind slipping wearily off the vexing paradox and back to Martha. Worry welled up in him. Would her captors treat her decently?

He tried to remember all he could about the two men who'd taken her—the one with the weal and the other, that bullnecked kid. What had their attitude been about him when they'd had him trapped in the alley? He could remember Jost's regret about having to kill him, but very little about the other two men. Were they good soldiers, idealists—

Or sadistic misfits drawn by violence?

Martha was a very attractive woman. What if they—

Elias' mind recoiled at the ugly possibilities, unable to bear thinking about them. He closed his eyes and thought, You will find her. She will be all right.

*And if she's not, I'll kill them both!*

He fought the bitter, savage fury that ripped through him. Opening his eyes, he caught Pendrake gazing at him with compassion. Elias said, "Know what I like about Cassiodorus? There're no mosquitoes."

Pendrake gave him an understanding smile. "Go to sleep, Elias. I will stand watch."

Elias came groggily awake, feeling a hand on his arm. He saw it was Pendrake and started to ask what was wrong, but the hand squeezed urgently, warning him to silence. He looked beyond Pendrake's dark silhouette to the mouth of the cave and saw another figure, half in moonlight, half in the shadow of the entrance.

Elias felt a cold shock of alarm, waking him fully. A man? No. The head was too large, the shoulders too narrow. The legs were massive and looked muscular, even in silhouette.

A sauroid! Elias thought. A thrill of fear shot up his spine. Holz had been right; it looked like the tyrannosaurus of ancient Earth, except it was much smaller—hardly bigger than a man. The creature stood very still, limned at the back edges with greenish moonlight, the front of its body dark.

Elias inched his hand toward the ruptor the marine had given him. Pendrake gave his arm another warning squeeze. Elias looked up at him, irked and unsettled, trying to read his face in the darkness. What the devil was wrong with Pendrake? Had his reverence for life suddenly extended to murderous animals?

Pendrake moved his head fractionally toward the sauroid.

Elias saw that it was moving, sidling across the mouth of the cave. It turned in profile, and Elias saw what was bothering Pendrake:

The sauroid was holding a club.

Elias stared at it, astonished. Dear God, the thing was *intelligent!* Holz hadn't said anything about that. The flesh crawled on Elias' neck. Tool-using, intelligent, and that would make it twice as dangerous. He raised the ruptor and aimed it. The sauroid went still again.

"Please, Elias," Pendrake whispered.

God, Elias thought with exasperation. It wants to eat us and Pendrake's worried about its soul. But he did not shoot. He saw that the sauroid was slowly backing away. It stood in full moonlight now, and Elias caught a glitter of red from its eyes. He shuddered, keeping the ruptor aimed at its chest. *You know what this is, don't you? You are a bright fellow. Good. Now go away.*

The sauroid slowly extended the arm holding the club out to its side. The arm was much smaller than the legs, just as the tyrannosaurus' had been, and Elias marveled at the uncanny resemblance. Parallel evolution? The sauroid opened its hand and let the club drop, a deliberate gesture of surrender.

"All right," Elias shouted. "Get out of here."

As if it understood his words, the sauroid wheeled and vanished with a speed that chilled Elias. If the thing was that fast, it might have been able to jump them before he could get off a good shot.

"Thank you for not destroying it," Pendrake said.

"You may be sorry," Elias growled. He blew out a long breath, shaking in reaction. "How long did I sleep?"

"I would estimate about four hours."

"Do you need a turn?"

"No. Resting has been enough."

"Then let's go, before that thing decides to come back." Elias felt the strength of adrenaline, the fright of the sauroid still coursing through him. He got up, wincing at the stiffness in his legs. The rest seemed to have helped, though. Walking hurt, but he could do it. He thought of Martha out there with those bastards and the pain lessened. He hitched the water sack to his belt, then hesitated. He'd planned to look for water in the cave. Should they take the time to do it now? No. They had enough water for two days.

He picked up the scope and the ruptor, then choked down a dry stimtab while Pendrake was busy shouldering the survival pack.

Elias stepped from the cave mouth and stopped, startled by the beauty before him. The land sloped downward gradually from the cave mouth between two other hills. The green moon—not visible last night— was now high in the sky, bathing the slope in a soft, phosphorescent glow. The air was still warm enough to raise sweat, but nothing like the brutal heat of the day. This was a face of Cassiodorus he could not have guessed at—a sensory respite from the harshness of day life. He could almost imagine being a colonist and living for these nights—developing an attachment to the monstrous planet because of them.

Almost, but not quite. Not with the gravity still crushing you, never relenting, bending your bones, stealing the marrow from your children.

Elias motioned to Pendrake and started down the slope, taking a quick reading from the scope. Because of the four hours they'd rested, Martha's signature was now six hours old. But at any minute that figure might take a sharp drop if they came to another place where Martha had forced a rest.

*Or we might even find them over the next hill.*

Elias felt an optimistic lift at the thought. It was good to be moving again, even through the pain.

Elias kept checking the scope every few steps. In the back of his mind, the sauroid lingered, disturbing him. Why hadn't Holz told them that sauroids were intelligent?

Oversight?

Or because he didn't want them to know?

Did sauroids somehow fit into what was happening on this planet—the secret for which three imperial inspectors had died? Part of that secret was almost surely a diversion of beta-steel ore, though he hadn't proved it yet.

But was there more? Perhaps something even more dangerous to the Imperium?

"Elias!" Pendrake hissed, stopping him in his tracks.

"What?"

"Listen." Pendrake held a hand up, cocking his head. "Do you not hear it? Someone running. Up ahead, over that rise."

Elias could hear nothing. He looked down at the scope, his heart bounding with hope. It still read about

six hours. Even so, Martha could be over that rise—
Martha running, escaping from her captors!

A scream pierced the night air.

Elias felt his stomach plunge down inside him with
dread and horror. He sprinted up the hill, unslinging
the ruptor, praying as he ran.

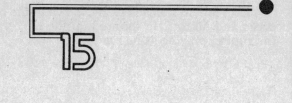

## 15

ELIAS FOUGHT TO KEEP RUNNING. THE HILL SEEMED to tilt up in front of him, the gravity dragging at his shoulders, turning his legs to lead. His muscles burned. Fear for Martha flogged him onward. He gasped for breath, unable to get enough air. He could feel himself slowing, his vision darkening. A nightmare, but he knew it was real: That scream, high-pitched with terror and pain—it could have been a man or a woman. His mind sent up ghastly images of Martha, hurt and bleeding.

Pendrake passed him at a lumbering run, a look of fierce intensity distorting his face. Elias cheered inwardly. He saw Pendrake top the rise and disappear over it.

The scream came again. *Martha, Martha, please, God!*

Elias topped the rise and collapsed onto his stomach, peering down the slope. Sweat poured into his eyes, stinging, blurring everything. Furiously he wiped it away. He saw Pendrake to one side, standing only a few steps down the hill, his face frozen in horror. He followed Pendrake's gaze to the moonlit valley below and saw two bodies. One was a man, lying face down.

A *man.* Elias felt a quick relief that it was not

Martha; then horror as he realized that the other body was not human, but a sauroid—and it was moving.

He watched, mesmerized, as the sauroid pushed up with its short arms and struggled to get its huge legs under it. It seemed weak, as though it was hurt—or terribly weary. It stood at last, weaving unsteadily, looking around the body of the fallen man.

It doesn't see us, Elias thought. His paralysis broke. He fumbled with the ruptor, trying to bring it to bear. He realized he was still gasping, each breath jarring through his shoulder to the ruptor's stock, wrecking his aim. He saw the sauroid bend over, then straighten again and realized that it had picked up a club, like the one the other sauroid had dropped back in the cave.

Elias saw the man stir feebly and hope sprang up in him. *He's alive! Hang on, man.*

Elias drew a deep breath and held it, steadying his shoulder, drawing the sauroid into his sights, then losing it as it circled around the man. He cursed and adjusted, but then the man clambered to his knees, his head hanging, swaying drunkenly and Elias was forced to hold his fire as the sauroid moved in, tapping the man's skull with its club. The man collapsed onto his face again.

Got you, now! Elias thought, but the sauroid collapsed at once beside the man, as though the effort of striking him had exhausted it. The two figures merged in Elias' sights. He cursed savagely. The sauroid lifted its head, its mouth gaping over the man's neck, saw-edged teeth glowing in the moonlight.

*I've got to shoot, or he's dead anyway.*

Elias began to squeeze the trigger, then stopped as he saw that the sauroid was not tearing at the man. Instead, it seemed to be nudging the side of the man's head with its own, as if with affection.

Elias' stomach squirmed with revulsion.

From the corner of his eye, he saw Pendrake break into a run down the slope. Worry for Pendrake filled him. The sauroid looked weak, but it still might be dangerous. Get down there and help him, Elias thought. He struggled to rise, making it to his knees, then freezing as he saw the sauroid spring up from the man's body to meet Pendrake's charge. It swung its club, but Pendrake raised a forearm and the club shattered over it.

The sauroid backed off a step.

Get him! Elias thought, but Pendrake only walked around the fallen man, putting himself between the sauroid and its prey. Elias groaned. He tried to aim the ruptor at the sauroid, but Pendrake was in the way. Using the ruptor as a crutch, Elias pushed himself to his feet and started down the slope. He saw the sauroid leap on Pendrake and was stunned by its strength and speed. Its earlier lethargy had vanished. Pendrake swept it off, but it leapt in again with blinding speed. *Dear God, how could anything living move that fast in this gravity?* With a sick feeling, Elias saw the sauroid's head darting, the wicked teeth slashing. A ribbon of blood streamed down Pendrake's shoulder, glittering green-orange in the moonlight. Pendrake broke the sauroid's grip and shoved it away.

"Run!" Elias shouted, but he knew Pendrake wasn't fast enough. The sauroid leapt in again, this time clenching Pendrake's chest in its short arms. It forced its head side-to-side against Pendrake's. Pendrake flailed at it with sudden, frantic energy, but the sauroid held on.

*It's killing him!* Elias saw with horror that Pendrake was weakening, dropping to his knees, the sauroid still clinging to him. Elias got up close to them and realized he couldn't shoot. He reversed the ruptor, holding it as a club. As he tried to swing it, the sauroid saw him and danced Pendrake away. Pendrake's knees were slack now; the sauroid was supporting Pendrake's weight, whirling him in a circle.

*So strong—incredible!*

Elias cut a wide circle around it, waiting his moment, lunging in, slamming the ruptor in fury against the sauroid's back. The blow did not faze it. With a curse, Elias threw the weapon down and leapt on the sauroid's back. Its tail lashed up, whipping him across the legs. Pain ripped through him and his vision blurred. *Hang on, don't let go.*

His sight returned; he saw Pendrake's face over the sauroid's shoulder. Pendrake's eyes were closed, his mouth slack. Elias could see flesh worming between the sauroid's ear and Pendrake's. Elias went cold with horror. He scrambled higher on the sauroid's back, digging his feet against the nubby, reptilian skin.

The eyes, he thought.

He jammed his thumb against the side of its head—again, again, feeling it sink into soft wetness. The sauroid shuddered under him. Elias yelled in savage triumph and gouged at the eye again. The sauroid roared and dropped Pendrake, backing up, trying to claw behind it and get at Elias. Its short arms could not reach him. The sauroid sprawled forward, then rolled over on top of him, flattening his lungs, pressing him down into the clay. He couldn't breathe. Panic flooded him. He pushed and kicked at the large, leathery body, but the sauroid was too heavy. He could feel his ribs pressing down into his lungs. A carrion stench filled his nose. He could not expel it or draw a breath. He tried to jab the eye again, but he was too far down the body now, the sauroid's head out of reach.

Everything began to fade.

He no longer wanted a breath. The ground softened under him, becoming a soft, slowly spinning cloud.

The pain came back, shooting down his throat, ripping at his lungs, and he heard himself gasping. Air flamed in his lungs, then sweetened as he sucked it in. He saw the sauroid above him, watching him intently. Fear rushed back into him, *get up, run!* but the sauroid's big, splayed foot settled on his stomach, pinning him. It prodded him, as if wanting to see if he was awake.

*It wants me alive.*

Elias closed his eyes and lay still, playing dead.

He felt the sauroid's foot bearing down on his stomach, squeezing pain through him, until he knew it would rupture his stomach. He bucked to life under the foot, squirming, beating at it with his fists. The sauroid pulled the foot away, then bent down to him with a vicious grin of triumph, its small arms reaching for his shoulders, man-like fingers spreading to clutch him. A phobic terror seized him. He struggled with desperate strength, but the sauroid held his shoulders easily. He smelled its stinking breath, saw the jagged teeth an inch from his throat, and then the sauroid pressed the side of its head against his.

He felt the cool flesh slide into his ear. *God, no!*

His mind opened in horrified revelation: the rebels' earphone weapon, the severed flesh—*a sauroid's!*

And then his strength plummeted away; the night and the sauroid blended together and vanished.

Elias opened his eyes and saw a blurred, grid pattern stretching up into a reddish circle of light. His mind felt slow and thick. *Where am I? What happened?*

His back hurt; his knees were jammed up near his face, his feet even higher. The grid pattern snapped into focus, and he realized he was staring at webbing; he was hanging in a cargo net. No, not net, vine—those ropy blue plants he'd seen on the hillside, woven into a crude net. Above him, he saw where the thing was attached to a rough, wooden pole traversing a rock ceiling. He realized they were in a cave. What in—?

*The sauroid!*

With a shock, Elias' mind cleared. He lurched and squirmed in the net, his heart hammering in panic.

"Elias!"

*Pendrake! He's alive!* Elias turned with delight, looking for him, seeing him hanging inside another net near the mouth of the cave. Pendrake's shoulder was encrusted with clotted, orange blood, but his face looked alert. "Are you all right?"

"Yes, Elias. How do *you* feel?"

"Like a ceiling decoration in Neptune's bar." Elias looked beyond Pendrake out the mouth of the cave. Outside, the reddish sunlight of Cassiodorus beat down, distorting distant hills in a shimmer of heat. The daylight gave him a sense of dislocation. "How long have we been here?"

"Too long," said another voice. Startled, Elias looked across the entrance from Pendrake. A third net hung there. Through its strands, a boyish face peered fearfully at him. It was "Bullneck"—one of the two men who'd kidnapped Martha.

Elias stared at him, fury surging through him. "What have you done with Dr. Reik?"

"She is safe—a lot safer than we. We be dead men, Inspector Kane."

Elias felt a quick relief for Martha, then thought of the sauroid again, and raw fear shot through him. He twisted in the net, trying to look all around the cave. On the floor he saw scattered bones. Some were from animals, but he realized with a sick feeling that some looked human. He became aware of an odor of rotting meat, and his gorge rose.

"Thou seest right, Inspector. Sauroids *do* eat the likes of us. But only when they be through with us."

Elias tried again to see into the dark interior of the cave, his heart pounding.

"The sauroid is not here now, Elias," Pendrake said soothingly.

Elias felt a thin relief. He stopped searching and turned back to Pendrake. "I'd like to get my hands on Holz right now. Sew the fork in his tongue together."

Pendrake grimaced. "He did tell us part of the truth. Sauroids *do* hunt humans for food."

"If that part had been a lie," Elias growled, "I'd have forgiven him."

Bullneck gave a hysterical laugh.

Elias ignored him and pulled experimentally at the woven vines, trying to pry open a gap large enough to drop through. He saw that each intersection of the net was bound together with clear, slightly sticky strands. He pulled with all his strength, but the strands neither stretched nor broke; the net retained its shape. He peered up at the top of the net, frustrated, hoping to see a gap, but there was no gap.

"There be no way out," Bullneck said in a dead voice.

Elias glared at him, angered by his defeatism, even as he realized the man must know what he was talking about. "What's your name?"

"Frez. Thou and Pendrake saved my life last night, Inspector Kane. I be grateful."

"That was you?" Elias stared at him, surprised, then realized that the man had lain face down, his features hidden. "If I'd realized it was you, I'd have let the sauroid kill you."

"Elias does not mean that, Frez," Pendrake said quickly.

Yes I do, Elias thought, irritated. How long have you two been awake, chatting? Are you buddies now?

"I don't blame him," Frez said.

"What were you doing out there?" Elias asked. "Why weren't you with the other thug and Dr. Reik?"

"I was sent back to check our trail. I thought it was stupid, but I see it wasn't. Lucky for me, thou *wert* close on our heels."

Elias was pleased but did not show it. Weal sent Frez back, he thought, because they were close to wherever they were going. Weal wanted to make sure no one followed them in. "I asked you where Dr. Reik is."

"I can't tell thee. But she be safe, with honorable men who will protect her."

Elias felt a grim satisfaction. Safe—and with *men,* not man. Her trek was over; they must be close by. *Now all we've got to do is get out of here and find them.*

"How *didst* thou manage to follow us?" Frez's voice was filled with respect.

"That's *my* little secret," Elias said, wondering

what had become of the K-scope. No doubt lying on the ground near the place they'd fought the sauroid. He didn't need it now, because he had Frez, and they were close. If we get out of this, Elias thought savagely, you're going to tell me exactly where Martha is, boy. And you can depend on that.

But right now, we've got another problem. Until we get away from the sauroid, Frez is going to have to be *your* buddy, too—whether you like it or not.

Elias shifted in the net, trying to move himself so that he could see Frez better. "You seem to know quite a bit about the sauroid," he said. "Tell me everything you know. Don't leave things out, like Holz did."

"There be nothing to tell," Frez said in a guarded voice.

Elias felt a surge of exasperation. "Listen to me, you bastard: If we're going to have any chance of getting out of here alive, I've got to know exactly what we're up against—this sauroid's patterns of behavior, everything you know about it. So start talking."

"It is futile. Thou can'st not save us."

"I 'can'st not' track you across this desert, either. But I did."

"You must tell him, Frez," Pendrake said kindly.

"There be nothing to tell," Frez insisted in a whining voice. "We be all dead men."

"What makes you so sure?" Elias said.

Frez did not answer.

He's hiding something, Elias thought. Just like Holz. Elias twisted in the net, turning his back on Frez, trying to find a comfortable position. The strands cut into his body no matter how he positioned himself. He ignored the discomfort and thought: All right, the sauroid had stunned them with the tissue from its ear— no doubt the same tissue that was embedded in the earphone weapon. Elias shuddered, remembering the horrible coolness squirming inches from his brain. It had stunned them, or paralyzed them—whatever you could call it. Then it had brought them here and immobilized them, planning to eat each of them as it became hungry—

No, wait, Elias thought. Did the sauroid stun Frez with its head organ or hit him with its club?

Both! It hit him, then lay down beside him and put its head against his, just like it does when it stuns. Why? If Frez was already out cold, why stun him again?

Elias felt his mind focusing, bringing back the details of last night. The sauroid was *weak!* he realized with dawning excitement. When I first saw it, it was lying on the ground. It barely had the strength to get up and hit Frez. So Frez must have put up a good fight— *Frez almost beat it.*

But how could that be? Frez was not as strong as Pendrake, and yet the sauroid had leapt up from Frez and handled Pendrake easily. Suddenly it was strong— incredibly strong and fast.

After it put its head against Frez!

*As if touching Frez's head had somehow made it stronger!*

Elias felt a fierce excitement. He closed his eyes, thinking furiously. What if, when the sauroid extended that stun organ into its victims, it didn't just destroy their energy but somehow was able to draw that energy into itself?

Could that be it? A neat, thermodynamic equation —energy lost equals energy gained? A chill ran up Elias' spine. If he was right, the sauroid would keep them, feeding on their energy over and over, until it took too much and killed one of them. Then it would eat that one and continue draining the others, for as long as it could, until they all were dead and had joined the bones on the cave floor.

Elias shuddered, understanding the fatalistic dread in Frez's voice. It's how the sauroid survives in this gravity, he thought. How it finds the strength to move around and hunt and kill. And it's got to have new energy regularly. Otherwise, it weakens. The gravity slows it, and it is no longer fast or strong enough to survive.

*Dear God in heaven! The strength of the colonists. The weakness of their children.*

A cold dread closed around Elias' heart, prickled into his mind. He thought of the children, sitting motionless in their classroom, their heads bowed in dull fatigue, and felt sick with horror. The earphone is *not* a weapon, he thought. The earphone is how the *colonists* survive.

He twisted in his net, filling with fury. "You *bastards!*" he shouted at Frez. Pendrake looked startled, but Frez just stared back at him, his eyes sick, and Elias knew it was true. He closed his eyes, groaning, realizing how it must have been: the first colonists settling this planet, discovering the native sauroids—probably the hard way. At first, the sauroids were just one more menace on a planet whose crushing gravity made survival difficult—and wrenching beta-steel ore from the mines almost impossible.

Then someone had had the malignant idea: *Find a way to do what the sauroid does to survive. Use the sauroids to do it.* So the earphone was made, not as a weapon, but as a means of drawing down the energy of a donor, transferring it to a recipient.

But why were the colonists draining their own children? It was monstrous. If the donors were adults, he could understand it, revolting and evil as it still would be.

Clearly, adults *could* serve as donors.

That's why they tried to kill me with the earphone, Elias thought. Instead of just bashing my head with a rock. *You've gotten so dependent on stolen energy, you never waste it, do you? It's the most precious commodity on your stinking planet. But you got a little too greedy; Pendrake got me away—and it's the biggest mistake any of you ever made!*

Elias felt a savage resolve building inside him. We're going to get out of here, he thought. Escape and put a stop to this. I'm going to find whoever's in charge —Cay Endor, or whoever it turns out to be. And when I do, I'm going to ask him if it was worth it, if he really needed the ore that badly.

*And then I'm going to kill the bastard, and no one's going to stop me.*

Elias realized that Frez was no longer looking at him, that he was staring in horror at the mouth of the cave. *The sauroid—it was back!* Dread filled Elias. The sauroid walked toward him slowly, teeth grinning, red eyes staring at him with terrible cunning. Elias tore in panic at the webbing even as he knew it was futile. Frez had been right; there *was* no escape.

He was not going to get out of here, not going to stop anything.

16

ELIAS STARED AT THE SAUROID WITH A SICK FEELING of helplessness. Don't come any closer, he prayed. As if it had read his mind, the sauroid stopped. It stood just inside the cave entrance, darkened and still against the blaze of sunlight outside. Slowly it raised its arm, and Elias saw that it was holding the carcass of a small, rabbitlike animal. He stared at it in dread fascination. I caught that animal, too, he thought. I was inside the sauroid, helping it kill. Elias felt a memory of motion in his legs, *sprinting across the clay, sensing the little animal's terror. Blood lust filled him as he matched its desperate wheels and turns, gaining on it. At last its small, darting form filled his vision. His jaws clamped down on it.*

Elias heard himself gasp, felt sweat break out on his forehead. The sensations were terribly real.

He saw that the sauroid was gazing at him in a strange reverie, as if it were tuned to his thoughts. Elias shrank back in the net, feeling soiled.

The sauroid broke its gaze from him and stalked to Pendrake instead. It tore a chunk from the carcass with its teeth and chewed deliberately. Blood poured from the carcass and dripped on the floor. Elias felt a twinge of nausea. He saw Pendrake turn away, his face a stoic

177

mask, but Elias could sense his disgust. *Is he seeing what I saw? Feeling what I felt? How much worse it must be for him.* Elias felt pity for Pendrake and anger at the sauroid. *Leave him alone.*

But it circled Pendrake's net, refusing to let Pendrake avoid it, holding the animal up in offering. Pendrake's lips curled back and he lunged against the webbing of the net with a hideous roar.

The sauroid leapt back as if shocked, dropping the carcass, hissing at Pendrake. Elias felt the same shock, his hackles rising at the raw bestiality in Pendrake's voice.

The sauroid retrieved the carcass and stalked over to Frez.

"No! Pul-please." Frez began to cry, to shake in sobs. Elias felt pity for him, too, and then his pity vanished as he remembered how willing Frez had been to use a piece of the sauroid against him.

Elias realized that the sauroid was heading toward him now. Fear surged through him; he struggled to rise and back up in the net. The sauroid offered him the carcass. Its eyes stared at him with a deadly, paralyzing message: *Eat, keep your strength up so I can feed on you.*

When he would not take the carcass, the sauroid dropped it and reached for him. Elias kicked at the sauroid in fear and revulsion, but it ignored his foot, reaching through the net, grabbing his arm, pulling him against the webbing. He fought with desperate panicked strength, but the sauroid was much stronger, drawing him tight against the vines, immobilizing him, moving its head toward his, and he knew he could not stand the stinking thing inside him again, he would go mad.

He heard himself screaming, and then the sauroid screamed too, and Elias smelled ozone, heard the sizzling aftershock of a blaster. The sauroid released him and reeled away; he saw a gaping wound in its back, and then it turned to him again, blood pumping through from a hole in its chest, spattering him.

It collapsed face down on the floor of the cave and was still.

Elias stared at it, trembling, his mind numb. He looked to the mouth of the cave, saw a big man pointing a hand blaster at the fallen sauroid. *Rescued!* Relief and gratitude rushed through him.

"Minc," Frez cried. "Thanks be to God. Thou saved us. Thanks be, thanks be!"

Elias wanted to shout too, but he could not find his voice. *God, that was too close!*

And then he recognized Minc. The man he'd known as Weal—Frez's partner; Martha's other captor.

"How didst thou find us?" Frez blubbered.

"Back straight, lad," Minc said, as if embarrassed. "In truth, I was about to give up looking for thee. But then I heard the roar of the orange man. That be not a sound I'll forget." As he talked, Minc took out a knife and sawed on the webbing, putting all his muscle into it. The vines parted grudgingly. Elias watched with foreboding. *What happens when he gets to us?*

*Just take me to Martha; nothing else matters.*

When Frez had clambered down from his severed net, Minc went to Pendrake. "Thy hands behind thee, please. Unless thou cravest to stay here."

Frez looked pained. "Must we—?"

"Yes, and thou knowest it. If they mind their manners, they have nothing to fear—at least not from thee and me."

Pendrake held his arms back and Minc clamped his wrists behind him. Elias saw that Minc was using a sens-arc and realized Pendrake might not be familiar with the cruel handcuffs. "Don't test them," Elias warned. "If you do, they'll shock you. The harder you pull, the greater the shock. It could kill you."

"Exactly right. Thou next, Inspector."

Elias held his hands back for the cuffs, outraged that he was still helpless.

"He saved my life," Frez said. "They both did."

Minc gave him a penetrating look. "Hast thou become too friendly with these two? Hast, perhaps, shot off thy mouth?"

Frez shook his head, but Elias saw his fear and knew with a sinking feeling that both men must be thinking of the sauroid. They knew it was the key to their ugly secret, and they were worried that the Earthie inspector had figured it out. He felt a rising fury at the two rebels, at their cruelty to their own children, their guilty efforts to hide what they were doing with the earphone.

No, not earphone. That was too innocuous a name for the hideous device. Vampire, Elias thought. The thing—and the people who use it. As Minc's hands touched his wrists with the sens-arc, Elias felt a deep revulsion. He did not want to be on the same planet with Minc and Frez, breathe the same air. He realized that it was more than revulsion: they scared him. How had human beings, men with a surface veneer of decency, given their allegiance to such depravity? Could Earth defeat people who would stoop to such depths to win?

Earth had to.

*But unless we can get away from these sick bastards, Earth won't even know the danger it's in.*

Elias watched for an opportunity as Minc cut him and Pendrake out of their nets, but Minc kept the blaster aimed at him. The blaster never wavered as Minc ushered them from the cave and down the slope to a waiting groundcar, motioning to them to crawl into the back. Minc got in the driver's seat and handed the blaster to Frez. "Keep it on them. If they try anything, shoot."

Looking miserable, Frez aimed the blaster over the seat at them. Elias was forced to sit forward awkwardly to keep his hands from being crushed against his back. Pendrake winced and then sat forward too. Elias realized from his face that, despite the warning, he'd tested the sens-arc.

"Thou wilt soon see Dr. Reik," Frez said hopefully. "She be well. I know she'll be glad to see thee."

"Shut up, Frez," Minc said from the driver's seat.

"Shut *thou* up!" Frez's face turned red, and for a moment Elias thought he might turn the blaster on Minc. Minc looked startled; his hands tightened on the wheel, but he said nothing further.

Elias knew he should try and exploit the rift between Minc and Frez, but his mind was full of Martha. From the moment they'd taken her, all he'd wanted was to see her again, to know that she was alive and safe and to hold her in his arms. And now he would do it. He felt a powerful longing—and then a sudden, sharp premonition of death.

He closed his eyes and visualized Martha's face, her lopsided grin, her unruly red hair, her gray eyes sparkling with wit and mischief. He could see her very clearly in his mind, almost *feel* her in his arms, and yet the sense of his death would not dissipate. He wondered if it had to do with the sauroid. Had an indefinable part of him still been trapped inside it when it was shot? *Maybe I'm already partly dead.*

He tried to fight off the morbid chill inside him. So what? he thought fatalistically. So part of me's dead. Before I even left the *Seraphim*, I got spooked about dying down here. So maybe now fate's satisfied.

Elias felt a sour amusement, then was annoyed at himself. Instead of brooding about death, he should be thinking, planning. He now knew how the colonists were able to survive here; how they not only survived, but how they were able to mine more beta-steel ore than anyone would dream possible. There could be little doubt what was happening to any extra ore. But figuring it out wasn't enough. He still must save the children. And—if it wasn't already too late—stop their fanatic parents from turning diverted ore into dreadnoughts.

The first step was to get to a radio, signal the *Seraphim*. The best chance for a radio was to go exactly where Minc was taking them: probably to a stronghold —maybe even to their headquarters here on Cassiodorus. Certainly, the place would have a subspace radio. So there was no point trying to turn Frez against Minc, even though he'd love to see the two bastards with their hands at each others' throats. Elias felt his hands clenching into fists, pulling involuntarily against the sens-arc cuffs. He barely felt the shock.

The groundcar coasted to a stop. Elias looked through the front screen and saw only a featureless mound of rock. And then the rock parted, two massive doors swinging wide. Minc drove the groundcar through into dim coolness, stopped and motioned for them to get out. As Elias slid from the groundcar, he felt the blessed relief of gravity suppression. He looked around, his heart racing, hoping to see Martha. His eyes adjusted to the dimness and he saw only a few guards standing around the perimeter of hollowed-out rock. He sagged in disappointment. When would they take him to her? *Now, I want to see her now!* He forced himself to be calm. Right now he must concentrate on observing, recording, remembering.

He looked around the room again and saw the elevator set into the far wall. The freight-sized doors filled Elias with foreboding. This little entry room was only the tip of the iceberg. They were in a stronghold all right—one as invisible to any orbiting spaceship as it would to a squad of soldiers passing by on foot.

And maybe they were in something else, too: *a mine.*

Elias' foreboding grew. Minc prodded him into the elevator; as he crossed the threshold, he got a faint, rubbery whiff of corside, the support material for mine walls. That's it, he thought with a sinking feeling. Please, let me be wrong. The elevator plunged, lifting his stomach to his throat. He swallowed and counted mentally. The cage slowed after a twenty-second drop.

They were deep into the earth—probably around 120 meters. He had no idea how many levels might be above, or yet below them. But he knew one thing: The place was huge—it had taken great effort and expense to build it.

The doors opened and Minc led them down a hallway lit by a chain of bulbs strung overhead. As they walked, Elias saw that the walls showed wide bands of corsided clay interspersed with the rock. A weight of depression settled over him. He glanced at Pendrake and saw from his grim expression that he realized it too: This was not just a rebel stronghold. It was a beta-steel mine, unregistered—totally unknown to the Imperium. He now had all the proof he needed that the colonists were diverting ore. But how long had they been at it? He could get no clue to the age of the excavation from the cut rockface. This underground warren could have been finished last month or ten years ago.

*Dear God, how long? How many dreadnoughts?*

A hall branched to one side. Minc motioned them into it. Elias saw that both walls were lined with steel doors set into the rock every few meters.

"Here," Frez said. "She be inside, Inspector."

Elias felt his heart leap and begin to pound. His dejection vanished; he forgot the dreadnoughts. Minc removed the sens-arc from his wrists and unlocked the door. She was standing against the far wall of a cell. She turned to him, her face lighting. "Elias!"

And then she was in his arms. Dimly he heard the door clang shut behind him. He held her, his heart overflowing with love and relief. He could smell her, a soapy scent and the sweet, natural oil of her hair. Her ribs, her flanks pressed against him, her arms tightly circling the small of his back.

He held her away, looking into her eyes, too full of emotion to speak.

"How did you find me?" she asked.

"Very squeezable."

"Oh, Elias. Nut! Nut nut nut!" Punctuating each

"nut" with a tap of her fist on his chest, grinning as she burst into tears.

He felt his own eyes draining. "They've treated you all right?"

"Even let me have a bath. Sent some musclebound woman along to watch me, of course. They act like I'm made of glass. It helped me slow them down."

"You did great." He felt his knees weaving under him.

She took his hands and led him to a cot hanging from the rock by straps. Gratefully, he settled onto it. "I'm tired," he admitted. "But I've found you."

"I love you." She kissed him.

He held her to him until he remembered Pendrake. With a guilty start he looked around.

"I saw him in the hall," Martha said, reading his mind. "I think they took him down to the next cell. Don't worry, they've been very civilized."

*Civilized?* No, that wasn't the word for these people.

She looked at his face in sudden alarm. "What's wrong? Are you sick?"

He sagged back against the rock wall. "Martha, I need your scientific opinion. But what I have to say isn't pretty. . . ." He stopped, realizing he was being foolish. She had probably dealt with more blood and pain and horror in her operating rooms than he would see in his life.

He told her about the children.

She wept as he talked. When he was finished, she dried her tears. Her face was white, her expression harder than he'd ever seen it. "We have to get out of here, Elias."

"Yes. How much have you seen of this place?"

"Not much." She closed her eyes as if reviewing an inner record. "When they took me to the bath, I passed a door with a guard."

"Tell me exactly how you get there from here."

Elias closed his eyes and concentrated as she described the route.

"Good. It might be an armory or, if we're lucky, a communications center." Elias pushed up, paced to the door to check the lock. He found only a thick steel plate on this side of the door—nothing to pick. His heart sank. Never mind—their moment would come; they would find a way out. As Martha had said, they had to.

He sat again beside her. "Does my theory about the vampire device make sense to you?"

"It fits perfectly with what's happening," she said.

"Yes, but what about the science of it? Something keeps nagging at me: We're assuming the sauroid—and the vampire device—draw down the neuroelectric energy of a person. Then that energy is pumped into a recipient. But what good would that do? It's our muscles that make us strong, isn't it?"

"Only partly," Martha said. "The more muscle, the stronger, of course. But the capacity of a given muscle to contract can vary widely, and nobody's ever entirely figured out why. There are documented examples of superhuman strength under stress—a little, fifty-kilo woman lifts a stalled groundcar off her child. But ask that same woman to lift that car when her child is not under it, and there's no way she can do it, no matter how hard she tries. So what's different? She's still got exactly the same muscles she had before. But the nerve pulse is quantitatively much stronger due to panic. Also, the endocrine system is kicking in with a potent stimulant, adrenaline."

Martha's eyes began to shine with the excitement of the intellectual chase. "This is fascinating. While I was in med school, I worked in a primate lab. Sometimes we had to take rhesus monkeys from their cages for injections or examinations. We had to have big, burly lab assistants for that job, because the monkeys—which only weighed around ten kilos—would put up a tremendous fight. Sometimes a rhesus would grab the bars of his cage, and it would take two lab assistants to pry it loose."

"OK, love or panic can enhance strength, but . . ."

"No, Elias. Those are only two of the things that enhance muscle power. So do certain drugs—all of which have serious side effects with steady use. But now there is this vampire device, transmitting natural neuroelectric energy, not some foreign substance. Clearly the device has no serious side effects or they wouldn't be able to keep using it." Martha frowned. "But that shouldn't be possible. Whether from stress or chemicals, superhuman exertion always takes a toll afterward."

"Maybe it's the *quality* of the neuroelectric energy that makes the vampire device different," Elias said.

Martha gave him an appreciative grin. "You're pretty smart, you know that?"

He felt a warm glow, absurdly pleased.

"That's got to be it," she said. "Stress and drugs act by overloading—flogging the muscle, forcing it. In the aftermath, there's torn muscle, adrenaline deficiency, and the body pays. The vampire device must stimulate extra muscle strength *without* overloading. It's the quality, not the quantity, of the neuroelectric energy that's different."

Martha's eyes widened. "*That's* why they use children!"

Elias looked at her, confused. But before she could say anything else, the door clanged open. Two big men entered, blasters pointed. "Dr. Reik, Inspector Kane. Come with us."

The men led them through a maze of corridors. Elias committed each twist and turn to memory, knowing he was about to meet the rebel leader—the person responsible for the mass abuse of the planet's children. Whatever Martha was thinking about why the colonists had used children, no reason could excuse what they had done. He was about to look absolute evil in the face.

He fought to hang on to his anger, but his heart pounded with dread.

The guards ushered them into a large, plain room cut from the rock. A man was sitting at a rough, wooden table, his back to the door, reading some papers. Even from behind, Elias noticed something familiar about him. Then the man turned to face them. Elias felt stunned recognition and then shock.

## 17

No! Elias thought, hoping he was wrong. The beard, the slight paunch—this wasn't Richard DuMorgan.

But it was.

Elias looked at Richard sickened. My friend, he thought. Even though we were on opposite sides. But we can be friends no longer. A terrible feeling of loss swept over him. DuMorgan's gaze became stark, as if he knew exactly what Elias was feeling.

"Hello, Elias, Dr. Reik."

Elias nodded, still too shocked to speak. Next to Gregory Amerdath, Richard DuMorgan was the most magnetic man he had ever known. Once, the finest of Amerdath's viceroys; leadership shone from his eyes, communicated itself in his walk, his voice, his straight back, even in the motions of his hands. Richard, leader of the rebels on Cassiodorus? Richard, responsible for the neurologic vampirism of the planet's children? Impossible!

And yet, wherever Richard DuMorgan was, he was always in charge. And he was here, now. The utter tragedy of it struck Elias like a blow to the stomach.

Richard stood and walked around the desk toward him, offering his hand. As he did, Elias saw movement in the corner of the room and realized that two other men were present; Dalt, Richard's chief lieutenant and bodyguard, stepping forward now to make sure Elias did not lash out at Richard. And next to Dalt, another man, still unmoving. *Jost!*

Elias made no move to take the offered hand. Seeing he wouldn't, Richard continued his motion smoothly, prodding his chest in a comradely way. "You've been lifting weights, Elias."

"And you've grown a beard," Elias said, uneasy at Richard's probing touch, then realizing there was no way Richard could guess the extra centimeters on his chest were plastiflesh. No way, either, for him to guess that the proof of his infamy lay under that skin.

*Under my skin.* Elias felt a bitter laugh welling up and dying in his throat. If Richard realized they knew about the children, what would he do? Elias felt cold fear for Martha.

Richard tossed Dalt and Jost a conspiratorial smile. "I get fat and hairy, and Elias gets musclebound. What are things coming to?"

"What *are* they coming to, Richard?" Elias said. *Careful.* He broke eye contact with Richard and looked over at Jost, saw that Jost's stillness wasn't voluntary— he was leaning on crutches. The leg Elias had shot with the needler was encased in an inflated splint, and the hand was gloved in bandages. Jost looked pale, and thinner than he remembered, but he was alive, and Elias was glad—he could not help himself—and his gladness unnerved him.

"No hard feelings," Jost said. "As a matter of fact, no feelings at all, in the hand or the foot. But I had it coming."

"Jost is one of our top people on Cassiodorus," Richard said.

Elias tensed. "Hold on, Richard."

Richard DuMorgan gave an impatient wave. "Come on, Elias. You've seen all this. You already know enough to hurt us badly. I want you to know enough to want to help us, instead. I want you to join us."

"You must be joking," Martha said. Her voice was hard. No! Elias thought, restraining the urge to grab her arm in warning.

"I have never been more serious in my life." Richard motioned to Dalt. "Let's sit down and talk. Will you at least do that?"

"Do we have a choice?" Elias said.

Richard did not answer. Dalt brought two chairs over. Elias met his gaze briefly, saw the same rigid dislike he remembered from the last time they'd met, back on Earth. He'd been Dalt's prisoner, Dalt thirsting for his blood, and yet Elias wished that he were back in that universe, where Amerdath had still been Imperator, and Richard DuMorgan his viceroy.

Where all Dalt would do was crack one of his bones.

"How be the rib," Dalt inquired as if reading his mind. His voice was oily with mock concern.

"Fine. And your head? Or is that a new one?"

Dalt's eyes flickered, just a hint of anger, then the cold composure again. He returned to Jost's side and Elias sat, annoyed with himself. Why irritate Dalt? he thought. Your position is shaky enough already.

Elias saw that Richard was peering keenly at him, as if trying to see into his heart. He gazed back, feeling the physical changes in Richard begin to sink in. What he saw disturbed him: That potbelly and the shaggy beard—both would have been unthinkable during Richard's days as viceroy of Alpha Centauri IV. They spoiled his lean, rugged handsomeness, making him look haggard and older.

And the beard hid his scars.

Elias' unease deepened. Richard had always been proud of those Andinaz scars on his cheeks. *What's happened to you?*

Elias realized he was still trying to deny the awful reality. The children of Cassiodorus had happened to

Richard—and he to them. The sick feeling returned, a queasy revulsion in the pit of his stomach.

"Elias," Richard said, "you and Martha have been loyal servants of the Imperium, just as I was. But it's time you realized the truth. You are serving the forces of repression."

You hypocrite, Elias thought. He contained his anger, tried to make his voice calm and reasonable. "The forces of repression. That has a nice, rhetorical ring, Richard. Too bad it's rubbish."

"It's the truth. And that tyranny must fall, Elias. The colonies must be free."

"You're free right now. Under law, every colonist has exactly the same rights I have."

"But you are *in charge* of us, and that's the difference. Come on, Elias. Earth has had the power right from the start. And Earth used it to try to strangle us. Remember the food monopoly?"

"Monopoly? I remember that each new colony in turn was unable to find enough arable land to support itself. Earth kept those colonies supplied with food *without fail* until hydroponics and terraforming could take up the slack."

"But at what price? We had to work ourselves into early graves to keep Earth supplied with the raw materials it demanded in return for that food."

"Graves, Richard? You've picked up a new flare for exaggeration. You know the truth as well as I do: Earth had to struggle too, and do without, to feed you. It had to learn agribusiness all over again, spend billions in incentives and support to get enough manpower recommitted to do the job. There's no way Earth could have financed that massive retooling without the help of the colonies. And the only thing the colonies had of value was raw materials."

"And meanwhile, you imposed your own laws and taxes," Richard said bitterly.

"Wait a minute. Not my laws, *our* laws—human laws—the product of over five thousand years of civilization. Did you expect to leave law behind when you went into space? And I pay taxes at exactly the same rate as a colonist."

"And where do those taxes go? To the comfort and advancement of Earthmen."

"That's bull, Richard. They go to maintain the civilization and the defense of all of us humans together."

"But, again, strictly under Earth control. Earth just loves monopolies. When we broke the food monopoly, you were ready with the next one: beta-steel."

"Ah, we're getting warmer now."

"Yes. I'm sure this place makes it obvious to you that we're squirreling away our own supplies of beta-steel ore. Just as obviously, we want it for dreadnoughts."

Elias listened acutely, every sense on edge. Is he saying that all he has right now is ore? Or is that just what he *wants* me to believe?

"The Imperium has tried to control the ore, mined with the sweat of our own backs, the ruptured hearts and broken bones of colonists. They've made it treason for the scientists and engineers of Earth to help us build and tie together the hundreds of technical systems necessary for the full functioning of a dreadnought. Earth controls the manufacture of beta-steel, Earth controls the making of dreadnoughts, and Earth controls the use of dreadnoughts. We, the colonies, are kept naked to our enemies so that Briana's fleet can maintain its mastery over us. But it can't work, Elias. Knowledge can't be stifled forever. Scientists are as capable of bravery and integrity as the rest of us. There are brave men and women who will risk execution for us."

Integrity? Elias thought. You dare use that word? "You are not naked to your enemies," he said. "You never have been. Those Andinaz scars—is that why you've hidden them under a beard? Maybe you no longer like to be reminded that Gregory Amerdath— and a lot of the rest of us Earthies—fought by your side to defeat the Andinaz? Damn it, Richard, if you think the colonies are naked to alien attack now, just wait until you've decimated yourself—and maybe Earth, too —in a civil war."

Richard looked offended. " 'Civil war' is the wrong term; it's a revolution."

Elias felt an immense exasperation. "Go ahead, Richard. Use the 'right' term. If you win, you can even put it in your history books—the glorious revolution, just like 1776. If you lose, it'll go down as a bloody and insane civil war. But win or lose, you'll end up weaker. Together, the human race beat the Andinaz—"

Richard slapped his desk. "We should not have needed that help. We should have been able to beat them on our own. And we would have, if we'd had the dreadnoughts."

"Maybe. But we have no idea what's out there beyond the Andinaz. The next bunch to come along might make the Andinaz look like a flock of doves."

"Your 'protection' costs us too much."

Elias shook his head. "I don't understand you, Richard. Is the Imperium evil because it saves your ass, or because it leaves your ass naked? Which is it?"

Richard flushed. "You're good with words, Elias. But we're determined to be free. You can help us, or you can go down with the oppressors."

The passion in Richard's voice touched and saddened Elias: Richard wanted to give himself up to a noble cause—freedom. The romantic fire in him was part of what had made him so special, but now it had inflamed and consumed his vision. "Oppressors?" Elias said gently. "Think, Richard: If Earth is such an oppressor, wouldn't we have stationed a couple of divisions of imperial marines on this planet? Wouldn't we have taken any means to make sure you couldn't betray us? Sure Earth has tried to control beta-steel—in the interests of all humanity. But you haven't felt the boots of imperial troops on your planet—only your own militia, which the Imperator has trusted to preserve the interests of us all. The only direct Earth presence you've felt is an imperial inspector every three months—poor, bookish fellows whom you've started murdering to hide your treason."

"You didn't need a garrison," Richard retorted. "Just one bad report from one of those 'poor, bookish fellows,' and you'd have sent your dreadnoughts."

Elias felt a weary depression. What was the use of this discussion? Richard, Richard, he thought. You couldn't have convinced me to betray Earth, even before. And now there are the children. How could you? If only we could talk about it. Is there any hope left for your soul? If so, I would risk it.

*Except that I'd be risking Martha, too.*

"I realize that it's hard for you to see this, Elias. You're one of the favored few."

"What does that mean?"

"It means I know about you and Briana."

Elias flushed. He was suddenly hyperconscious of Martha sitting beside him. He saw a smirk on Dalt's face, and felt the overpowering urge to leap up and smash it away. "What is it you think you know?" he said in a calm voice.

"I know that she is carrying a child, that it might be almost anyone's—even yours—and that she means to own you as surely as she does the baby when it comes."

Elias was stung—and strangely angry on Briana's behalf. "What have I done to make you insult me like this? I once thought we were friends despite our differences."

"I *am* your friend, Elias. More than you know."

"Is that why you kidnapped Martha? Why you're now holding us and Pendrake in cells under armed guard?"

Richard gave him a calm, triumphant look, and Elias knew that somehow, he'd been led directly to this point. "You want to know why we kidnapped Martha?" Richard said. "We did it because of your Imperator, Briana. Except that she wanted us to kill Martha outright."

Elias felt the blood draining from his face. His mind spun in shock. He was too appalled to think. Dimly he felt Martha's hand gripping his arm. "Liar," he said.

"Briana got word to the rougher elements on Cassiodorus that a hundred thousand imperial credits would go to whoever killed Martha Reik. Fortunately, some of our people were among that group and got word to me. I had Martha kidnapped to save her. I knew you would follow her—yeah, Elias, I know all about the imperial navy's new trinket, the K-scope. I let you find us—I even brought you here, so you could know the truth."

"After you tried to kill me."

"I never wanted that, Elias." Richard glanced at Jost, then quickly away again, but Elias knew he was meant to see the look—and interpret it. "Not everyone knows you as I do," Richard went on. "Unlike your Imperium, we are not a dictatorship led by a tyrant. But now you are here, and it is exactly what I have wanted and hoped for from the start. Join us, Elias. It's where you belong. You owe Briana nothing—but death."

"No," Elias muttered. He pressed his hands against his face, trying to suppress his horror and rage and think: Would it make sense for Briana to offer a bounty on Martha's head to colonists, knowing full well they might be rebels? It would be a huge gamble. If they killed Martha—and kept their mouths shut—she would win twice over: She'd be rid of her rival, and assured of his implacable hatred of the rebels.

But if she lost the gamble, she'd lose the father of her child—the *possible* father—to Martha and the rebel cause, a double defeat that would be utterly galling to her.

Elias suppressed a groan. An impossible position: He must either trust Briana, a powerful woman, capable of total ruthlessness, or Richard, a man who had once been noble, but who had now proven his own horrifying lack of principle.

But why would Richard lie? Elias wondered. If he's

sunk as far as I think, why doesn't he just kill us? I'm the most dangerous man in the universe to him right now.

*And I could also be the most useful. I've been at the heart of power. I know a lot that would benefit him.*

Abruptly, Elias made up his mind. He would believe in Briana—for now at least. He could not be sure. He might never be sure. But he must choose.

Richard spread his hands in appeal. "Elias, Martha, join us."

"A man who drains the lives from his own people's children?" Martha said. "I'd die first."

Elias felt a cold rush of dismay, then pride in her courage. Richard stared at Martha with a shocked expression. "What did you say?"

"Don't deny it, Richard," Elias said. "We know all about your little vampire device; how you got the idea —and the tissue—from the sauroids and converted it to use with the miners. You wanted your beta-steel ore and you've got it, and your miners had enough energy left over to kick up their heels all night too. God, you disgust me."

A look of anguish crossed Richard's face. He slumped back on propped arms, gazing at the ceiling, shaking his head slowly. He looked at them again. "Do you think I don't disgust myself?" he said in a low voice. "All of us disgust ourselves. It's only one of the burdens we must bear."

Elias remembered the "pleasure alley" of Neues Eisen—the people throttling each other, binding each other with ropes, and suddenly it all made sense. The awful image of children, arms at their sides, slumped over their desks, merged with their parents, bent and immobilized in the rope parlors. A dread awe possessed Elias. They were punishing themselves, he thought.

"Let me tell you something," Richard said. "I always thought I had courage. But a point comes in your life when you realize that courage isn't just doing what everyone thinks you ought to do." Richard gave a bitter laugh. "Oh, it's *easy* to come down on the side of the angels, Elias. So easy. But if a moment comes when you must come down on the side of the devil, that's when you'll find out if you have courage."

Elias stared at him in disbelief. "Tell me, Richard: If doing wrong is so hard, how come it's so popular? According to your theory, child molesters and ax murderers must be the most courageous people in the world."

"Could you molest a child, Elias, so that generations of other children could grow up in freedom?"

Elias felt revolted. "If I ever thought I had to molest a child, I'd know something was very wrong with my thinking."

"How convenient for you," Richard said scornfully. "You would decide you were insane. You'd opt out."

"You're right," Elias said. "I'd opt out of any life that required me to molest a child. Pretty gutless, I guess."

"You've been around Pendrake too long," Richard said.

Martha said, "Richard, I could understand consenting adults. But, damn you, as soon as you realized it had to be children, you should have stopped."

Richard looked startled, then impressed. "You've figured out why it had to be children? God, if only you'd join us. We need you, Martha." His face became tormented. He closed his eyes. "We tried to use animals, the way the sauroid does. But it didn't work. Adult humans *do* work, but it was self-defeating to take the energy from one miner and give it to another. Not only that, the energy taken is vastly inferior to a child's."

"Why?" Elias asked. "Will someone tell me that?"

Martha took his hand. Richard opened his eyes, gave him a sad look. "Have you ever watched a baby, Elias? Seen it lie on its back and kick its arms and legs for hours at a time? True, its legs are tiny, but so are its muscles. Your muscles are much bigger. But just try it sometime. If you can do it for even five minutes, you are very strong."

Elias felt Martha's hand grip his suddenly with

fierce strength. Her face was appalled. "You use *babies?*"

"No. We could not bring ourselves to go that far."

"Congratulations," Elias said acidly.

"Fortunately, the quality of neuroelectricity in young children is extremely high."

"That's because they need it to grow and learn," Martha said.

Richard ignored her. "The sauroids have taught us a wonder of biology, Elias. A dark wonder, yes, but a wonder all the same. Based on our new knowledge, we've achieved real breakthroughs in the area of physiology—things that will one day benefit all mankind."

"That puts you right up there with Dr. Mengele and his Nazi buddies," Elias said.

Richard looked stung. "No, damn it. The Nazis were sick sadists. What *we've* discovered has *positive* value. It's not the muscle alone that determines strength, but the brain. We've learned that, like man's brain, his muscles are content to operate at around ten percent efficiency. It took this planet, our need to be free of tyranny, and the absolute commitment of all our people—including our children—to teach us that it need not be so."

"Oh, good. You *asked* the children," Martha said sarcastically.

"We are very careful about how much we take. When . . . when the need is past, they will return to normal."

"Damn you!" Martha shouted. "You can't know that. We saw them one day, when their yokes had been taken off for a few hours. They stumbled and flailed. They were too small for their ages. They couldn't even speak like normal children. They're being stifled through the critical periods when their brains are designed to learn important skills. Once those periods are past, the learning is a hundred times harder—if not impossible. They'll never be right."

"And you can't know *that*," Richard snapped.

"Are you willing to gamble I'm wrong?" Martha shot back.

"Yes, Dr. Reik. I am. I have no choice."

"You're worse than disgusting. You're *evil.*"

Elias saw Richard stiffen. Elias glanced over at Dalt, saw death in his eyes. Jost had turned away.

"We could have taken Earth children," Richard said with soft menace. "Thousands go missing each year anyway in the normal course of events. A few more wouldn't have been missed. But that *would* have been evil. And so the children of our oppressors frolic, while our own pay the price of freedom. It is *our* sacrifice."

"This be useless," Dalt said. "Thou can'st see that they'll never be with us."

Elias looked at him again, saw the blaster in his hand.

"They must die," Dalt said. "Now."

Elias pulled Martha to him, looking to Richard for help, filling with a cold, sick dread as he saw Richard look at Dalt and nod.

# 18

*If I had to choose between betraying my country and betraying my friend, I hope I should have the guts to betray my country.*

E. M. FORSTER

---

"I'LL SEND FOR THE IMPULSER," DALT SAID.

Elias realized he was talking about the vampire device. Fury boiled up in him. "You will not touch any of us with that thing."

Jost gave Dalt a hard look. "He be right."

"But the waste—"

"Enough, Dalt. It's bad enough we must kill these people, without profiting from their deaths, too."

Elias looked at Richard in disbelief. Why was he so silent? Didn't he have anything to say about this? Richard looked back at him with an agonized expression, and Elias knew that Richard *couldn't* save them, no matter how great his power over the rebels. He knows that if we get away, he'll be fighting a new enemy, Elias thought. Since Amerdath had abdicated, Briana has been establishing her control over the Imperium with diplomacy, keeping her militaristic tendencies in check. But if Earth learns about the children, it and the colony loyalists will rise up together in horror and indignation. There will be war—not when Richard decides he's ready, but right away.

*Dalt's right. Richard has to kill us.*

"Well, it's been great, Richard," Elias said bitterly, "but I'd trade it all for never having met you."

"You saved my life," Richard said brokenly. "And now I must kill you. I'm running out of courage."

"It's not courage you've run out of," Elias said. "It's perspective."

"Thou be not fit to carry Richard DuMorgan's coat," Dalt snarled. "Thy empire makes all this necessary, including the children. Thy death is at thine own hands."

"Stow it, Dalt," Jost snapped.

Richard pushed the intercom button on his desk. "Bring Pendrake—be sure and keep the cuffs on him. Send in the physician and the . . . the other."

Elias felt his life draining away, the dread feeling of seconds counting down. He took Martha's hands and looked at her. She gazed back as if trying to memorize his face for all time. Her eyes were glossy with tears, crushing his heart with sorrow. "I'm sorry," he said. "I should never have let you off the *Seraphim.*"

She jerked in a silent, convulsive laugh, tried to say something, but nothing came out, and he knew that her throat had gone dry with fear. She tried again. "Elias, I'd never have forgiven you if you'd died without me."

It was what he'd thought out in the wilderness. *Martha, don't die before me.* So he could believe she meant it, but he felt himself going wild with grief. If he died, she could survive it and love again. He knew that. *Oh God, please help me save her.* His mind circled feverishly, trying to find a way, but he could think of nothing. He could not control this, keep her alive, any more than he had Beth. He felt a massive weight of despair.

Pendrake entered, hands cuffed, Minc behind him with a blaster. Elias' grief expanded, spreading through him with paralyzing force. Martha and Pendrake, both here because of him. *I'm sorry.* On the heels of Minc and Pendrake came a tall man who looked like another miner, except that he was holding three syringes. Elias felt a bitter recognition: *You were ready, weren't you, Richard? You knew you'd kill us. But now you can tell yourself you tried.*

Elias heard a rumbling sound. Three coffins being wheeled into the room. They gleamed with a poisonous, quicksilver shine, striking him cold to the bone. His senses thinned, turning the room distant, unreal. How could this be happening? He looked toward Dalt, saw the man's eyes fixed eagerly on him, wanting him to try something so that the blaster could hiss, and his body could spatter the room in blackened bits. And then Martha and Pendrake, too, butchered in flame, because once unleashed, Dalt would not stop.

Elias straightened and gave Dalt a contemptuous stare, determined to have one small, final victory. He turned back to Martha. "I'm going to see you forever."

Tears rolled down her cheeks, paining him beyond endurance. His throat ached. He took her in his arms, holding her close, feeling her heart pound against him. "Together always, Elias. I know that. I only wish . . ."

"Someone else will find out," he said. "They can't hide it forever. The children will be saved." But he could not believe it.

He felt Pendrake beside him and turned.

Pendrake gave him a gentle smile. "I take it you have no plan, Elias."

"No. How about you?"

"I could try roaring, but I think they are used to that now. And it is so undignified."

Elias nodded, unable to speak.

"My life has been immeasurably better because of you, Elias. Thank you."

Elias took his hand, felt the unwavering strength of the three curling fingers. He tried to draw that strength into himself and failed.

He felt another hand on his shoulder—Richard's. "Elias, would you like a priest or something?"

"Or something."

Richard nodded. "Could . . . could you and the others get into the coffins?" His voice broke.

Elias fingered the satin lining. The nerves of his stomach trilled with nausea. He saw that one of the coffins was huge. It must have been made especially, perhaps while he and Pendrake were staggering through the wilderness with such fierce hope. He tried to think of something to say to Richard, some last witticism to show how uncowed he was. His mind yawned open, a huge dark abyss. He saw that Martha was climbing into the end coffin, Richard helping her as if she were getting into a canoe for a Sunday paddle. The cruelty of it broke Elias' heart. He went to the middle one, stumbling as he climbed in, feeling Richard's hand on his arm. He was too numb to shake it off.

He lay back in the chill, slippery fabric, seeing Martha's hand above the edge, taking it, and then Pendrake's on the other side. Is it my baby in Briana's womb? he wondered. The tears began to roll down his cheeks. He'd never see it or hold it in his arms. He'd die without knowing.

The man with the syringes moved between the coffins, his head a malign, floating presence. Dimly, Elias felt rubber tubing constrict above his elbow, the distant prick of the needle.

"Elias?" Martha's voice was high with fear.

"I'm here." The tubing let go. Coolness slid up his arm. The room dissolved into a gray, nether world. He heard his father's high voice singing, a homely tenor, soft and without vibrato:

> *I come to the garden alone*
> *While the dew is still on the roses*
> *And the voice I hear*
> *falling on my ear . . .*

## 19

IT WAS DARK. ELIAS SMELLED ROSES. HE BECAME aware of the dampness of tears on his cheeks.

*Father?*

No, he was gone.

Elias ached with sorrow. His mind vibrated with the chords of the hymn. How Father had loved it. I felt you close, Elias thought. I heard you singing. Did you know I was there?

*I was dead too.*

I was with Father, and now I'm back. He felt a powerful, bitter regret. I *miss* you.

*Martha! Pendrake!*

Elias remembered the meeting with Richard. Anxiety flooded him: *Richard ordering them into the coffins, the needle sliding into his arm. Were Martha and Pendrake alive again too?*

Suddenly the darkness horrified him. *God, are we all buried alive?* He strained his eyes wide, fighting panic, groping the lid of the coffin above him. Then the panic took over and he bucked and thrust his knees against the lid of the coffin.

It popped open.

He gasped with relief, squinting against a flood of light. Above him he saw a rock ceiling, like the one in

Richard's meeting room. He grabbed the sides of the coffin and pulled himself up. He saw Pendrake, sitting slumped in his open coffin, a look of confusion on his face. Hope swelled inside Elias; he turned to Martha's coffin, saw with alarm that it was still closed. Dread seized him. He clambered out of his coffin and sprung the lid on Martha's. Her eyes were closed, her hands on her chest.

*She was breathing!*

Elias' heart leapt with joy. He gazed down at her, transfixed by her face. She was smiling. It was the tenderest expression he had ever seen. His throat knotted. He reached out to touch her, then pulled back, realizing she was having a beautiful dream. *Let it finish.*

After a minute, her eyes opened. She seemed to have trouble focusing on him. Then she said, "Oh, Elias. I saw Mom."

"Yes." He took her hands, choked with feeling for her.

"I thought I was on Cephan." Pendrake's voice was sad. "But we were dead."

Elias felt Martha's grip tighten on his hands. "Did you see things too, Elias—important things? You did, didn't you? Was it real, or was it just in our minds?"

Elias' mind whirled in confusion. "I don't know. I only know we've lost it. I don't think we can have it and live too."

Martha pulled him to her, kissing him on the lips. He could feel her trembling.

"Elias, Pendrake, Martha."

Elias whirled, startled. Richard! No, Richard's voice. He realized the sound had come from a recorder sitting on a table. He saw that they were in a small room carved from rock. On one wall were shelves stocked with food packets and water jugs, as if someone had provisioned the room for a long siege. The thought filled him with foreboding.

"Do I have your attention?" the recorded voice asked, and Elias realized the message was on an interactive chip. It would not proceed until one of them responded.

"Yes."

"Good. I know you despise me, but I have not forgotten my blood debt to you, Elias. You saved my life, so I owed you yours, and the lives of those you love. Maybe you'll grant I have a shred of honor left after all. Or maybe it's just that saving you is an act of honor I can afford—so long as you remain exactly where you are.

"I had hoped you would join us, but I also knew I'd be forced to destroy you if you would not. Only my physician and I know you have not stayed dead."

Martha shivered. Elias pulled her close.

"By the time you hear this, other coffins will have been buried in the desert. I'm sorry I couldn't give you any hint of what I was up to, but I couldn't risk it in front of Dalt and Jost. Instead of a lethal injection, my physician gave you a cataleptic, mixed with one of the new biostasis washes. You were dead about an hour. The biostatic kept brain decay from taking place, so don't blame any future stupidities on me."

Elias looked at Martha, surprised. She nodded and he felt his mystic wonder at what had happened fading, leaving him with a sense of loss. We were dead, and now we're alive, he thought, and it was all done with drugs.

*But I heard Father singing.*

He realized that that was fading too; he could no longer be so sure. Depression settled over him.

"You have enough food and water," Richard's voice went on, "for a long stay. The walls are solid rock. The door is not beta-steel, but it is too thick for you to break, Pendrake—even if you meditate into the tropos trance. When I had the door installed, I remembered what you did to the steel door in another of my strongholds. I can't claim I knew our paths would cross again, but we humans always close the door after the cows have escaped. Elias will explain."

Elias glanced at Pendrake in time to catch his baffled expression. Elias almost laughed, but then what

Richard was saying penetrated with sobering force: *We're trapped in here, no hope of escape.*

"When the time is right," Richard's voice went on, "I'll come back and free you. I know I've done the right thing on Cassiodorus, terrible as it is. I hope you can forgive me—as I shall never forgive myself."

The recorder went silent.

Incredible, Elias thought sourly.

"A 'long stay,'" Martha said. "I wonder what that means. Will he let us go when his dreadnoughts are ready?"

"I doubt it," Elias said. "In the first place, he may already have dreadnoughts."

Martha paled. "Here?"

"No. It would be too risky to try to hide a shipyard on the same planet where they're trying to conceal the theft of ore—they'd be putting all their eggs in one basket, and Richard's too smart for that. If I know him, he's hollowed out some obscure asteroid and is ferrying the stolen ore there to build the dreadnoughts. The point is, we may be in for a long stay. Richard won't want what we know getting back to Earth—not until the war is over and it's too late for it to make a difference."

Martha looked glum. "You're right. Elias, we've got to find some way out of this place, save the children."

"What do you mean about saving the children?" Pendrake asked, and Elias realized he didn't know. He told Pendrake what the vampire device was used for. Pendrake turned away with an appalled expression. Abruptly he settled cross-legged to the floor, folding his arms over his chest in the tropos stance. Elias almost stopped him—if Richard said the door was too thick, it was too thick.

*No, Martha's right, we have to try.*

While Pendrake sank into the tropos trance, Elias further inspected the room. The desk that held the recorder also contained paper and pens. In the ceiling he saw a ventilation shaft far too small to crawl through.

Behind the privacy of the food shelves he found a door leading to a water closet, complete with the vital waste reconverter. Also behind the shelves was a box of dishes and cutlery and a roll of foam cushioning big enough for several people to sleep side by side. The foam would be necessary, Elias realized grimly: Like the walls, the floor was chopped unevenly from solid rock.

Elias saved the entry door for last. As he inspected it, his hope faded completely: The door was a single piece of steel that slid across in thick steel tracks to seal off the opening. There was no lock access from this side.

We're going to be here for a long, long time, Elias thought. A bitter frustration filled him. He had never needed more in his life to act, and he could not act. If he didn't get out of here, a planet full of children would be destroyed.

And after them, the Imperium itself might fall.

Pendrake rose and approached the door.

"Good luck," Martha said hopefully. Elias said nothing, knowing it was futile. Pendrake turned his side to the door, pivoted on one leg and smashed the other foot against the steel. It rang dully; Pendrake staggered away, regained his balance and ran at the door, launching himself at it feet first. He rebounded onto the floor, rolled and sat up.

Elias winced; Pendrake's expression remained stoic. He backed up to the door, knelt and found handholds against the uneven, rock floor. Gripping these, he pressed one foot then the other against the door, suspending his body between floor and wall in a modified handstand. Pendrake's back and arm muscles bunched. The massive muscles of his thighs bulged. The door bent slightly, then would move no further.

The tropos trance was not enough.

Elias shook his head, hating the feeling of defeat.

Pendrake dropped his feet from the door and stood. "I am sorry, Elias. The steel *is* too thick."

Elias roused himself and patted Pendrake's arm.

"You did your best. Too bad we don't have the strength of those miners—"

He stopped, startled, remembering the vampire device hidden against his chest. *One of us—Pendrake—could feed on me.*

The thought revolted him. *But we have to do it.* His gorge rose. He ran to the water closet and threw up into the toilet, gagging and retching, dimly feeling Martha's hand soothing the nape of his neck. *No, no, I can't.*

He pushed away from the toilet and stood, taking the towel she offered.

She looked at him with concern. "What is it, Elias?"

"We have to cut me open, get the vampire device. If it'll work, I'll feed Pendrake. It's our only chance."

"No," she said.

"Don't argue. We can't stay here. You said it yourself; the children—"

"I'm not arguing with the plan. But you're not going to feed Pendrake, I am."

Elias looked at her in horror. "Absolutely not. I won't let you."

"You have no choice. You're a better fighter than I am. And if you can get a weapon, you're a much better shot. If this works and Pendrake breaks out, you will have to fight your way to a radio."

With a sinking feeling, he realized she was right. "You don't understand," he said. "It . . . it's a filthy thing."

"I'm an adult, a physician. I can handle it." Her eyes had an odd light, and he realized that she *wanted* to try being a donor. It had engaged her scientific curiosity.

But she had never felt it inside her, sucking at her brain, *her soul.*

"What if something goes wrong?" Elias protested. "These things can go too far. We've never used one. It could take everything, kill you—"

"Stop it, Elias. Let's go. Let's get it out of you."

He looked down at his chest with a sick feeling. "How? You don't have your medkit."

Her face fell. "Damn!"

"The cutlery," Elias said. He rummaged through the box, thumbing each blade. They were all dull. As long as Martha was cutting the nerveless, bloodless plastiflesh, he'd be all right. But when she got to the meld of the plastiflesh and his skin, she'd have to sever thousands of surface nerves and capillaries that had bonded through the skin with the gel undercoat of the plastiflesh. His skin crawled. It would be like being skinned by a stone-aged ax.

He handed the knife to Martha.

She looked at it with horror. "Elias, I can't operate on you with a butter knife."

Elias pulled his shirt open. "Just don't try and cut with the handle, all right?"

Pendrake looked sickened. He walked away from them to the door, leaning his face against the steel.

Martha took Richard's recorder off the table and helped Elias lie down. She cut a shallow ring in the plastiflesh, outlining where she'd placed the vampire device. "Cut wider," Elias advised.

She frowned. "The wider I cut, the more skin you lose. If I could get right around the device—"

"Forget it. If we don't get it out undamaged, it's all for nothing."

Martha widened the circle and began to cut. Elias tried to compose himself, waiting for the knife to hit real skin and nerve. He closed his eyes, trying to will himself into another plane, where the pain would not come, where he could float serenely, *holding his baby, looking into its dazzling, curious eyes*—

Pain stabbed through him, swelling, ah—*God!* Too much—

*feeling its soft, downy hair*—

God, *God*, Martha; stop it. Elias bit his tongue, keeping silent as the pain burned across his chest, seared the backs of his eyelids, breaking the sweat from his forehead.

"Got it!" Martha's voice was bright with relief.

He sat up, glimpsed the raw, bleeding hole in the middle of his chest, and lay back again, dizzied. He gritted his teeth, and tried again, this time making it.

"Hold on," Martha said, "I've got to patch you up. She tore his shirt into strips and wrapped his chest in a makeshift bandage. He could feel the blood soaking it. The wound throbbed viciously.

He thought of what Martha was about to endure, and his pain receded. He watched her carve carefully at the bloody plug of plastiflesh she'd removed until the cone of sauroid flesh was exposed. Before he could say anything, she pushed the cone into her ear. He hurried to her side, drew her to the table with him, but she resisted lying down.

"No, Elias. Wait . . ." She gazed at him, her eyes widening. "Elias . . ." she whispered. "Oh, poor Elias."

He realized that the switch in the plastic base must be in the sending position. She was not giving up strength to the device but *drawing* it—*his* energy, stored when Jost and the others had tried to kill him. He felt a grim excitement—the bloody thing still worked. It had held his energy all this time, waiting for another brain, another central nervous system in which to dump it.

His excitement grew as he realized that Pendrake would now have both of them to draw on. It would be enough—it had to be.

Martha reached a hand out to him, tracing his face, her eyes wide with wonder. "Oh. You're so beautiful," she whispered.

A thrill passed through him, tingling in his stomach; he felt a swell of sexual arousal; a rapport with her that he could never have imagined. It was beautiful, but dangerous, too—seductive, to think of losing himself in her, to *be* her.

He turned away, shaken, wanting the device so he could draw from her—frightened at his hunger.

"Elias?" He turned back, saw that she'd taken the device from her ear. She grinned at him. "I love you."

"I love you, too," he said softly, but he was still afraid.

"Watch this!" She took the table by one leg, lifted it high above her. He knew that it must weigh sixty kilos, and yet she held it aloft as easily as an umbrella.

She laughed. "I feel like I could smash that door out myself."

Cold fear expanded inside him. She was not herself now, but something both more and less. "Martha. Get hold of yourself."

She closed her eyes, grinning, and a chill went up his spine, but then her grin faded.

"All right," she said. "All right." She opened her eyes and turned the switch at the base of the sauroid tissue, thrust it into her ear again. She gasped and sank to her knees. Elias rushed to her, easing her down to her back. "I feel it going," she said. "I'm getting weak."

Elias was breathless with fear for her. "Can you still move? Move your hands, Martha!"

She complied, flapping her hands, then wiggling her fingers.

"Talk to me."

"Elias . . . I felt . . . you. . . . Your essence . . ."

Her eyes rolled back and her eyelids fluttered. He grabbed the vampire device from her ear, handed it to Pendrake and bent over her in an agony of fear, his mouth dry. "Martha? Martha?"

"I'm here," she whispered without opening her eyes. "So tired. Hold me. I want to feel you."

He scooped her to him and held her, full of pained love. He realized his blood was staining her blouse, but he could not let go.

"Perfect!" Pendrake's voice startled him, low, resonant with power. Elias looked up at him, saw that his face was alight, the black eyes glittering like onyx. *Pendrake, too.*

"You are perfect for each other, Elias."

Elias felt a lump in his throat. He was filled with dread and awe. *What was this thing doing to them? Was what they were feeling beautiful—or obscene?*

The rebels, he thought. When they use it, they are drawing the essence of children. How does it affect them? They have the pure, prime energy, yes, *but they have a part of the child in them too.*

Suddenly he was more horrified of the device than he had ever been: children, sweet undeveloped children—

*And nothing in the universe could be more cruel.*

It was the cruelty of innocence—of morality and ethics not yet learned—but cruelty all the same. Did the rebels understand this? Yes, they must have, but they'd drunk of the cup anyway—perhaps so much so that they no longer thought of it, no longer saw the erosion of their own morality—no longer felt the infusions of child energy changing their honor, their judgment, their mercy, their *perspective!*

Elias shuddered. "The door," he said to Pendrake. "Can you do it?"

Pendrake paced to the door. He turned and knelt, grabbing the rocks, planting one foot against the steel. He pushed. The door buckled and crashed away.

ELIAS GAZED AT THE SHATTERED STEEL WITH AWE. HE cheered inwardly: *Now we've got a chance!*

Pendrake rose and dusted his hands. His face was troubled. "Elias, I have a terrible feeling inside. I want to kill these rebels."

Elias felt a twinge of guilt. "It's not you, Pendrake. You got that feeling from me, along with the strength."

"Then this device may be even more dangerous than we think."

"You're right. So let's get it stopped." Elias knelt beside Martha, taking her wrist, finding a slow pulse. She opened her eyes and winked at him. Reassured, he squeezed her hand and rose again. "We've got to figure out where we are," he said to Pendrake. "Wait here with Martha a minute."

Elias hurried through the shattered door into a small, spartan bedchamber containing a single cot and a trunk. At the foot of the cot was a door, standing open. He eased his head and shoulders through and recognized the meeting room—empty now—in which Richard had condemned them to death. He felt a grim satisfaction: he knew where he was, and that was half the battle. Now all he had to do was get to a radio. That guarded door Martha had described earlier would be his best chance.

But first he must get Pendrake and Martha out of here.

A sudden indecision gripped him. How was he going to get them out and get to the radio room too? To escape, they'd have to get past the guards in that surface entry room. Once they'd made it—*if* they made it—the alarm would be raised all through the stronghold. If he wasn't already in the radio room at that point, he'd never make it back there. Frustration and anxiety filled Elias. There was no way he could go with Martha and Pendrake first, make sure they were out safely, and still get word to the *Seraphim* about the children.

He'd have to rely on Pendrake to save Martha.

Elias hurried back to the cell and told Pendrake where they were. "I want you to carry Martha out," he said. "I'll go for the radio room. Do you remember the way Minc brought us in?"

"Yes." Pendrake gathered Martha up in his arms. Elias was wrenched by the limp way her arms and legs dangled. "She is all right, Elias. I see her breathing."

Elias tried to push his anxiety aside. "Come on."

He hesitated in the small bedchamber. We need weapons, he thought. He threw the trunk open and rummaged through the clothing. His hand hit something hard, and he drew it out, hoping, but it was not a weapon.

It was a medal—the Legion of Mars.

The medal Gregory Amerdath had pinned to Richard's chest after the defeat of the Andinaz. *You were a hero, Richard. Might you also be a victim?* Elias looked at the medal, grieving for the man who had worn it: Richard DuMorgan, undone, because a viceroy must never have the conscience of a child.

Elias put the medal in his pocket. *I'll keep this for you, Richard.* He dumped the trunk over; from the bottom tumbled a blaster and a stunner. Pleased, Elias turned back to Pendrake. "Would you be able to stun a man?"

Pendrake swallowed. "Possibly, but if I take the

stunner, then you would have the blaster. And I know you would kill."

"Not if I—"

"I *know* you would, Elias."

Elias felt a chill along his spine, and anger at being invaded—

No, it was not Pendrake's fault. It was the vampire device. If it took from you, it stripped you naked. He's feeling my rage at Jost and the others, Elias thought. He's seeing things in me—dark things—that I can't see in myself. Elias felt a deep shame. He held the blaster out to Pendrake. "You're good at roaring, maybe you could fake it with one of these?"

Pendrake tensed, making no move to take the blaster. He's really afraid he might kill someone, Elias thought. *And he might need to.*

Elias realized that he must make sure it did not happen. Pendrake could not live with it afterward. He removed the powerpack of the blaster and held it out again. This time Pendrake took it.

"Once you get out, head due west as far as you can make it, so I'll know what bearing to find you. If I can get to a radio, there are going to be airstrikes here. I'm going to turn this place into one big tomb. . . ." Elias stopped, seeing the dismay on Pendrake's face, aware again of the reservoir of violence in himself. I *need* it, he thought defiantly. Or I'll never get inside that radio room.

"Let's go, damn it!"

Elias followed Pendrake from Richard's bedroom, out through the meeting room where they had died. In the corridor outside, Pendrake froze. Damn! Elias thought, knowing there must be a guard. He swung out behind Pendrake, saw the man, face surprised, hand going for his blaster. Elias popped the man with the stun beam, watched him toppled over backward. Elias looked both ways—good, no one else in the corridor.

"Pendrake, that's not a banana in your hand. If you see anyone else, point it at them. *Mean* it."

Pendrake nodded, looking sheepish.

"Here's where we split up. Save her, Pendrake."

"I will." Pendrake loped off down the corridor. When he was around the corner, Elias scooped up the fallen guard's blaster. He dragged the guard into the meeting room and popped him again with the stunner. He weighed the blaster and the stunner in his hands and, remembering what Pendrake had said, stuffed the blaster into his belt.

*I'll use it only if I have to.*

He hurried down the corridor, feeling the drag of gravity through his thighs. His exertion opened the raw wound in his chest; fresh blood soaked his bandages. He ignored it, reciting Martha's instructions to himself. He came to a fork in the tunnel, rounded the corner—

—and came face to face with four miners.

He beamed them with the stunner. Three fell, but the one in back leapt at him with ferocious energy, and Elias whipped out the blaster. The man stopped with comic abruptness, almost overbalancing.

"Just feed, did you?" Elias snarled. "A nice juicy kid? Yours or someone else's?" The man's face reddened. Elias walked up to him, his legs springy with rage, and stuck the stunner against his temple. "Eat some of this."

The stunner popped. The miner groaned and sank down.

Elias found the elevator Martha remembered. When it opened, he sprayed the insides with the stunner. Two women and a man slumped to the floor. Elias could feel a furious blood lust pumping in his veins. He wanted to drop all of these bastards, and he knew it wasn't just the children—it was Martha and himself and Pendrake. These big, hoggish people had tried to kill them—over and over, they'd tried. *But we're still alive, and I'm going to beat you, shut down your heavy, stinking hellhole of a planet.*

The elevator registered level two. He leaned halfway out, looking down the corridor. Twenty meters away he saw the door with the guard, just where Martha had remembered. He felt a surge of confidence. This *had* to be the radio room, the electronic nerve center of the stronghold. Why else would they guard it? But they'd been smart, too, putting it too far from the elevator to rush. The guard was already looking at him with suspicion. And he was well out of range of the stunner.

Elias stuffed the stunner in his belt and switched his hand to cover the blaster butt. He staggered the rest of the way out of the elevator, waving at the man, pointing at the blood on his chest. "Need help, friend. Just took a drill rod in the chest"—walking toward the man as he talked—"who be on the subspace?"

"What want'st thou with subspace? Stay back!"

The guard drew his blaster, and Elias fired from the hip then fell flat as an answering beam of energy sizzled over his head and the guard screamed and spun down, thrashing. Elias pushed to his feet, ran toward the door, panting, feeling the rock floor jolt him. He tried the handle. *Damn, locked!*

And it was controlled by a sequencer—to get in, you had to punch in the right digits in the right order.

He looked down at the guard, who was writhing in pain, holding his wrist. His body was unmarked. Must have caught a refraction from the wall. *You're lucky, punk—and so am I.* Elias kicked the guard's blaster away, grabbed him by the collar, jammed the blaster into his mouth. The man stopped writhing and looked at him, bug-eyed.

"You're going to open that door for me."

The man shook his head, gargled something. Elias grabbed the burned arm, and the man bucked in pain, coughing around the blaster muzzle. Elias felt the skin oozing under his fingers. A wave of sickness passed through him. He gritted his teeth and showed the guard the stunner.

"The numbers. When you give me the right numbers, the pain will stop."

The guard gasped out the numbers.

Elias punched in the sequence; the door slid back. He stunned the guard, cutting off his warning scream, and rolled into the room, spraying the stunner around him. The man at the radio slumped over. Elias saw that he was old—too old to work the mines—and felt a pang of remorse. He eased the unconscious man to the floor and grabbed the radio, dialing the *Seraphim*'s frequency, praying silently:

"Elias to *Seraphim*, come in please."

Elias shoved a tall, metal cabinet over, adding it to the makeshift barricade. He checked the door, saw that it was glowing a cherry red now. He could feel the heat of the melting steel on his face even through the protective shield of the gas mask. Sweat soaked his bandages, stinging the raw wound in his chest. In a minute, they'd break through. He thumbed the subspace switch.

"It's getting warm in here. Your marines planning on joining me or not?"

"Hang in there." Captain Streetham's voice was calm—as clear as if he were in the radio room instead of on the bridge of the *Seraphim*. "I thought you disabled the sequencer."

Elias looked at the tangle of wires and smashed chips dangling from the access panel beside the door. "This is a *mine*, Captain. They're used to getting through things."

"Understood. I can't tell you the progress—unfriendlies are monitoring us and you don't know our codes. But we'll try not to let you down, Mr. Kane. You say these rebels have superhuman strength, but Colonel Teegarten's marines are strong, too. He's had them drilling in 1.5 G's since you touched down. They're all megastimmed to the gills. And best of all, they're imperial marines."

Elias realized what the captain was doing—sending a message to the listening "unfriendlies," playing with their minds.

"The point is, Captain, these people have got to be *stopped*."

"I've got three kids, Elias." Streetham's voice was hard.

"Right."

"And anyway, we've got a nice surprise lined up for these bastards. You'll like it, Kane."

Elias looked at the door. It had edged from red to white hot. The room was a furnace. Fear yammered inside him. They'd kill him the minute they got the chance—that was certain. He was supposed to be dead already. But they had to get to him first, and there were certain limits on what they could do. This was the most important room in the stronghold, filled with high-tech equipment that would be hard to replace, including one of the new, interplanetary-range radios. Even if the command center weren't so valuable to them, they'd not dare use explosives for fear of collapsing the tunnels below. Gas was no good either, not with him wearing the radio operator's mask.

They'd have to shoot him.

The fear bubbled up in him again. He hunkered down behind the jumbled barricade, propping his blaster hand over the top, watching the steel in the door begin to sag. He thought of Martha, and felt a gnawing worry. Had Pendrake gotten her out? He didn't dare ask Streetham, for fear of putting the rebels on Pendrake's trail.

*Get her out, Pendrake. Just get her out and I'll die happy.*

A disc of molten metal blew inward, scorching a path across the floor toward him. Then the white foam of a fire extinguisher sprayed through, sizzling around the edges of the rupture.

"Here we go!"

"Good luck!" Streetham said.

A blaster thrust through the hole, firing at the barricade. Elias fired back. For a second the firing stopped, then a man's head and shoulders sprang at him through the hole. Elias fired, wincing at the man's scream. The blackened head and shoulders bumped against the ragged edges of the opening as the body was dragged back through.

Dear God, Elias thought, appalled.

He saw the door redden again and knew they were enlarging the hole. Elias checked the charge on his blaster. Half full. He felt a blistering upsurge of heat through the mask as the door hit melting point again. The center of the door sloughed away. The fire extinguishers hissed again, a snowstorm blowing at him through the glowing halo of seared steel. The hole was big enough now for a man to jump through easily. Elias felt a scrape of panic deep in his bowels. He shouted, pumping himself up.

A man came through the door firing, blowing away a piece of the cabinet. Elias shot him down, and the next man and the next, bodies sprawling, piling up. A savage fury possessed Elias. "You want some more? Come on, you bastards. Or maybe you'd rather push your kids in front!"

Two more men, firing, a sear of heat along his shoulder as he blasted them down, then more men hit the barrier, smashing it back against him. He tried to lunge back, but the cabinet fell on top of him, crushing pain through him. He lay, frozen in agony, breathless, the room spinning above his head. He heard them tearing at the rubble, felt the weight on him easing. One hand was numb. He squeezed the other hard, felt the butt of the blaster, still there. A space cleared, a face leaned in over him, teeth bared. Elias shot it. He kicked along the floor, pulling free of the shelves, crawling on his side.

"There he be—shoot him!"

He saw the blaster swinging toward him, then the rebel holding it flew forward, his body arching in the middle, spraying blood from the sternum. Elias saw the blue of marine jumpsuits pouring through the ruined door. The remaining rebels dropped their blasters and raised their hands.

Exhilaration pumped through Elias. He sat up and thrust a fist into the air, shouting incoherently. A young lieutenant walked over to him. "Mr. Kane?"

He let the marine help him up, then grabbed him in a bearhug. "You can call me Elias."

Elias sat in the co-pilot's seat of the lander. All around him thin red lines sliced up the night sky as imperial attack ships dueled with renegade militia fighters. The desert below flickered under the man-made lightning storm—he almost didn't need the infra-red scope.

He returned his gaze to it, scanning the desert, filled with restless, burning anxiety. They were almost back to the stronghold now. They'd flown much farther out than Pendrake could have walked. If he'd gotten free with Martha, he had to be back along this line somewhere. *Pendrake, Martha, where are you?*

The lander swung in an arc.

"Keep it east!" Elias shouted.

"Damn it, Mr. Kane, we're under attack," shouted the pilot. Elias heard the gunner cursing behind him. Something about the automatic tracking scanner being disabled. He turned, saw the youngster frozen, hands hovering uncertainly over the control console. He leapt from the co-pilot's chair, pushed the gunner aside and popped the manual release. The two sculpted guide-handles sprang up into his palms. Through the clear shield of the gunnery bubble he saw the ugly V-winged shape of a rebel fighter bearing down. He gritted his teeth and swung the handles, squeezing, tracking by sight, knowing he had about two seconds. Red lines sprang from his laser cannon and converged on the rebel ship; it ballooned into a searing red-orange smear that faded quickly against the black sky.

Sweat poured into Elias' eyes. He felt his hands shaking on the gun handles.

"Mama Satan," the young gunner breathed.

"Now get us back on vector," Elias snarled.

With a scared look, the pilot complied. Elias returned to the infrared scope. "Take us lower," he said.

"But—"

"Lower, damn you, and drop the airspeed. If you can't fly this thing, I can."

"Yes, sir."

Elias' stomach churned. The flat desert floated up to them, unfolding at a creeping pace. The engines of the lander whined in protest as the craft vibrated in the effort to part the thick air. *Please God, let me find them —alive!*

"Whooeee, look at that!" the pilot said excitedly.

Elias looked up through the forward viewscreen, hope bursting inside him. He saw that they were back at the stronghold; a long line of rebels was streaming from the entrance, hands on their heads in surrender, flanked on either side by lines of imperial marines. Elias returned his eyes to the scope, disappointed, wanting only to find Pendrake and Martha. Could Pendrake somehow have walked farther than he thought?

*Or could he have driven?*

Elias remembered the groundcar that Minc had used to bring them back. It might still have been in the entry cave. If so, it would be the best way to get clear— Pendrake would have taken it! Elias felt renewed excitement.

"Reverse to the west," he ordered. "Top speed, damn it!"

The pilot looked at him as if he'd gone crazy. "Top speed, aye, sir."

Twenty klicks out, Elias spotted the groundcar. It wasn't moving. He shouted with glee. "Take her down, pilot."

"We're under attack again," the gunner bleated.

Elias swore and jumped into the gunnery bubble, grabbing the handles of the laser cannon. It was a lone rebel fighter, and it was attacking all right, but not them. It was coming in abeam, nose down toward the groundcar in an obvious strafing approach.

"Oh, *Christ!*" Elias felt sick sweat popping out on his forehead. He gripped the handles in desperation, firing on the fighter as it cut loose on the groundcar, seeing the red lines converge with awful slowness, exploding the fighter at last, but it was too late. The groundcar was in flames.

"Take it down," Elias gasped, nauseous with dread. *Don't let them be in it, don't let them be in it.*

The lander settled, Elias pounded the hatch with his foot in an agony of impatience. It cycled open and he clambered down the ramp, every muscle aching with the fierce exertion of horror. The groundcar was still ablaze. He ran toward it, stumbling in the heavy gravity, feeling hands grabbing at him from behind. He tried to fight free, cursing himself with bitter vehemence: *If he'd thought of the groundcar in time, he'd have been here already, made the rescue.*

"Damn it, let me *go!*"

"Elias, it is me. We are safe."

*Pendrake!* Elias whirled, looked into the smiling orange face; he saw Martha behind Pendrake, walking toward them—slowly, but walking! An incredible joy filled him. He squeezed Pendrake's arm wordlessly, then ran to her, feeling no gravity, no pain, nothing but love and a vast relief.

"Elias," she said, and fell into his arms.

He sat with her on the desert floor, holding her as the pilot and the gunner walked up.

"Uh, we'd better get back to the ship, sir."

Elias looked up at him, dazed with happiness. It doesn't matter, he thought. Nothing could go wrong now.

And then the black sky flamed in dazzling rainbow colors. Elias stared upward, stunned, recognizing the radiant, swirling aurora of a dreadnought dropping out of paraspace. *A dreadnought!* Elias' heart leapt to his throat. He scrambled up, horrified, then saw that the pilot was grinning.

"Well, there she is!" the pilot said. "Isn't she beautiful, sir."

"What?"

The pilot looked at him in surprise. "Haven't you heard? That's the imperial flagship. Briana herself, five centuries of praetorians and twelve legions of marines. These beanos have had it now."

Elias gave Martha a long kiss in the back of the groundcar, knowing Pendrake wouldn't turn around in the front seat, and not caring about the praetorian chauffeur.

Martha nuzzled his ear and whispered, "Is this what they used to call necking?"

"No, I think they called this earing."

She dug him in the ribs, then gasped. "Oh, I'm sorry. That's right where the cabinet fell on you."

"It's all right. I'm recovering fast."

"Good. All you did last night was sleep."

"Isn't that what beds are for?" he asked innocently.

She ran a hand up his leg, and this time *he* gasped. "Why do you think Briana wants to see you?" she asked.

"Who knows? She just occupied the viceregal buildings an hour ago. Probably wants me to witness her triumph."

"I hope that's all," Martha said.

He sensed her worry and was panged by it. He remembered what had happened when he'd left Earth —pulling away from Martha at the spaceport because he was afraid of what Briana would think. He felt a brief, powerful disgust for himself, then dismissed it. He had done what he thought he must.

Things were different now.

Elias put his forehead to Martha's, cradling her face in his hands. "No one is ever going to take us away from each other," he said.

"Oh, Elias." She hugged him to her. "But she *is* Imperator."

"Don't worry," Elias said, but he could not stop the anxiety inside himself, the gnawing unease. Why *did* Briana want to see him, so soon, the battle hardly over?

Had she received the genetic report on her child?

The groundcar eased to a stop. Pendrake cleared his throat, then looked back over the seat. "We are here, Elias. Good luck."

Elias reached up, grasped the big hand, feeling a tide of affection. "I'll be back before you know it. We'll catch the next lander up to the *Seraphim*. In a week, we'll be on Cephan."

Pendrake's face lit in a broad smile. "Are you sure you want to go to another heavy-gravity planet, Elias?"

"Hey, I'm as used to it as I'll ever be."

The chauffeur stepped out and opened the rear door. Elias kissed Martha. "Trust me," he murmured.

The chauffeur escorted him as far as the anteroom to Cay Endor's office. As they arrived, two black-suited praetorians led Endor through the huge double doors. His hands were cinched behind him in a sens-arc. His fringe of hair was ruffled, and his eyes looked half crazed. Elias felt an instant, instinctive pity for him.

Endor recognized him. "Kane? Kane, do you see what she's done to me? This is her thanks for all the years I served her father. I had nothing to do with the rebels—"

The praetorians jerked him past.

Over his shoulder he shouted, "Nothing, I swear it. Tell her."

Elias watched them take him out, embarrassed for him, sorry for his humiliation. Amerdath would not have done it that way, he thought.

He felt a tap on his arm and turned to find a praetorian major facing him. The man saluted sharply, surprising Elias—Briana's personal guards were known for their arrogance. A feeling of foreboding awakened inside him.

"Mr. Kane, the Imperator is waiting. May I show you in, please?"

Briana was sitting at Endor's desk. Beyond her the corpse of Subrath, Endor's Ornyl bodyguard, sprawled on the thick carpet in a circle of greenish blood. Elias could not find pity for the warrior, and knew Subrath would not have wanted it. He looked back at Briana, stricken by her beauty. Her face was flushed, her eyes had a look of mystic ecstasy. He was strangely stirred as she stood, hesitating, feet apart in front of the huge alien's corpse. Did she shoot Subrath herself? he wondered with dread fascination.

She hurried to him, taking his hands. "Elias! My hero!"

"All I did was stay alive."

She laughed. "You're far too modest, as always. We've kicked their asses on this planet, Elias. They had six frigates. My flagship blew them up in space. The only things that got away were a few scoutships and fighters."

"Did you capture Richard DuMorgan?"

"Not yet. He may have escaped."

Elias did not know if he was glad or sorry. But he knew it would make the future harder.

"Resistance is ending," Briana went on, undaunted. "It's all over but the mopping up. The kids are free of the vampire devices, thanks to you, and on their way back to Earth. They'll get the best care and rehabilitation Earth can provide. I promise you that."

Elias felt a huge lift of satisfaction. The children were saved. And Briana was going to go to the limit for them. Seeing the humanity and concern in her face, he warmed to her. Then he remembered Endor. "Do you have any proof against the viceroy?"

She dropped his hands. "Elias, Endor was in charge of this planet. Whether he was with the rebels or not, he failed me—failed us all—in the worst way possible."

"What will you do with him?"

She shrugged. "If I find he was with the rebels,

execute him. Otherwise, a jail term for gross dereliction of duty." She nodded to a chair in front of her desk and pulled another around to face him. As he sat, he noticed the thickening of her waist. Her pregnancy was starting to show. His foreboding returned. He could feel his heart hammering against his chest.

She settled across from him, gazed at him with intense concentration. "I was worried about you, Elias. You might have sent me a report or two, you know. Finally, I subspaced the *Seraphim* from Earth. But when Captain Streetham couldn't raise you at the viceroy's quarters, and Endor said he didn't know where you were, I was afraid they'd killed you too. I wanted to smash them."

Elias nodded, feeling awkward. Was she trying to profess her affection? He felt touched. He saw that she was still looking at him, still intense, and he knew there was more.

"Elias," she said softly. "The test results are in. You and I are going to have a son."

Tears of joy sprang to Elias' eyes and rolled down his cheeks. *A son! I'm going to have a son!*

*And Briana is his mother.* His joy refused to fade.

"How are things between you and 'your friend' Martha?"

"I love her," Elias said.

Briana closed her eyes. Her face went impassive. "And me?"

"I'm sorry."

She opened her eyes, glared at him. "You haven't tried, Elias. What have you got against me? I'm beautiful, I'm strong, I'm smart. The sex was wonderful between us, you know it was."

"All that is true," Elias agreed, feeling a pained sympathy for her hurt.

"I could make it very hard for you."

Elias stared at her, against his will feeling a smile tugging at his mouth. She looked nonplussed, then burst out laughing. He laughed too; he could not help himself.

She took his hands again, leaning into his shoulder. "Oh, damn you, Elias Kane. That's not what I meant."

"I know," he murmured. "Richard DuMorgan claims you put a bounty on Martha's head."

She straightened and stared at him, wide-eyed. "Did you believe him?"

"No," Elias said. "He would say anything, do anything to defeat us. You are better than he. You know that you can't save yourself by destroying yourself. It's what makes you worth fighting for."

"And yet you cannot love me?"

Elias said nothing. *The mother of his son.* He felt sorrow that he must be the cause of her pain.

"What are we going to do?" Briana said softly. "He will be the next Imperator. Turn against me now, and he will be lost to you forever."

Elias yearned to make peace with her, to convince her. "I won't turn against you, Briana. I want to be a father to my son and a right arm to you. Will you let me?"

Briana bowed her head. For a long time she said nothing. Then: "I'll try, Elias."

He stood and walked to the tall windows, avoiding the fallen Ornyl warrior. He looked out on the red daylight of Cassiodorus, feeling a mixture of hope and fear for the future. He had Martha and he had a son, and somewhere into that he must fit Briana, proud ruler of the Imperium. Meanwhile, Briana would keep trying to have things her own way—there could be no doubt of that. Somehow, he must fend her off.

And he must help her.

Resolve flowed into him. The struggle was not finished. Just let him give his heart to Martha, and he would give Briana his intellect, his allegiance, his determination.

Because somewhere out there, beyond the awful red sky in the black reaches of space, he could sense the rebel dreadnoughts.

## ABOUT THE AUTHOR

STEVEN SPRUILL is the author of three previous science fiction novels. *The Psychopath Plague* and *The Imperator Plot* feature the recurring characters of Elias Kane and Pendrake. His other science fiction novel is *Keepers of the Gate*.